T0007120

BLOOD
IN THE
HOLLER
What would you
do to survive?
DAVID SANGIAO-PARGA

BLOOD
IN THE
HOLLER

DAVID SANGIAO-PARGA

woodhall press
Woodhall Press | Norwalk, CT

Woodhall Press, 81 Old Saugatuck Road, Norwalk, CT 06855
WoodhallPress.com

Cover design: Jessica Dionne
Layout artist: LJ Mucci

Library of Congress Cataloging-in-Publication Data available

ISBN 978-1-954907-90-4 (paper: alk paper)
ISBN 978-1-954907-91-1 (electronic)

First Edition
Distributed by Independent Publishers Group
(800) 888-4741

Printed in the United States of America

For Daniel,
DCW Tag Team Champs for life, brother.

Prologue

Release

July 6, 1991
Mount Olive Correctional Complex, West Virginia
2:33 p.m.

There were a lot of things Lester Goode was pissed off about as he waited in the summer sun. He was pissed about the heat. He was pissed that Norm had forgotten today was release day. He was pissed about the hole in his shirtfront that he was certain had not been there eight years ago. But the thing irritating him the most was his pants. He never would have thought it possible to actually gain weight in prison, but somehow in the past eight years he'd managed to outgrow his size 34 Levis. Even with the top button undone, he could barely sit comfortably. His legs felt like they were in spandex. He sat on a concrete bench at the start of the access road to the prison, reclined as much as he could to relieve some of the pressure.

Les had walked almost three miles to reach the bench, and he would have been happy to walk even farther if needed. No one wanted to stay near Mount Olive once they got out, not one second longer than necessary. Putting a bench here was the only real act of kindness he'd seen come from the prison.

He heard an engine coming from the northbound lane. Les tried not to get his hopes up. With his luck, his ride home was somewhere off in Virginia right now. It was only a thirty-minute drive from the farm to Mount Olive, but he didn't trust Norm not to get lost. He stared down the road as a white Ford Econoline van came rattling around the corner. It had a grimy windshield and rust stains all along its body. Les shook his head sadly as he saw Norm come into focus behind the driver's side.

This was not the car he was expecting.

Before going away, Les had given the keys to his Chevy 2500 to his cousin Louanne. The Chevy was his most prized possession, the most expensive thing he owned, and he treated it like a goddamn show car. Louanne he trusted to take care of it. Her husband, Norm, on the other hand . . .

The van came to a staggered halt in front of Les's bench. Norm rolled down the window, grinning at Les and showing off his missing incisor.

"Hey there, Cuz, you need a lift?"

"I ain't your cuz," Les growled. "And you shoulda been here three fuckin' hours ago." He stood up and walked awkwardly to the open window. "Where's my truck, Norm?"

"What, you don't like the ride? I got it for a steal."

"Where's my truck?"

"You got better options?"

Les glared at Norm, but the man was unfazed by the look. He went on, "If not, you best get on in, 'cause we ain't got all day." Les didn't reply, chewing his bottom lip and considering his options. He had none. The rest of his family was all gone now. He went around to the passenger side of the van and hopped in the back.

"Damn, Les, you put on some pounds, huh?"

"You'd'a known if you ever came to visit."

"I didn't know you wanted me to visit."

"I didn't." Les looked at the rider in the passenger seat. "Jesus, Nate, I hardly recognized ya." Norm's son Nate was tall—at least about a foot taller than Les remembered—broad-shouldered, and strong. He sat with a blank expression, which suited Les fine because Nate never smiled for anything good.

"He wanted to come," Norm said. "Tol' me he was anxious to see ya. You know, the last time you saw this guy, I think was three years ago. He was only fifteen. Hadn't quite sprouted yet."

"Well, where's Mark then?" Mark was Norm's son with Louanne. Nate's half-brother. The only person left that Les had any family ties to.

"He's watchin' over the farm. Can't really leave it unattended." Norm wasn't making eye contact with Les anymore. He made a show of watching the road as they rolled downhill away from Mount Olive.

"Watchin'?" Les asked. "Watching what, exactly? The pigs fuck?"

"We ain't doin' the pig thing no more," Nate said. He had no inflection to his voice. Like a robot. For a moment Les worried that Nate had killed all the pigs for fun.

"Son, shut the hell up! We ain't even made it home yet." Norm turned to look at Les. Les stared hard at Norm, trying to intimidate him. Eight years ago that might have worked, but Nate's presence changed the nature of the relationship considerably.

"Before we go any farther," Les said, "I wanna know what happened to my Chevy."

"Sold it," said Nate.

"Goddamn it, Nate!" Norm shouted. Les leaned forward between Nate and Norm. He'd heard enough of their bullshit.

"Norm, I just wanna know what the hell happened to my truck. I'm tired of all this pussyfootin' bullshit." Nate started to say something, but Les whipped around and cut him off. "Not from you, son, I wanna hear it from your daddy." Nate stared back with a blank look.

"The farm was goin' to shit," Norm said. He tried to sound defiant, but there was a tremor in his voice that Les knew very well. "We had to sell the Chevy to cover Louanne's funeral. I'm sorry." He was quiet then, but Les couldn't argue with what he'd said. He would have done the same thing. Norm sighed and met Les's eyes. "You don't know, Les, you been inside too long. The whole state's goin' to shit. Everyone's leaving. Buncha miners got laid off last year, you know. Not just from one company. From all of 'em."

"Okay, but I still gotta make money. How the hell am I supposed to support myself if I ain't got a ride?"

"Well, that's something we need to talk about," Norm said. "We got something going on already that you can help us out with." They rounded a curve and entered a wall of green on the right side. Les could hear the river to his left, dashing over the rocks and splashing sparkling droplets in the afternoon sun. It was too peaceful, too pretty, to even think about anything shady.

"Whatever it is, I'm not doing it. I'm on parole; I ain't goin' back."

"You sound like you got it all figured out. 'Cept, your name's still shit in town. Dunno who's gonna hire you."

Les considered his options. As the van traveled round the mountains back to the farm, Les thought about how alone he was. He knew that Norm was right: If he didn't find work fast, he'd be back at Mount Olive. He sighed and listened to Norm's offer as they passed a small waterfall on the way to town.

Part One

Marking Out

FRIDAY, OCTOBER 24, 1997

1

Louisville, Kentucky
7:00 p.m.

Jeers and boos rained on Julie Sandusky as she emerged onto the walkway to the ring. She kept herself in the dead center of the aisle, just out of reach of prying hands on either side of the barricade. It was a motley assortment of men, boozed up and worn out from a night of bell-to-bell action. She ignored their catcalls and focused on the ring ahead of her, where a kiddie pool of sloshing brown pudding sat waiting in the center. A tarp laid out underneath it would keep the rest of the ring clean for the main event immediately following this "match."

Julie used every ounce of acting ability she had to sell the crowd on the seriousness of the situation. Instead of rolling her eyes at the debased debauchery of it all, she instead climbed the stairs to the ring, stopping to do her traditional pose of hooking a leg over the top rope and hanging upside down while firing off devil's-horn hand signals. The boos intensified as she did this, coming to a crescendo when the announcer finished introducing her by her ring name: "Goth Girl."

Julie watched from the far end of the ring as her opponent came out next. The obvious babyface, Kirsty came bouncing out in little more than a string bikini, her bosom bouncing in a way that Julie's own minor endowments never would. She grinned ear to ear, soaking up the whistles and catcalls from the crowd, but Julie noticed that she too was reluctant to get too close to those grasping hands.

As soon as Kirsty began to slide seductively into the ring, Julie slid out on the other end. She could her the play-by-play guys wondering what she was up to, and as she seized an empty metal folding chair from next to their table, she was sure Jack Mayer was screaming his head off in the back, wondering what she was doing.

She slid back into the ring, where Kirsty had finally noticed her after taking some time to prance around the kiddie pool for the audience. Benny Russell, the ref, came up to Julie and grabbed at the chair.

"Jack's telling me to get that chair outta here," Benny said in a hushed whisper. Julie could imagine the expletives Jack was using over the earpiece in Benny's ear.

"Just go with it. If you try to take this chair from me, I swear to God, Benny, I will use it on you first."

Benny hesitated, then looked over his shoulder as Kirsty approached.

"Come on, babe," she said to Julie; "let's make this shit look good."

Kirsty threw a weak-looking punch Julie's way, giving her an opening to ram the top of the chair into Kirsty's midsection. Kirsty gave an overexaggerated *whoof*, and Julie raised the chair high in two hands, preparing to bring it down on Kirsty's back. She left herself open for Kirsty to lunge forward into a spear tackle, and Julie fell backward with the chair. Benny leaned forward toward both of them, appearing to check on Julie.

"Jack says if he sees any blood from you two, neither of you is getting paid tonight," he whispered harshly. "Now get in the damned pudding!"

"Throw me in there," Julie said as Kirsty pulled her to her feet. Kirsty obliged, seizing her by the waist and shoulder and hurling Julie face-first into the kiddie pool. From there, the match went just the way Jack had wanted. Five minutes of two women rolling in pudding, with plenty of sexual innuendo played up as Julie put her hands all over Kirsty's mostly-exposed body. The fans who hadn't chosen to go the restroom beforehand were getting the best smut you could see on public access TV.

It ended with Kirsty holding Julie under the pudding until Julie flailed her arms in a pantomime of something between passing out and tapping out. It was a far cry from the type of wrestling Stu Hart had trained her to do, but she'd be fifty dollars richer by the end of it. For a minute-to-minute basis, that was a good bit of money. At least that's what she told herself.

She wasn't more than two steps backstage when Jack accosted her. He reached for her pudding-streaked arm, but then thought the better of it. He'd already made that mistake once.

"Goddamn it, Julie, what was that shit? A fucking chair, really? For a pudding match?" He was red-faced, balding, and smelled of Winston cigarettes. Julie wondered for a minute what would have happened if she'd actually bladed out there. A heart attack, maybe?

"What's the big deal? I got one shot with it, then it was right into the pudding, just like you wanted. Excuse me for wanting to put a bit of actual wrestling into a wrestling match."

"No one watches you girls for the wrestling. Besides, Kirsty barely knows how to throw a worked punch. Things like that pudding match protect *you*, Julie, because otherwise it's gonna look like the Hardcore Queen got her ass handed to her by a fucking cheerleader."

"Gee, thanks Jack," Kirsty said as she came around the corner. She wiped pudding away from her mouth. "By the way, this pudding tastes like shit. What did you make it with, tap water?"

"Well, you aren't supposed to eat it," Jack said. "Anyway, Julie, you're lucky I'm paying you at all after that stunt. Instead, I'm just taking a tenner off your rate."

"Are you serious? How the hell am I even going to afford a hotel room, let alone gas?"

"You should've thought of that before you grabbed a fucking chair," Jack said. "I let you get away with that shit, next thing you know someone's doing a goddamn suicide dive off the balcony or some other crazy thing for cheap pops. No, I gotta put my foot down. Sorry."

Julie tried to object, but Jack waved her off as he looked past her. "Get to the showers, okay? I gotta talk to Brick." He walked past her, catching up to the beefy ex-marine who was getting ready for the main event. Julie shook her head.

"Fuck him," she muttered.

"Don't worry about it," Kirsty said. "I'll give you some of my cut."

"You only got sixty," Julie replied.

"Yeah, so I'll make it fifty-five. Come on, let's get this shit off of us." She put an arm around Julie and steered her forcefully towards the showers.

"A collect call? Really?"

Eric Johnson winced at the sharp tone of Cynthia's voice. His ex-wife knew the perfect pitch to make his ears ring.

"I don't have enough quarters on me." Eric gripped the receiver tightly, reigning in his own irritation. "Look, I'll cover it on the next child support payment."

"You'd better," she said.

"I will." Eric gritted his teeth. "Anyway, the *reason* I'm calling is because I still haven't gotten an answer from you about Thanksgiving."

"I don't have one yet. If you can keep up your good behavior, *if* you don't remind me why I divorced you in the first place, then maybe yes. But that's a big if."

"I ain't even there to cause any trouble."

"That's the idea, Eric. So you'd better watch your tone. If I even think you're still volatile, you won't be seeing Lillian for the holidays. As it is, you're lucky I'm even considering it at all. Hell, you're lucky you're not in jail. You should be thanking me, asshole."

"Yes, thank you, hon . . . uh, Cynthia." Eric winced, aggravated with his own slipup. It was still too easy to fall into old patterns with her. "Listen, I got to go; I've got a match, but just keep an open mind, okay? I miss my daughter." He waited for a moment, then girded himself to ask, "Can I at least talk to her?"

"Uh, no. It's late, and I don't think this is the best time anyway. You have a match, right? Main event? Jack'll dock your pay if you screw that up."

"Right, right." Eric said. "It's just that I haven't talked to her in so long, you know? What's it been, like, a year?"

"So call back tomorrow. If you're normal, if I don't think you sound like you're going to snap, you can talk to her for a minute. It's a Saturday, so she won't be in school."

Eric's heart catapulted in his chest. "Thank you, hon; Jesus, thank you!" He didn't bother to correct himself this time. "I gotta go, but I'll call tomorrow!"

He hung up and spun around, almost right into the chest of Brick Lamar, Midwest American Wrestling champion and Eric's opponent for tonight.

"Hey there, Jiggolo," Brick said, calling Eric by his ring name. "Jack wanted me to make sure you've got your head on straight before we go out there."

"Yeah," Eric said, a tinge of irritation in his voice. "I'm fine."

"Yeah, you seem real fine." Brick gave him an appraising up-and-down look. He raised an almost-invisible eyebrow. "It's going to be a bruiser out there tonight."

"We still doing the table spot?"

"Yup." For the big finish, they'd planned to have Eric take a power-bomb from Brick onto the announcer's table, which would hopefully smash to pieces on impact.

"Okay, well, just don't slam me onto the monitors and we'll be good. Right in the middle, okay?"

"Are you sure you don't want me to just throw the monitors out of the way first?"

Eric shook his head. "That always looks silly. Like, oh, you're gonna make sure you don't hurt your opponent too much before you put him through a table? Nah. You got this."

It was dumb, and a good way to seriously hurt himself, but that's how TJ Azz did his table bumps, and Eric was *not* going to get shown up by TJ Azz.

"Come on, it sounds like they finished cleaning the pudding out of the ring. They'll be calling us out there any minute." He clapped Brick on the shoulder, which was about as high as Eric could comfortably reach on the big man, and they headed toward the ring entrance.

Burt Knox winced as Ricky Chalmers dabbed at his back with an alcohol-soaked cotton swab.

"Yeah, I bet it hurts," Ricky said. "What the hell, Burt? Why'd you let that asshole hammer you like this?"

Knox stood, stepping away from Ricky and turning to face him. "I didn't let him, okay? It was just a receipt from last week."

"A receipt for what?" Ricky asked.

"I kneed him in the head by mistake. It happens." Knox shrugged and turned again to look for his shirt.

"Terry just likes to hurt people," Ricky said. Knox had been in a feud with Terry "TJ Azz" Jones for the past month, and Ricky had never seen Knox so bruised and battered. "He's a bully, and it's ridiculous—you could lay him out with one punch." Ricky wasn't wrong. Knox was close to seven feet, by far the tallest wrestler in MAW, but he was still the new guy, and the new guy had to pay his dues. Sometimes he had to take a receipt.

"It won't be long before I'm getting pushed, Ricky. And once I'm main-eventing, where's Terry gonna be? Still jobbing out on the mid-card. So who gives a shit if he stiffs me with a chair sometimes?"

"I thought it was Brick's turn at the top right now."

"Brick's a flavor of the month, and you know it. He'll be a big, black monster for someone like me to conquer. I mean, come on, the fans are already throwing shit at him when he comes to the ring. If Jack leaves the belt on Brick, we're gonna have riots before too long." Knox put on his shirt, wincing as it rubbed against the welts from Terry's chair shots.

"Maybe I should ride with the two of you to Richmond," Ricky said. He adjusted his glasses as he said this, something Knox knew as a sign of irritation from him.

"No. We talked about that already." Knox walked over to Ricky and put a huge right hand on his shoulder. "I appreciate the concern, but I can handle a few hours in the car with Terry."

"There's no one else you can go with?"

"Not unless they've got a car big enough for me to fit in. Terry's the only guy who has an Excursion." Knox winked and gave Ricky's shoulder a squeeze. "Maybe when I'm champ, I can afford to get one of those for myself. Then we can ride in style."

Ricky was about to say something, but they stepped apart when they heard the locker room door open. Terry walked in, a towel wrapped around his neck and nothing else. Knox consciously averted his eyes.

"What's the matter big guy? Jealous?" Terry asked. He marched between Knox and Ricky, rummaging in his own bag for a pair of undies. "You're gonna be ready to go soon as the show's done, right? I don't want to be waiting on your ass all night."

"You're the one who's still naked," Ricky said.

"No one asked you," Terry replied. "What the fuck you doing in here anyway? It's not like you need to change." He looked between the two of them, then shrugged and pulled on a pair of jeans. "Fuck it. I need to take a shit." He walked past them again, still talking. "I hate when that happens. I just cleaned my ass." The door closed behind him, and Ricky looked at Knox once more.

"Well, I'd better get going. Jack said he wanted to talk to me after Jiggolo's match."

"Yeah, okay. If I don't see you before I leave, I'll catch up in Richmond, okay?" Knox smiled, and Ricky returned the gesture before leaving as well.

Eric waited next to Brick Lamar near the entry to the arena floor. The crowd was cheering, fired up after Goth Girl's match and ready for some real action. He glanced toward Brick, who was taping off his massive wrists.

"You think we could use some color tonight?" Eric asked. Brick shook his head.

"I don't blade. Didn't think you did, either."

"No," Eric said. "Not anymore, at least." Eric hadn't used a razor blade in a match since he'd accidentally nicked an artery in his forehead. The practice of blading was a more old-school thing now, but wrestlers still did it if they thought the match needed some "color," as the wrestlers called it.

"Then what you wanna do?"

"Maybe you can bust me open the hard way," Eric said. He'd been debating whether to even bring it up. To make someone bleed "the hard way," you had to actually injure them. Smack their forehead into a ring post, bash them too hard onto the steel entry steps, something like that. It was dangerous, it was stupid, but after that phone call with Cynthia, he was feeling particularly nihilistic. Brick finished the tape and stared at Eric.

"There's no fucking way I'm doing that. Especially not for a damned house show. Are you serious? In two days we're gonna have a regional televised match, the whole East Coast can watch if they want. You think Jack'll be happy if his top guy shows up with a stitched-up forehead?" Brick shook his head. "Get your head straight, Jiggy. Let's just do what we planned. The table spot's plenty enough. You want more than that, let's save it for the TV, okay?"

Eric sighed, embarrassed he'd even brought it up. He shook out his whole body, limbered up, and turned to the tech guy. He gave Eric a countdown from five, and when the music hit, Eric braced his shoulders and walked out with Jiggolo's swagger.

The match itself went fine, although Brick's concern over the monitors turned out to be valid. Eric's ass landed hard on the edge of one as Brick powerbombed him onto the table. Normally, a table was actually a more comfortable spot to take a slam like that, as it broke your fall, but Eric grimaced in real pain as the monitor first bruised his right cheek and then fell on his groin. The ref checked on Eric to make sure he wasn't seriously injured, but Eric waved him off. He stood, stumbling slightly as Brick taunted him from inside the ring, and slid in there himself just as the ref counted to nine on a ten-count disqualification.

Eric traded a few blows with Brick in the ring, but the match was nearing the end. Brick put Eric in a headlock, and Eric whispered to him, "I'm gonna throw you off the ropes, then go for a Stunner. You counter and give me a Hangover." He pushed Brick from the back, throwing him into the ring ropes, and Brick bounced off. Eric went for a kick to the abdomen, the setup for his signature move, but Brick caught Eric's foot with his left hand and then did a stiff Clothesline with the right arm, knocking Eric off his feet. From there, Brick hoisted Eric bodily off the floor and, to a chorus of boos from the audience (with more than a few cheers, Eric noticed), held Eric upside down and fell to his knees, appearing to drive the top of Eric's skull into the mat.

In the hands of someone as large and strong as Brick, it was one of the safest moves you could do. But it looked absolutely devastating, and the crowds loved it. Eric went limp and crumpled onto his back. Brick covered Eric for the pin, and Eric stared at the lights as the ref counted to three. Brick's music cued up, and he seized the title belt from the ref, heeling it up as he paraded around the ring with it over his head. Eric rolled out of the ring and slunk back toward the locker room, all but forgotten as Brick posed on the top turnbuckle.

—

Julie sat in the locker room, digging through her bag as she made a grim inventory. Most of the other wrestlers had cleared out, either getting ready to leave or already taking off for Richmond. Her options for finding a ride were limited, her funds even more so. She'd have to share the cost of gas, but she also needed to pay for food and the motel in Richmond. She had enough for two, but not three. As she scoured her supplies, she found several protein bars, at least one of which was considered a "meal" bar, and a half-empty bottle of Coca-Cola. She sighed and zipped up her bag. Time to start conserving. Her stomach rumbled in protest.

"What's the matter?" Kirsty asked as she passed Julie. Her bags were in hand, and she eyed Julie with concern. "Are you still pissed about Jack?"

"No," Julie said. "Well, yes," she corrected, "but that's not it, really. I'm just running low on cash."

"Couldn't find anyone to split a room with in Richmond?"

Julie shook her head. "All the other girls are already paired up. I'm still looking for a ride too."

Kirsty looked back and forth, then set her bags down and sat next to Julie. "You know, Terry hasn't left yet."

"Terry?" Julie asked. "How much does he want for gas? He's got that big-ass SUV; it's gonna cost a lot."

"Not for you," Kirsty said. Julie cocked her head, waiting for Kirsty to go on. "Listen, I don't talk about it much, but sometimes, especially early on when some of the rest of us were real hard up, Terry would give us rides for free."

"Free? Why?" Although Julie felt like she knew where this was going.

"Not 'free' free. He would expect certain things."

"No." Julie said. "Nuh-uh; I am not going to sleep with him." She began to stand up, but Kirsty put a hand on her elbow.

"Wait," she said. "You don't *have* to; he's just got to think you will, you get me?" Kirsty raised her eyebrows, waiting for Julie to get the hint.

"Somehow, that seems even sleazier. I'm not that kind of woman."

"Look, as long as you aren't planning to make a habit of it, he's a good . . . how can I put this . . . he's a good resource to have. Once or twice he'll let you ride free, at least until he catches on that you won't put anything out for it."

"Does anyone ever put out for it?" Julie asked. Kirsty stared at her.

"That's not something anyone's gonna talk about, sweetie."

Julie looked at Kirsty, through Kirsty, and out the locker room and into the parking lot. She could see the other wrestlers loading their cars, talking about where they would eat dinner. Julie could go for anything right about then, even a gas station egg-salad sandwich. She could see, out in the parking lot, Terry with his Excursion, almost beckoning to her. Her stomach gave one more painful twist, and her mind was made up.

"Okay, I'll go talk to Terry. What should I say, exactly?"

"Just, you know, ask if he has room for a ride. Tell him you're happy to chip in for gas. He'll feel like a big hero when he tells you he'll let you ride for free. Men like him are so, um, so . . ."

"Gullible?"

"Yes!" Kirsty said with a laugh. "I was trying to think of a nicer way to say it, but that works." She leaned over and gave Julie an unexpected hug. This felt important to Julie. She didn't make friends easily, especially female friends, and she hadn't been particularly close to anyone on the roster since starting with MAW four months ago. But this hug, this moment, felt like a bond to Julie, one she hoped she'd be able to strengthen in the coming weeks and months.

"Thank you," Julie said, patting Kirsty awkwardly on the back.

"I'll see ya in Richmond, honey," the former cheerleader said as she snatched up her bags and practically danced out of the locker room. Julie reached into her bag, pulled out a protein bar to take the edge off, then quickly raced out the door to catch Terry before he left.

Eric looked for Brick in the parking lot after his shower, but the champ had already taken off in his BMW. Brick never stayed long after the shows, preferring to take off and do his own thing. Eric thought Brick might want some dinner, but he'd known that would be a long shot before he even got out of the shower.

He turned and headed toward the Nissan Altima that belonged to "Big Fig" Donnie Figueroa. Eric and Donnie had come up through the territories together, had debuted as a tag team in MAW, and were still the best of friends. After Eric had lost his car in the divorce, he'd become a more-or-less permanent driving partner for Donnie. As he neared the sedan, though, Donnie came up behind him and steered him away with a meaty arm around the shoulders.

"Uh-uh, not tonight," he said. Donnie looked like he might be soft, but he had the build of an Olympic weight lifter. It was like being hugged by a rock.

"What are you doing?" Eric asked. He still limped slightly on his bruised ass and had been looking forward to getting off his feet.

"Tonight you're riding with the great journeyman, TJ Azz!" Donnie replied. Eric pulled back then, stopping them both in their tracks.

"Terry? What? Are you fucking serious?"

"Dude, just tonight, trust me."

"I can't fucking stand that guy, Fig."

"No one can. But listen, do you know who's riding with him tonight?"

"Who?"

"Fucking Goth Girl, man!" Donnie's eyes gleamed. "Seriously, dude, she's putting her bags in the car right now." Eric followed Donnie's gaze and saw he was right. Julie was loading her suitcase into the back of the cavernous Excursion while Terry looked on.

"Oh, God, she's riding with him?" Eric knew the rumors about Terry. Most of the roster did. But no one had ever confirmed how true they were.

"Yeah, so you know what's up. But, dude, if you're there, you can cock-block it."

"You're dreaming if you think I have a chance with her. She's what, seven, eight years younger than me? Why the hell would she be interested in an overweight, middle-aged has-been?"

"Hey, you're not a has-been yet. You're still main-eventing Sunday night."

"Yeah, only to put over Brick. Then I'll be free-falling down the card."

Donnie nodded, then winked at Eric. "Okay, but until then, you aren't a has-been. So come on, take your shot; what do you have to lose?"

Eric considered this. He thought of the long, lonely nights since his divorce. While he'd been away from home more often than not when he was married, it felt different now that Cynthia was no longer his wife. The beds felt emptier, the nights longer. He wasn't using downers to get to sleep anymore, but even without the uppers they'd been counteracting, Eric still had mostly restless nights. Donnie was right. He should take the shot. He had nothing to lose.

"I don't know if Terry will even let me ride," Eric said, the last bit of protest he could muster. Donnie waved it off.

"He'll want the money. That Ford's thirsty, and you know he won't be asking Julie to cough up. Not cash, at least." Eric elbowed Donnie half-heartedly, then nodded. "Okay. So what should I tell him about why I'm not riding with you."

"I dunno. Just say we had a fight or something. He'll love that; he can get out all his pent-up gay jokes. And if he gets too carried away, just remind him of the time you fucked his sister."

Eric chuckled and clapped Donnie on the back. "Good idea. Okay. I'll see ya on the other side, man."

Burt Knox was loading his bags into the back of Terry's Excursion when Julie approached him with her own suitcases.

"Is there room for my stuff in there?" she asked, although the answer was obvious. With the third row seats folded down, Terry's cargo space was cavernous. Knox decided not to point this out.

"No problem," he replied. "Want me to grab those bags for you?"

"Maybe this one," Julie said, pushing un ugly green suitcase toward him. To say it had seen better days would be complimentary. Knox smiled as he hoisted it up with one hand and set it down next to his own much newer suitcase.

"So, where should I sit? Is it just the three of us?" Julie asked.

"Yeah. Usually I take the front with Terry. So you'll have the back all to yourself if you like." Knox gestured expansively toward the back seats past the suitcases. "Good way to get some sleep."

"Yeah, it sure is," Julie said. She hoisted her other bag higher onto her shoulder and moved to the passenger-side doors. Knox watched her as she opened the back door and set her duffel on the seat. He didn't notice Ricky approaching from behind until they were side by side. Knox jumped back half an inch in surprise.

"Ricky? What're you doing here?"

"Talked to Jack. Decided I'd tag along with you rather than ride with him this time."

Knox peered down at Ricky. He had more than a foot of height on the man. He raised his hand to Ricky's shoulder then pulled it away. Instead, he crouched a bit and lowered his voice.

"Why? You don't think it's gonna look weird?"

"I think it's going to be fine, since I have cash. You and I both know he won't be asking Goth Girl for any money."

"This is a bad idea. This is a bad idea." Knox stood back up, shaking his head as he turned away from Ricky.

"I'm sorry; I thought you might like being able to ride with me for once," Ricky said. Knox could tell he wasn't really apologizing.

"It isn't like we're gonna sit with each other, or talk or anything. He'll expect me in the front like always, not sidled up in the back with you."

"Maybe he'll like the idea of Goth Girl being in shotgun next to him."

Knox turned and gave Ricky a thin-lipped stare. "I'm not putting her in that position. Bad enough she has to ride with him as is."

"Your chivalry is wasted," Ricky said. "But really, it's too late to back out now anyway. If I go back to Jack, he'll realize something's up, and he's a lot smarter than Terry."

"Is everything okay back there?" Julie asked. She was already sitting in the rear passenger seat, staring through the open rear door at Ricky and Knox. "Oh, hi, Ricky!" she said with a polite wave. "Are you riding with us too?"

"As a matter of fact, I am," Ricky replied. Knox turned his back to Julie and rolled his eyes. He opened his mouth to argue the point some more but was interrupted by the approach of Terry and Eric. They appeared to be in a heated discussion as they walked, and as they got closer, Knox could hear them better.

"You should be thanking me for chipping in on the gas, not busting my ass over it."

"I figured it was Fig that busted your ass most nights," Terry replied with a forced guffaw. "But I guess your little lovers' quarrel is good news for me, at least."

They made it to the back of the SUV, where Eric nonchalantly chucked his bag in next to Julie's. He made an effort to avert his gaze from her, but Knox noticed it. He smirked a little, amused at the direction this ride was taking. If nothing else, it would at least be more entertaining than most of the rides he took with Terry.

"What're you doing here?" Terry asked as he muscled in between Knox and Ricky. "Ain't you supposed to be riding with Jack?"

"Jack had some other business he wanted to take care of tonight. Said I should hitch a ride with you. Said something about putting this thing to good use finally."

Terry scowled and slammed the rear door shut. "I'm not a fucking Greyhound. You're gonna pay up for gas, right?"

Ricky nodded. "Sure. Whatever you think's fair."

"Well, we'll sort out the math on that later. For right now, why don't you hop in the bitch seat?" Terry walked around to the driver side, opening the door. "Hey! Come on, Jiggy, you're in Rick's seat."

Eric turned from Julie, whom he'd just begun conversing with, and glared at Terry. "You have assigned seats? What is this, kindergarten?"

"No, it just makes sense, damn it. Why's Julie gonna want to be squeezed up against your fat ass when Ricky's such a pipsqueak? Come on, get out and let Ricky in." Eric simply stared. "I mean it; you either sit behind me, or your ass is walking to Richmond."

"Terry, it's okay, really," Julie said. "I've got plenty of room."

"That's nice of ya," Terry replied, "but I ain't buying it." He looked at Eric and motioned with his thumb. "Out. Now." Eric begrudgingly complied, sliding out so Ricky could get in.

"Oh, yeah," Knox whispered to Ricky. "I don't see any problems with this *at all*." Ricky elbowed Knox in the hip before walking off. Grinning, Knox went the opposite way and hopped in the shotgun seat.

"All right," Terry said, turning the key in the ignition. The V8 engine roared to life in the rapidly-emptying parking lot. "Next stop, Richmond."

SATURDAY, OCTOBER 25, 1997

2

US Highway 60, 27 miles northwest of Chimney Corner, West Virginia
1:07 a.m.

As Eric Johnson woke, he panicked as he tried to remember where he was. After a moment it came to him; he was in Terry's car, heading to Richmond for Sunday's show. He squinted into the light punching at him through the rear window. The sulfurous glow of the street lamps punctuated the darkness in slow-moving sweeps through the car. In his head, Eric could hear them humming.

Whoosh. Whoosh. Whoosh.

He rubbed his eyes reflexively, sitting up in the back seat. There were five of them crammed into the SUV. Eric was lucky to be in the back with Ricky Chalmers, who was the smallest person in the car, and Julie Sandusky, one of MAW's five female wrestlers. It meant he had some space to move. Burt Knox, an almost seven-foot-tall giant of a man, sat in the front while Terry Jones drove. Eric's ass was sore where he'd fallen wrong on that monitor earlier. It would be one hellish-looking bruise for sure. Ricky stirred next to Eric but didn't wake. His head was canted at an odd angle that would surely cause him some trouble come morning. On the other side of Ricky was Julie, staring out the window while she chewed on half a protein bar.

He watched Julie out of the corner of his eye, examining the way her jaw moved as she ate. In the brief flashes of light he could see the outline of her face as she chewed slowly. When she glanced his way, Eric averted his gaze to the window by her head, looking at the vague, tree-lined landscape they were speeding past.

The view outside the window was of a two-lane backcountry road, carved into a mountainside and wandering through sheer, man-made cliffsides. This was not Interstate 64. Eric didn't know what road it was, but he knew they weren't still en route to Richmond. He looked toward Terry, who was tapping the steering wheel to the steady beat of "Turn the Page."

"Where are we?" Eric asked. "This isn't 64."

"I-64 is fucked with a pileup," said Terry. "I decided to take us down US 60, cut through West Virginia, and reconnect with 64 past the accident."

"Is that really better than going through the traffic? US 60 is a winding piece of shit road."

"I told Terry that," said Burt from the passenger seat. "He's convinced this is faster, though."

Eric leaned forward and rested his hands on the two front seats. "You don't think you should've asked anyone before deciding that?"

"My car, my rules. You don't like it, you shoulda hitched a ride with Fig like usual. Or maybe even Brick," Terry said with a chuckle. Knox laughed at this, his barrel-chested bass tones rumbling the car. He gestured over his shoulder toward Eric.

"Eric's way too white for Brick. He wouldn't let 'Jiggolo' here within twenty feet of his pimpmobile."

"You got that right," Terry said. "Ask me, Brick's the one shoulda been called Jiggolo. That guy gets more tail than any other dude on the show. Guess the groupies got themselves some jungle fever."

"I wish you wouldn't say things like that," Julie said. Her voice was so quiet, Eric wondered if Terry even heard her. His shoulders dropped in response as he let out a long sigh.

"Aw, shit; I'm sorry Julie. You know I like Brick just fine. Old habit, that's all."

Eric knew better than to say anything. There was no point. Midwest American Wrestling, like most wrestling companies, only had a handful of Black wrestlers. Normally they'd be cannon fodder for someone like Terry, but Brick Lamar was anything but normal. He was a rising star, and the current MAW heavyweight champion. Eric was well aware of Brick's talents. He'd been the one to drop the belt to Brick after a long and well-received feud. As much as the crowds loved it, Eric didn't like the beatings he'd had to take. Brick worked as stiff as they came, barely pulling his punches, and he loved showing off how he got his nickname. Eric knew all too well that those hands felt like balled-up concrete.

Everyone anticipated Brick as the next big thing, Eric included. He'd had his time on top with multiple runs as the MAW champion, but that time had passed. He was too old, too fat, and no one was buying him as a credible challenger anymore. It was almost laughable to ask people to believe he could last five minutes with Brick, let alone the twenty-minute war zone they'd put on tonight. Brick was the find of the century for MAW's owner and promoter, Jack Mayer. He was the perfect specimen to strap a rocket to for a monster push to the top.

Physicality was one thing, but Brick's race was something else. Being Black was a great heat magnet to draw a crowd on their tour routes, but it got a little too hot in some of the smaller towns on the circuit. Eric wasn't sure how Brick tolerated the slurs the crowd yelled at him most nights. Terry's laid-back attitude was a much more benign sort of prejudice in contrast, the kind that didn't see a problem with racism as long as no one was burning crosses. While Brick didn't let those things bother him outwardly, he wasn't about to give a ride to any "honky motherfuckers" either. No surprise then that Terry's roomy Excursion only had white passengers. Eric didn't care much for Terry, but he appreciated having the chance to get close to Julie.

"You know, that name was supposed to be a joke." Eric hated his gimmick name, Jiggolo. He'd made it up before he even really understood what it meant. It wasn't until long after that someone explained that "gigolo" didn't mean "lady's man." He hadn't even spelled it right, but by the time anyone noticed, it was already on all the flyers. So it stayed. It made sense when he was younger, leaner, and sexier, but nowadays he was starting to see the name as a curse.

"Yeah, you're laughing all the way to the fuckin' bank," Knox said. "You're the most over guy in the company. Besides, we all got dumbass fuckin' names. Fort Knox? TJ Azz? Fuckin' Goth Girl?" He laughed heartily at his own point.

"Everyone has stupid names at some point," Julie said. She crinkled the empty wrapper of her protein bar and threw it on the floor. "People used to call the Undertaker 'Booger Red,' for God's sake. No one outside of Texas can take that seriously."

Eric turned toward her and smiled, desperate to think of an appropriate reply. None came to him. Julie went back to staring out the window. Ricky still dozed heavily next to Eric, and he envied the way Ricky could sleep through just about anything. You could dangle Ricky out a car window and he'd still be snoring away. Usually the movement of the car was enough to lull Eric back to sleep, like a baby in a rocker, but this time he sat wide awake, and soon he started to feel hungry. He looked out the window at the blackness beyond. No town lights, no twenty-four-hour McDonalds, no 7-Elevens. Now that he'd noticed the rumble in his belly it was becoming more insistent.

"You gonna need to stop for gas soon?"

"Maybe in about an hour. Why?" Terry asked.

"I'm hungry as hell. We're already going to be late. Why not let us get some food?"

"I can stop sooner. Won't really make much difference if I fill up with half a tank or a quarter of one. Don't know if the station will be open, though. I think if you want food, you might have to shoot yourself a squirrel," he said with a loud, barking laugh.

"I'll let you know if I see any raccoons on the side of the road," Knox said. Normally, Eric might have laughed with the ribbing, but he was becoming uncomfortably hungry. He couldn't remember when he'd eaten last. Maybe before the show earlier that night. It takes a lot out of you, being thrown around like a toy, and Eric wished he'd packed more snacks for the trip. He hadn't been expecting to detour through the middle of nowhere, though.

He found his thoughts wandering, as was often the case for him now, to his daughter. He hadn't seen Lillian for more than a year, and that time was supervised. All his fault, Eric knew; he accepted that now, but it was still hard to live with. When he got to Richmond, he would let Brick beat him bloody, from post to post, until someone would have to carry him out. An inglorious end for "Jiggolo," but it meant Eric would have to time to rebuild things with his daughter. A wrestler in his mid-thirties was already past his prime, but Eric still had a lot of years left to rebuild the bridges he'd burned back in the real world.

Soon enough, they passed through what could only generously be called a town, with only a handful of worn-down structures on either side of the road. A sign read "Welcome to Chimney Corner, Home of the Mystery Hole!" as they passed into the downtown area.

"Mystery hole?" Knox asked. "Isn't that what Eric calls Fig's ass?" This got a couple of laughs out of Terry, but that was all. Eric tilted his head.

"You gonna get in on that shit too, huh? I'll remember that," he said. Knox promptly closed his mouth.

Ricky snorted in his sleep, and Eric stared at the diminutive manager. It was another mystery that Ricky had decided to squeeze himself into the car with them at the last minute. Eric was resentful that Ricky was here, wedged between him and Julie, but he tried not to let it bother him. There must be some reason Ricky wanted to ride with Terry, and it certainly wasn't a particular fondness for the man. Eric assumed he probably had a thing for Julie as well.

Terry slowed down as the road expanded from two lanes to four, scouring the area for a gas station. The street lights barely illuminated anything past the road, which made the dull lights of a run-down diner visible as they passed it.

"Turn around," Eric implored. "That place is still open." Terry swung around in the middle of the road, unconcerned with finding a proper intersection, and pulled up to the diner's meager parking lot. A dim "Open" sign flickered in the window, while a few upturned lights illuminated a sign that said "Good Eats All Day All Night."

"Somebody wake up Ricky," Terry said as he turned off the engine. "Otherwise, we gotta carry his ass inside." That wouldn't have been hard to do. Ricky wasn't a worker; he was just their carnival barker, the manager, the one who talked everyone into the show. He was good; he knew how to rile up a crowd and sell just about any match. It helped that the fans loved seeing a skinny, spectacles-wearing know-it-all get tossed through a table every other night. He woke up after some insistent prodding from Eric, wide-eyed but groggy.

"Huh? What? Why are we stopped? Where are we?" He pulled his glasses from his shirt pocket and pushed them up his nose. "Are we on I-64 still? What time is it?"

"We're on US 60," Eric said. "There was an accident on 64. We're just stopping for some food." He opened the door and hopped out. "Are you coming or what?" Eric started for the door without waiting for a response. He was too hungry to wait on everyone else to stretch their legs.

Julie started to come after him but stopped when her purse fell from the car and to the ground.

"Dammit," she muttered, crouching down to scoop up the contents that had spilled. Eric hurried over along with Terry to help her collect the items that had fallen out of its open compartment. Eric was agitated with Terry for coming, but bit that down. Julie didn't give either man a chance to lend her aid, though.

"Thanks guys, but I have it," she said. Her gruff tone stopped both men mid-crouch, and they moved out of Julie's way as she hurriedly bundled up the items. "I didn't even mean to bring it. It must have fallen out of my bag." She carried everything in one big handful, her other hand clutching the purse by the sides, and pulled open the door to the diner with her pinky. Once she was inside, everyone else quickly followed.

Eric opened the door and stepped inside, happily taking in the grease-pit smells of fried potatoes and fatty burgers. Just what the doctor had ordered.

The diner looked like it had come out of a stereotypical mold. It had one long bar, dinged and rusted over, that was buttressed with stools held together with duct tape. A smattering of tables lined the opposite wall, with two ratty booths at either end of the place. It was bright inside, lit up with cold fluorescents that Eric was sure didn't do anything for the look of the food. It was the sort of place you ate at if you were low on options.

There was one patron at the bar, sitting on the center stool. He turned to look at the wrestlers as they walked in, his eyes narrowed menacingly. Eric wasn't sure if the man was genuinely irritated about having to share the diner or was one of those people that just seemed perpetually angry. A battered blue baseball cap covered most of his hair, but what did poke out underneath was a brown, stringy mop of oily strips. He looked like he hadn't shaved in four or five days, and probably hadn't bathed for that long either. Eric didn't want to get close enough to find out. He was wearing a stained cotton tank top, a "wife-beater," and an equally dingy pair of jeans and work boots. Eric couldn't be sure, but he thought they might be steel toed. Was he in construction? What the hell was being built out here? And why was he just now eating dinner at two in the morning? This didn't seem like a town that had a large number of night-shift workers who ate at odd hours.

The MAW wrestlers stood silently just inside the door, unsure of where to sit. The man at the bar made a garbled noise as if he was getting ready to hock a loogie, then turned back around.

"Mason! Ya got customers. Prob'ly more'n you've had all night." He looked back over his shoulder. "Ya'll just go ahead and sit wherever ya like. Mason's the only one here tonight, an' he's a little slow at the best of times."

"Thanks," Terry said. He led the way to the booth in the back. It had room for four normal-sized people, but only Julie and Ricky came close to that. Burt Knox could have filled one side all on his own. Terry slid in first and motioned for Ricky to slide in next. He didn't immediately move to do so, instead eyeing the table behind the booth. Eric wondered why Terry wanted to sit at a booth, then caught him motioning to Julie to sit across from him. Terry was apparently more self-confident than Eric was about his animal magnetism. Eric wondered if the forty-five-year-old Terry would really try to play footsies or something with a woman more than twenty years his junior. It made Eric question how he must look pining over Julie, even if he kept his intentions strictly to himself.

“What are you doing?” Terry grumbled at Ricky, who was still moving toward a table. “Just get in the booth. I wanna order and get goin’ already.”

Knox stepped between them, sliding into the booth opposite Terry. Eric smirked at the inadvertent foiling of Terry’s grand scheme. Knox shook his head ruefully. “While you guys argue, I’m gonna look at the menu.” He picked up the grease-stained laminated sheet, turning it over slowly. “Well, what they have of one at least.”

“I don’t think we’re all going to fit,” Julie said. She looked toward the table behind the booth as well. “Why don’t Ricky and I sit there?” Ricky looked back over at Terry and Knox, but before he could answer, a voice interrupted all of them.

“Hey guys, it’s okay; ya’ll can just slide the table up to the booth, see.” A disheveled young man in a ragged white apron came out from the back, hurriedly scooting the table behind the booth into position. “Holy cow, you’re some big guys. Bet ya’ll can eat like crazy.” He slid the chairs up to the table he’d moved. “Name’s Mason, by the way.”

“Thanks,” Eric replied. Julie sat at the table next to Eric.

“Can I get a coffee, black, please?” Ricky asked. The rest of the table asked for coffee as well. Mason stepped back and smiled at them.

“Tell ya what; how about I just bring the pot out to ya. It’s quiet right now, and Les don’t even like coffee.”

“I don’t think those people really care what my name is or whether I like coffee, Mason.” Les said the man’s name with pointed irritation. If he was trying to imply anything, Mason showed no sign of understanding.

“Oh, yup, yup, just bein’ polite’s all. Don’t ever see people like ya’ll. Usually it’s just truckers and stuff. And people like Les, but he ain’t so talkative.” He headed to the back to fetch the coffee. Les continued to glare until he was out of sight, then went back to his burger.

Burt looked over at Ricky. “Hey, man, shouldn’t we call the hotel?”

“Why you wanna do that?” Terry asked.

"Just trying to be safe," Burt said. "How much would it suck if we rolled in late just to find out they've got no rooms for us?" Burt looked at Ricky, who handed Burt his cell phone. He flipped it open and dialed, but after a minute put it back down. "No signal," he said. Ricky nodded.

"I'm not surprised. Cell service is spotty at best out here in the mountains. I saw a pay phone by the front door you can use. I've got some change." Ricky slid out of Burt's way and passed him a few coins as he went by. Burt smiled warmly and made his way to the phone. The man at the counter followed him with a turn of the head before going back to his burger.

Eric looked over the menu. It had breakfast on the front, lunch and dinner on the back. There was a star-shaped blurb on the side that advertised "home-made sausage and pork products." He couldn't decide if he should go for breakfast or not. Even after all these years, he didn't think it was "normal" to eat at two in the morning.

"Don't be going too carb-heavy, Eric. You're main-eventing against Brick."

"Yeah, in a day and a half, Ricky. I think I'll be okay with an order of pancakes."

"Now see," Terry said; "that is why you have the physique you have. Me? I'm ordering a T-bone." He proudly pounded on his toned midsection as Burt returned to the table. Ricky smiled and nodded.

"Any luck reaching the hotel?"

"Yeah; they said not to worry. The rooms will be ready when we get there." He returned Ricky's smile as Eric responded to Terry.

"I don't really care too much about whether I've got a gut or not. I'm never gonna be main-eventing WrestleMania, so I'm not gonna add insult to injury with some crazy diet." Eric looked over at Burt. "Now you, on the other hand, have a real shot, hoss. I hear there were scouts from Atlanta at our last show."

"Yeah, and maybe a few from New York on Sunday. They're probably looking at you, Burt." Julie smiled in his direction, but Knox didn't seem to notice. He was singularly interested in the menu. Eric wished he could get a smile like that from Julie, but she barely acknowledged him. Eric reckoned he was about ten years and twenty pounds out of her range.

Eric normally didn't ride with Terry. Eric had snorted at the idea when Donnie Figueroa suggested doing so. It would take a miracle, not luck, to draw Julie's eyes to him. But he took the spot anyway. He could at least pass the time admiring the long legs, toned arms, and raven-black hair that had drawn so many men's eyes to her already. She was self-conscious about her face, with its strong jawline and angular features, but to Eric they were beautiful in an almost classical way. He was falling deeper into an admiring reverie when Ricky's voice jolted him back to reality.

"It's pretty serious. You know Jim Ross has been on the phone with Burt?"

"J.R.?" Terry asked. "J.R." was how most people referred to Ross, the VP of talent relations at WWF. If he was talking to Burt, a contract was almost a guarantee.

"Yep. Burt's just what Vince McMahon wants. A nice, big meaty babyface. Like Hogan or Sid Vicious."

"I'm surprised they aren't talking to Brick too," Eric said.

"Well, Brick's what, thirty-five? Too old for WWF at least," Ricky replied. "Besides, they've already got Farooq and Ahmed Johnson. Their quota for big Black badasses might be full."

"I can't believe we're calling Brick old just because he's in his mid-thirties," Julie said.

"Well, he's not exactly the most electrifying guy to watch," Terry said. "Guy barely leaves his feet. I think he's got bad knees or something."

"Undertaker never leaves his feet either," Julie retorted. "Or Hogan, for that matter. And they're both older than Brick too."

"How'd you find out about Burt talking to J.R.?" Eric asked Ricky. Ricky shrugged, abashed, and glanced sideways at Burt.

"He just overheard me on the phone," Burt said quickly. "I'd asked him not to say anything, though." He glared at Ricky, then softened his expression when Ricky looked away.

"I wonder if they're scouting Burt or if they're scouting Jack," Terry said, taking a sip from his coffee mug. Eric thought that made no sense. Jack was a fiercely independent promoter who despised the big-name wrestling leagues.

"What the hell are you on about?" Eric asked. "Neither WWF nor WCW needs a promoter."

"No, they need a facility, a pipeline," Terry replied. "I've heard things. Rumors from friends in Ohio and Florida. The big boys are looking for someplace that can make new stars. They take the best guys, train them up early, and have them exclusively."

"Yeah, well, with the way everyone's been jumping ship from WWF, it isn't too surprising," Julie said. "Lex Luger, Madusa, Hall, and Nash; it's been crazy."

"This is the hottest wrestling's been since '85. I mean, hell, they've even managed to make Hogan a draw again with that New World Order stuff, which I never thought I'd see." Burt held up his hand with the middle and ring finger touching his thumb, the NWO "Too Sweet" hand signal Hogan had popularized, then turned the menu over once more. "As for the food, well, I think I'll go out on a limb and try the biscuits and gravy."

"If wrestling's so fucking hot," Terry said without looking up from the menu, "then why are we sitting in a diner in the middle of nowhere at 2:00 a.m.? Why are you guys hitching a ride in *my* truck?"

"Everyone starts somewhere. Some of us just end up nowhere." Burt pointed at Terry as he said that, prompting a guffaw from Eric and Ricky. Eric felt a twinge of regret from laughing. He wasn't too much younger than Terry, and he didn't have any illusions about going further than where he was right now. But then again, Terry had never even made it to MAW champion. Eric wondered sometimes why Terry was still plugging away at it, but he could probably have asked the same question of himself. The truth was, even if the money was mostly shit and they had no hopes of climbing any higher, none of them could really give up that feeling you got when you had the crowd going for you. Whether they were booing or cheering, it was like a drug to know they were there to see you. It's why someone like Koko B. Ware was still wrestling in school gymnasiums. You couldn't get it out of your blood. And God Almighty, what else could any of them possibly do?

Eric watched Terry fuming over the joke about his career path, thinking he was on the way down as well. It was a choice for him, at least. Settling down, easing out, and hopefully spending time with his daughter. He'd called his ex-wife earlier in the day to confirm the tentative plans for Thanksgiving, but hadn't been able to get ahold of anyone.

Their conversation was interrupted by Mason's reappearance at the table. He moved real damn quiet, but Eric thought that maybe they were just being too raucous, especially for the time of night. Easy to miss someone when you're having a good time.

"Hey there, ya'll ready to order?"

"Yeah, yeah I think we are," Eric said. "I'm gonna go with a short stack, side of sausage, and over-easy eggs." Terry coughed loudly, and Eric glared at him. "Also, I'll have a *diet* soda, thank you."

"Oh, diet, very nice."

"Screw you, Terry." Eric glanced at Julie. "I don't like hot drinks, you know? Coffee, tea; never really been a fan."

"Yeah, I get it," she replied. "Mason, I'm gonna have a turkey club, no mayo, with a side salad."

"See, Eric? She knows how to keep that killer figure," Terry said. "They'll be snatching her up for the big time too; I'm sure of it."

"Oh, please don't," Ricky blurted out. "Women's wrestling in the United States is a dumpster fire. Neither WWF or WCW even *have* a women's championship. Madusa dumping her belt in the trash on Monday Nitro should tell you everything you need to know about women's wrestling in America."

"I know. I really don't want to be doing pudding matches or shit like that," Julie said. "I've been thinking of maybe wrestling in Mexico or Japan instead."

"Oh, hey, you guys are wrestlers? Hell, I thought you looked pretty big." Mason looked over them now with newfound respect. "I don't s'pose any of ya'll know Dusty Rhodes by chance?"

"Ah, no, sorry; none of us are quite that big," said Ricky, pushing his glasses up the bridge of his nose. "We're actually with Midwest American Wrestling."

"Oh, yeah, I know that one; I seen it sometimes on Channel 2. Gosh, I never had any celebrities in here b'fore!" He paused for a minute, building his courage. "Listen, can I get ya'll's autographs, here in this booklet?" He handed over his order book, flipped to a blank page. At first the wrestlers hemmed and hawed, but finally Julie took it.

"I don't see why not." The other wrestlers gave her a look, but Julie shrugged it off.

"He's a fan, and he's sweet. What's the problem?"

The other wrestlers grudgingly went along, quickly signing the booklet as it was passed around. As Burt Knox finished, a harsh voice came from the counter.

"Mason!" Les barked from his barstool. "They're hungry, and you've only taken half their orders. I reckon they ain't here for fun."

"Yup, yup; I'm sorry about that, guys. And gal. Sorry. Um, what would you like, fella? You look like you could eat everything we've got here."

Knox put down the menu and rubbed his hands eagerly. "Nah. I just want a ham-and-cheese omelet. With water."

"I'll have the BLT, with plenty of mayo," Ricky said.

"T-bone on the hoof, and flop two with it," Terry said. Mason raised his eyebrows.

"Hey now; we got a fellow fry cook here! Nice!" He finished writing down the orders and gave an extra nod to Terry. "I'll be right out with your food, guys." After he left, the rest of the table turned toward Terry.

"Yeah, I was a short-order cook in high school. So what?"

"On the hoof?" Julie asked.

"Rare. Don't ask me; I didn't make this shit up."

The front door swung open then, and a scraggly young man barreled in. He wore mechanics coveralls and a bright orange baseball cap spotted with oil stains. Like his counterpart at the counter, he looked as if he hadn't shaved in at least three days, though his hair was much shorter and hidden under his hat. Eric watched them out of the corner of his eye with curiosity, straining to hear.

"Hey, Les," the newcomer said as he sat down on the stool to Les's right. "How're things?"

"You're late," Les said, not looking up from his burger, which had only two bites left to it.

"Jesus, sorry. Ran into some trouble's all."

"Trouble?"

"Nuthin' serious. I took care of it. Jesse tells me when I get there—"

"That's enough," Les barked. The young man shut his mouth instantly. "We ain't gotta advertise our whole lives to the world, right?"

The younger man looked toward the wrestlers at that point, his eyes at first barely acknowledging them but then stopping on Julie.

"Hey now, wait a sec . . . ," he said. "I know you, right? You're uh, you're . . ."

"She's a wrestler!" Mason said as he came out from the back. Eric cringed at the cook's pronunciation of it as "wrassler."

"Really?" said the man. "Yeah, yeah, I do know you! You're Goth Girl!"

Les groaned. "Mason, they're still waiting, okay?" Mason nodded and retreated quietly as Les turned to his companion. "Mark, these people are just tryin' to get some food. They don't wanna be bothered."

"Oh yeah, I bet! They've got a big event comin' up on Sunday!" He paused, staring now at Eric. "Holy shit, that's Jiggolo!"

"Jiggolo?" Les asked. He sounded like he could barely hold back a laugh. Eric winced.

"Yeah, he was the champ, but that Black piece o' shit Brick beat him for it. But you're gonna get it back, right Jiggolo?"

"Uh, right," Eric said. He hated this part. You never knew who was aware of professional wrestling's scripted nature and who still thought they were really beating the piss out of each other every night. Eric had a feeling that Mark was the latter. "I'm gonna make him pay for taking my title."

"Well, I hope you do. Bad enough those guys are taking the other sports away from us. Football, basketball, baseball; it's all just Blacks now. We gotta keep something for ourselves, right?"

Eric nodded. He was pretty sure Mark wouldn't have the gumption to talk like that if Brick was here in all his 325-pound glory. Thankfully, Mason came through the kitchen door with Ricky and Julie's sandwiches.

"Hey there, I got the cold stuff done; just gonna be a few more minutes till the hot food's up." He set the plates down in front of Ricky and Julie, sidestepping around Mark.

"Mark, why don't you come sit back down, let those folk eat in peace?" Les asked.

"Wait, wait, Les; I just wanna get an autograph!" He snatched a napkin from the nearest table and pulled a chewed-up Bic pen from his front breast pocket.

"They already done for Mason," Les said. "I bet they fuckin' hate getting asked for that everywhere they go."

"No, no; it's okay," Julie said. "I don't mind signing for him. And I'm sure none of the boys do either, right?" The other wrestlers all shook their head. Eric, for his part, would be happy to give the kid what he wanted so they could be left alone.

They all took turns signing the napkin Mark had given them, and once that was done Mark grinned widely, showing off teeth that Eric thought needed some serious dental care.

"This is so awesome!" Mark cried. "I watch you guys every weekend."

"He does," Les said, turning to face them. "Loves you guys."

"We love seeing the fans," Ricky said. "I hope you guys have a great night."

"Wait a second," Mark said. "I have an idea." He turned towards Les. "Do you think you could take a picture of me with them?"

"If you got the camera, might as well," Les said. He started to get down from the stool. "We already done this much, right?"

"Uh, hold on for a second," Knox said. "An autograph, you know, that's one thing; but taking pictures and stuff, you know, that's something different."

"Different how?" Les asked.

"Well, we get paid for photo ops, for one thing," Ricky said.

"Yeah, and you get paid for autographs too, I thought."

"At the shows," Ricky replied. "We gave you guys free ones, to be nice. But this isn't a show, and we're in the middle of a long trip. We'd really just like to eat up and get going now."

"I don't understand why I can't just take a pic with ya'll. I've got a disposable Kodak in the van. Won't take no time at all." Mark's voice was plaintive, whiny. It was starting to grate on Eric.

"Tell ya what, kid. Come out to the show Sunday and we'll all take pictures with ya. Sound good?" Ricky, ever the salesman. Les sneered in response.

"Drive a few hours outta state, pay to see you, like we got endless money?" He turned back to Mark. "Come on, son, let's go. These people ain't got no love for their fans." He paused and turned back to look at Burt in the eye. "Even the one's don't know it's all fake."

Terry's face turned red at this, as did Knox's. Eric took a deep breath. If there was one thing wrestlers *hated*, it was being told what they did was fake. Just ask John Stossell.

"You know it ain't fake," Knox said.

"Come on, don't bullshit me." Les turned toward them once more, staring them down. "I watch enough with Mark to know that you ought to be spittin' mad just to be sittin' next to him," Les said, pointing at Terry. Knox had been feuding with Terry on TV for the past several weeks. "My nephew here just don't wanna hear it. But if you wanna prove me wrong, just let us take a damned picture."

Terry shook his head slowly.

"I'm not gonna take pictures with someone who calls what we do fake."

"It ain't for me, it's for the boy." Les looked at Julie. "He's especially excited about you. Maybe he'd be happy with just a picture of you."

"I, uh, I don't see why not," Julie said.

"Julie, you don't have to do that," Knox whispered to her.

"What does it hurt?" she replied. "I don't know about you, but I'd rather just give him a picture than potentially cause an incident with someone in the middle of nowhere."

"I'll get the camera!" Mark said excitedly, racing out the door.

"I wonder how much longer our food's gonna be," Eric mused.

Mark came running back in with a battered and torn Kodak disposable. "Here we go," he said breathlessly, thrusting the camera toward Les.

"Perfect," Les said. "Get on over there with him, sweetheart, and we'll wrap this up." Julie stepped toward Mark gingerly, putting on her most charming smile and draping an arm very lightly over his shoulders. Les raised the camera up, counting down from three. As he reached "one," Mark's hand suddenly slipped around Julie's midsection and landed very prominently on her right breast. The flash went off as Julie's face morphed from a smile to an open-mouthed grimace. She swatted Mark's hand away like it was the world's greasiest wasp.

"What the fuck was that?" she cried. Eric was stunned. He'd never seen her swear like that before. Les was laughing too hard to respond at first, but he finally managed to.

"Relax darling; Mark's just a teenage boy havin' fun. No harm done, right?"

"No harm done?" she replied. "He just grabbed my tit!"

"Well, honestly, ya ain't got much of 'em to grab. Don't know why you're so upset about it." Eric watched the color rise in Julie's cheeks, the shame cloud her eyes, and he felt a slug of white-hot rage dig into his guts. He'd seen men leer at her before; he'd even seen a couple of handsy fans squeeze her ass and one time even try to force a kiss on her. But he'd never seen Julie react this way, with such rage and humiliation. It lit a fire inside Eric that he'd rarely experienced before, a protective push that overran his normal judgment in a moment of what he later tried to believe was noble concern.

"Give me the camera," he said. Les gawked at him.

"Are you fuckin' with me? There is no way in hell that I'm giving you my camera." He moved to pocket it, struggling to make it fit. Eric didn't even think; he just moved, reaching forward and grabbing Les by the wrist.

He knew immediately he'd made a mistake.

Eric had put a lot of people in wrist holds over the years. Some, like Terry's, were hard, knobby wrists and you could feel the tension within them. Others, most others, had give to them, like a thin oak branch, pliant and malleable.

Les's wrist, however, was corded steel. Eric had never grabbed someone with such strength in his life. He hadn't paid much attention to the man when he came in, but that was a mistake. The bare arms rippled with muscle as Les flexed them. He sneered, yanking his arm back and throwing Eric off balance. With his other hand, he shoved Eric the rest of the way over, smacking his face onto the table and sending him sprawling onto the grimy linoleum.

From the floor, Eric saw Ricky move in next, seizing the camera itself in an attempt to wrench it free. Les tugged it back and forth a few times before rearing back and slapping Ricky full across the face. Ricky staggered backward, his glasses askew. Les looked like he was about to step forward and follow up on that slap, but Knox seized him at that point, spinning him around by the shoulder.

Knox stood a good five or six inches over Les, but Eric knew that wouldn't deter the man in the slightest. This was getting out of hand very, very fast. Terry was up and moving as well now, coming up on Les from behind. Eric didn't see any way this would end well, no matter who won the fight.

Everyone was so focused on Les that none of them had noticed Mark. The fight happened fast enough that no one had any time to think, only to react. Mark reacted too. He seized the glass coffeepot on the table and, with an inhuman screech, swung it as hard as he could into the back of Knox's head.

Eric had seen various glass objects shattered over a wrestler more times than he could count. Sugar glass, it was called. Looked impressive when it smashed into a million pieces on impact, but you barely felt it hit you.

He'd never seen someone use real glass before.

It didn't shatter, like most might expect. It cracked into large jagged pieces as it struck Knox in the base of the skull. The flow of blood was almost immediate. Incredibly, Knox managed to stay upright, his eyes glazed with dull surprise. Hot coffee soaked his shirt, and Eric was sure that it must burn like hell itself. Within seconds his blue polo was saturated with blood as it poured out of his head and down his back. Mark backed away slowly, dropping the remnants of the pot. Coffee and blood mixed as they traveled down his face.

Finally, Knox fell in complete silence, slamming his head against the counter on the way down. He lay in a heap on the floor, not moving.

"Burt!" Ricky bellowed. He wrenched away from Les's grip and rushed to Knox's side, falling to his knees as he cradled the large man's head. "Hey now, look at me, okay? It's gonna be just fine, you hear? We're gonna get an ambulance out here and get to a hospital right away, okay?" Knox made no reply, save for the trembling that was overtaking all his limbs. Les stared at the situation, glared back at Mark, and immediately made for the door. No one tried to stop him.

"You piece of shit!" Terry yelled, pushing Mark over the table. He landed hard on his ass, staring up at Terry with bewilderment.

"No, no, that ain't right," Mark said. "It don't work like that; I seen it done. He's taken harder hits than that an' been fine! He's fine!"

"That's not real glass we use, idiot!" Eric grabbed Mark by the neck as he lay prone on the floor. "They're props!" Terry stepped forward as well, fists raised. "Terry, back off!" Eric said. "What I need you to do is get to a phone and call 9-1-1, got it?"

"No one's doing anything like that at all," said a voice from the door. It was calm, authoritative, and cold. Les was standing in the doorway. He held the largest pistol Eric had ever seen and was aiming it straight at him. "Come on, Jiggolo; let Mark go and back up slowly. You too, tough guy." Terry glared at Les. "You're close to losin' those eyes. Only reason I haven't shot yet is 'cause Mark watches you every damned Sunday. I want all of you against the wall, right now. Especially you," he finished with a nod toward Julie.

Ricky didn't move. He had taken off his own shirt to use as a pillow and compress for Knox. It was saturated with gore, but the pressure would hopefully keep the blood loss from getting any worse. He'd extracted a ragged shard of glass from Knox's skull, which now lay at his side.

"He needs an ambulance," Ricky said. Eric sympathized, but he knew what Les would say.

"He'll get what I decide he gets," Les said. He looked at Mark. "I need you to get the zip ties from the van." Mark scrambled to his feet and ran out the door.

"What are you trying to do?" Julie asked.

"Well, honey, you and your friends have put me in a hell of a spot. Couldn't just leave the camera be, could you? No, you had to push it."

"If you don't get Burt to a doctor, he's going to die," Ricky said. His eyes were wet with tears. He'd had to take off his blood-stained glasses.

"Shorty, I think he's probably gonna die no matter what. I've seen men hit like that before, and it ain't lookin' good for him." Next to Eric, Julie made an involuntary retching sound. Les turned toward her. "You're gonna want to control that, sweetcakes. I don't like the smell of upchuck." Mark came back inside with the zip ties. Eric felt his guts knot as Les nodded toward Mark.

He'd just wanted some fucking pancakes.

"Everyone just stay calm," Les said. He sounded like his mind was half a mile away from here. Les kept his focus on Mark. "Take those zip ties and tie our new friends here together, wrist to wrist. You understand?" Mark nodded. He appeared dazed, but followed Les's orders without hesitation. He approached Eric slowly, pulling a long plastic zip tie out of the bundle in his pocket. "I don't want none of ya giving Mark a hard time. I ain't afraid to blow you're fuckin' heads off one by one if I don't like how you're acting." Eric held up his left wrist, around which Mark cinched the first zip tie hard enough to pinch Eric's skin. He tried not to wince; he didn't want to give Mark the satisfaction.

Next, Mark cinched one around Terry's wrist and connected Eric to him with a tie looped through each of their wrists. He did the same for Julie, then motioned for Ricky to come over. Ricky shook his head defiantly.

"It's not a choice," Mark said. "You get on over here, or we'll drag you ourselves."

"Mark," Les said. "Get over here for a minute." He pointed at the shirt wedged under Knox's head as he pulled a flattened roll of duct tape from one of his pockets. "Wrap that shirt around his head with this." He looked back at Ricky. "Your friend's best bet is that you do what we say, and we'll take care of him. You got it? Otherwise, we'll just let him bleed out on the floor. He's close enough already." He motioned with the gun toward the other wrestlers. Behind him, Mark was gingerly wrapping the duct tape around Knox's head, avoiding the eyes, nose, and mouth as best he could. Ricky slowly stood up and joined the others against the wall.

"Tighter," Les barked. "It won't do any damned good if it's too loose." He looked over at Ricky. "Wouldn't want him to die right here."

Once Mark was done with Knox, he approached Ricky. Taking his wrist, Mark tied him to Julie, and then led him around to Eric and tied them together as well, forming a circle.

"It seems like you've done this before," Eric said as Mark looped the last tie between him and Ricky.

Mark only grunted.

When Ricky was attended to, Les backed up to survey the scene in the diner. Mark had already flipped the sign in the diner to "Closed" from "Open" and shut all the blinds. He approached Les, speaking with him urgently.

"I'm sorry, Uncle Les. I didn't mean for this to happen."

"Yeah, well, your impulse control is total shit. You know what we have to do."

"I don't want to kill 'em all, Les."

Les stared at Mark, his hard features softening under the young man's plaintive gaze. "You're young. You haven't done hard time. These people have seen us, they know our names, and there ain't no way around that."

"If that's true, then why are we takin' 'em out of here? Why do that at all?"

"Think, son! You wanna carry five bodies into the car? You wanna clean up this diner more than we already have to? Wanna risk leaving even more evidence here? No, we finish them at the farm." He looked back at the door to the kitchen. "Now, I'll go in the back and tell Mason to take off early. He ain't seen any of this, and if it stays that way, we don't have to do anything to him."

"What?" Mark raised his voice, and Les clamped a hand on his arm to calm him down.

"It don't matter how long he's been your friend. He'll talk if anyone asks. At some point, probably soon, someone's gonna look for those guys. The less Mason knows, the better. Otherwise . . ."

"All right," Mark said with irritation. "I get it."

"I'll let him know I'll talk to Bud. He won't get in no trouble on that end." Les pushed past mark, gun steadily pointed at the wrestlers. Ricky's eyes fixed on Knox while the rest stared fearfully at Les.

"This is what we're gonna do now." Les's voice broke through the silence in the diner like a gunshot. "Mark, you drive their Excursion back to the farm behind me in the van." He looked at Eric and the others, eyes narrowed, contemplating. "You four are gonna ride along with me. We'll load your friend into the back of your truck. More comfortable for him, though I don't think he's gonna notice."

"Wait!" Ricky demanded. "He needs to get to a hospital!"

"Not one more word, or all ya'll's gonna die right now. I ain't gonna tell ya again." He turned back toward Mark. "Get the place straightened up, son. I'm gonna have you come back later to finish too. Mopping, bleach, the whole deal." Mark scowled but went to work setting the tables and chairs back in place. Les picked up his burger and finished the last two bites.

"Damn, this got cold real fast. Still good though." He looked over at the wrestlers. "You guys had to fuck up my dinner too. Thanks for that." He went into the back. Mark had just finished with the last chair by the time Les came back. Les motioned toward Terry. "Get the keys to that truck out of his pockets," he said to Mark. Mark gave a warning look to Terry, then bent down to get the keys.

Eric watched carefully as Mark rifled through Terry's front pockets, pulling the keychain out. There were several keys on it, connected with a "Ford" logo on the ring. Mark held up the Excursion key as he looked Terry over.

"Yeah, you look like the Ford type," Mark said. "Fuckin' Ford. They ain't never made nothin' worth shit." Terry's lips tightened, but Eric was relieved when he stayed quiet.

"That's enough," Les said.

"What's the matter?" Mark asked. His petulance, the whiny questioning of a teenager, was starting to really grate on Eric.

"No reason to be talkin' to anyone. Especially not the guy what already gave you that bruising."

Mark's skin was already purpling where Terry had decked him, which was no surprise to Eric. Terry was the hardest man Eric had ever met. The very definition of what it meant for a wrestler to be hard. Terry wrestled stiff with anyone he worked with, barely pulling his punches. Eric hated having to work matches with him, but at least Terry liked his opponent to work stiff too. He wanted to have welts on his skin and blood in his hair. He wanted those slams to shake the ring. He was dedicated to making everything look real. And God help anyone who complained about it to him.

Eric knew Terry could handle the kid. It was the older one, Les, that gave him pause. Eric thought of the iron bar Les's arm had become when he grabbed it, the ease with which Les had slammed Eric to the floor. It had been a long time since anyone had manhandled him the way Les had. Eric doubted Terry would have fared better.

Les motioned toward the front door with his gun. "Okay, let's get you guys into the van." When no one moved, he stepped forward and pointed the barrel at Julie. "Let me make something clear: I am the boss, okay? You will do what I say, when I say, without questions." Ricky, Eric, and Terry all nodded. Eric thought Julie might scream with a gun in her face, but she stood resolved and firm, fixing Les with a steely gaze.

Eric imagined breaking free of the zip ties, taking both Les and Mark down at once, overpowering them with the sort of ease one might expect from a legitimately trained fighter. Of course Eric hadn't been trained for real martial arts, but he'd always been tough. He could work stiff; he could take a potato as well as he could throw one.

The problem was, Terry was right when he said Eric could be in much better shape. He was on the wrong end of his thirties and hadn't felt comfortable wrestling in just his briefs for at least ten years now. He liked to joke that he was the poor man's Mick Foley, but he didn't have a missing ear and a dozen other injuries to lean on as a crutch. Eric hadn't ever broken anything, not even a finger. He wondered if that was the difference between him and someone like Terry. A heavy-handed shove brought reality back into focus. "Move." Les pushed open the door with his boot. They shuffled awkwardly as they were herded outside.

It was dark. Sunrise was still several hours away. The faint glow of the streetlights barely illuminated the parking lot. Eric could see the outline of Terry's SUV and the van parked next to it as well. Eric watched as Mark held up Terry's keys and fumbled to unlock the back doors. He swung them open, paying no attention as one of the suitcases, Eric's suitcase, tumbled to the asphalt.

Mark reclined the back seats enough to accommodate Burt's near-lifeless body. Their suitcases were haphazardly piled in the front seat to accommodate this. Eric felt a heavy thud of finality as he watched the careless way they were being handled. This was not a good sign.

Les opened up the rear doors to his Econoline van. Inside, it was all cargo space with a metal barrier between the front seats and the back. There weren't even any windows. Eric saw at least five propane tanks in the back, most with an unusual blue coloration to the fittings. Rubber tubing, painter's masks, and bedsheets littered the area around it. Les climbed into the van first, swearing under his breath. He gathered the loose items together with the tanks at the front of the van, covering all of it with a bedsheet that had red stains on it.

Eric shuddered. Were those bloodstains?

He saw Julie looking at them too and started to say something, but she shook her head at him and looked away from the sheets.

Eric understood, but he couldn't stop looking. Everything felt somehow like a dream, almost like it was too real. This can't be happening, he thought, absolutely not. You read about this happening to someone else, or you watched it on TV. It's not real life.

He snapped out of it as Julie nudged him, indicating with her head that he needed to climb into the van now.

They settled down uncomfortably in a circle, trying to adjust for their bound wrists. The doors were closed behind them, and Eric heard the click of a padlock being latched onto the outer handles.

"Gun or not, we gotta try to take this guy out soon as he gets into the car," Terry whispered. "He's not gonna let any of us leave here alive." Then he looked over his shoulder, evaluating how easily he could vault over the piled-up debris and gain access to the driver's seat.

"He's expecting us to do something like that," Ricky said. His glasses sat crooked across his nose and sweat dotted his sinewy upper body. Eric had never seen Ricky without a shirt and had no idea he had any kind of physique to speak of. "He's a criminal, clearly. He'll shoot all of us dead before we get through that wall." Ricky couldn't help but sneer as he eyed Terry. "I don't care how hard you are, a bullet will rip through you same as anyone else. And he'll probably shoot you first."

"I'm surprised you aren't egging me on to do it, then. I know you never liked me much."

"Whether I do or not doesn't mean I want to see you get your head blown off. If we do get a chance to run, all of us need to work together."

"Ricky's right," Julie said. "We have to be careful, and we have to be on the same page."

The driver side door opened and Les hopped in, eyeing them with caution. "We're headin' out now. Ya'll stay quiet; don't do anything stupid." He made a show of passing the gun from his left hand to the right, resting his arm on the windowsill. "Yeah, jus' keep everything nice and calm."

He started the van, and as it rumbled away from the diner, Eric could feel his stomach gurgling. No food, no sleep, and he doubted he'd ever get a chance to enjoy either again. He lowered his chin to his chest and did something he hadn't done since grade school. He began to pray.

3

Bud's Diner
2:45 a.m.

As Les left the kitchen and headed back out with the wrestlers, Mason wondered, not for the first time that night, what was going on. Mason already had the dishwasher going when Les came in the back unexpectedly. He'd pulled off Mason's headphones, giving him a hell of a surprise. Bud would have complained about Mason listening to his Discman while he cooked, but Les didn't care. He did seem to care, though, when Mason cut his finger on the knife he'd been using to prepare the rest of the food..

"You're bleeding all over," Les said. Mason expected Les to be furious, but he seemed thoughtful instead, almost pleased.

"It ain't nothin', Les. I'll just wrap it up and keep goin'."

"No, no," Les countered. "Those are big-time TV stars out there, Mason. They aren't gonna want to see some backwater kid bleeding all over their food, for Christ's sake." Les shook his head. "No, just head home. Clean it out with alcohol. But go out the back. I don't want those guys to see you had to leave."

Truthfully, Mason didn't mind getting a chance to go home. He'd been working extra hard to keep things in top condition for Marcy in the morning, with perfectly cleaned counters and fresh dishes. Anything to take some stress off her. But he was ticked about not getting to see the wrestlers again before he left, and said so.

"Look, you already got their autographs. Just go on home. I'll finish cookin' the food then close up when the others leave. I'll let Bud know what happened so you don't get in any trouble."

Mason wanted more than anything to stay and spend more time with the wrestlers, but he knew that when Les made up his mind about something, that was that. Arguing would only piss Les off. He considered saying goodbye to Mark but decided against it. Les was pretty clear about staying out of the dining room. It still felt weird not to see Mark at least before leaving, though.

At one time, Mark and Mason had been joined at the hip, to the point that people in high school often joked they were a couple. At least they joked about it till Mark heard; then someone ended up with stitches. Mason never cared as much; he was always more easygoing than his best friend. In fact, Mason couldn't recall a time he'd ever actually thrown a punch.

The whole evening had been strange ever since those wrestlers had come in. Les hadn't been in a pleasant mood earlier, but he'd turned downright ornery as soon as they'd sat down. Mason wasn't ever quick to anger, but Les's barking had irked him something fierce. It wasn't like Les was the boss of this diner, though he sure did act like it sometimes. Mason wondered why Bud tolerated the way Les acted. Like tonight, for instance. Shutting down the whole diner. So they got to hang with the wrestlers and he had to go home. It wasn't fair.

Mason had felt nervous when Les suggested closing up the diner for the night. Bud wasn't gonna like that. The diner was always open, even on Christmas, Thanksgiving, and Easter. It didn't make any sense to Mason that Bud would be okay with this just 'cause Les said so. Sure, Les had been friends with Bud since they were kids, and Bud bought all his pork products from Les to boot, but that shouldn't give Les any say over whether the diner was staying open for the night. Mason was also sore that he wouldn't see Marcy on his way out for the day.

As far as Mason was concerned, Marcy was the hottest gal in Chimney Corner. He reckoned she was about fifteen years older than him, but that didn't matter none to Mason. A good-looking woman was still a good-looking woman, no matter how old she was. Mark always teased Mason about his inability to just make a move on her, but Mason couldn't imagine she'd be interested in him when she probably had the entire town to choose from. Chimney Corner was pretty damned small, but even here, Mason wasn't at the top of any woman's list.

Mason had nothing else to do before heading home. He made his way out the back entrance, where his car was parked under a dim streetlight. The car had been his mother's, much like almost everything else Mason owned, a pale blue 1986 Chevy Impala. He actually preferred the hard edges of the late '80s model to the softer curves of the newest Impalas, but he would have loved some of the automatic features they came with. He was tired of having to lean across the football-field length of the front bench seat every time he wanted to roll down the passenger-side window.

You never saw much of anything brand new in Chimney Corner, so Mason didn't feel any shame in driving around in a car more than a decade old. He'd seen Les driving a newer Firebird around town, but tonight for some reason, he and Mark were going around in that dumpy old van of theirs. He glanced at it as he drove past, wondering what they were doing inside with the wrestlers. They hadn't left yet, even though the shades were drawn and the sign in the door now read "Closed." Mason felt a twinge of jealousy, picturing everyone having a good time together in there without him.

Since Les had come back into the picture, Mark's friendship with Mason had suffered. Mark had more money than ever, but no time anymore for them to hang out. He was sure Les was something of a hard-ass to work for, especially since, at one point, the farm had been going so bad that Mark said they were fixing to close it. But that all changed once Les got there.

Maybe Les knew more about hog farming than anyone else out there. It would make sense, Mason supposed. Mark's father, Norm, had only married into the business. Probably Les wasn't keen on letting the family farm go to pot. The Goodes had been an institution in Chimney Corner for as long as Mason knew. Les was the last Goode left, and Mason guessed he was pretty protective of everything that went with that name.

The Impala turned over hard as usual, sounding like it could barely get up the energy to start. Mason knew the alternator was going bad; the transmission probably would need a complete overhaul before too long as well. Mason sighed with worry, not sure how he'd ever get enough money for a new transmission. He could take it to Mark's brother, Nathan, he knew, but . . .

Mason had been best friends with Mark since grade school, but Nathan was a different story. Nathan was older, sure, but he was also just plain scary. He was different in a way that made people nervous. Mason's mother used to insist that he have Nate do the repairs on the Impala because he was cheap, but Mason never felt good about using him. And after what happened to Mark's mother, Mason had put his foot down for the first time and told his mother no, he wasn't gonna let Nate work on their car anymore.

The drive back to his mother's house was quiet as always. Mason saw absolutely zero cars on the road, which was the norm for Chimney

Corner before sunrise. His mother's house was a simple home set back from the road about a hundred feet. It had three bedrooms, but Mason rarely used anything but the common areas and his own childhood bedroom. His mother had passed on three years ago now, but Mason still couldn't bring himself to move into the master bedroom. Hell, he couldn't even stop thinking of the place as his mom's house. He missed his mother something fierce, and he couldn't bear to erase any part of her that was left.

He sat down in the living room, sinking comfortably into his prized La-Z-Boy recliner. He spent nearly as many nights sleeping in it as he did his bed. He turned on the TV, which was already tuned to MTV. This late at night, it was mostly reruns of *The Maxx* cartoon. He watched it disinterestedly, contemplating how to spend the rest of his evening.

Mason glanced at the old rotary phone sitting on the end table by the sofa. He noticed Dante's card next to the phone and made a mental note to throw it out when he got up. He'd gotten the man's number from Mark about a year ago. Mark's idea had originally been to boost Mason's confidence with women, to break him in and give him some experience, but Mason hadn't lasted long enough for the woman to get all her clothes off. It was humiliating. After that, he'd decided, never again. And it was just as well; money was too tight. Especially now—he'd need every cent to fix the car.

He could go to Ansted. There were a couple of all-night bars out there, and he knew the bartender at Chelsea's at least. But with the car having trouble, he didn't want to risk driving any farther than he needed to. He heard a faint scratching to his right and looked over to see Scrappy, the little stray cat he'd befriended, coming in through an open window. It paced back and forth, mewing loudly, and Mason ran to get a can of tuna from the pantry and set it down. He stroked Scrappy's tangled fur as it ate, listening to the loud purr that vibrated through its rib cage. "Yeah, it's good to be home early," Mason told the cat.

After a few minutes, Scrappy was done and hopped onto the couch. It was their normal routine to snuggle up like this, and Mason was only too happy to lay down on the couch next to Scrappy. The cat kneaded at the cushion by his head, something his mom called "makin' biscuits," then laid down for the night. Mason petted the cat gently.

He'd get some sleep and then make his way back to Bud's for lunch. Marcy would be there, waiting the tables, and he could plunk himself down at the bar and kill a couple of hours drinking coffee and eating a ham steak. It was better than nothing, and maybe this time he'd even have the balls to see what Marcy was doing after her shift ended. He laid his head down and closed his eyes, thinking of Marcy's smile as the lights of *The Maxx* flickered across his darkened living room. In a few minutes he was snoring softly, oblivious to the outside world.

4

Goode Farm, West Virginia
3:07 a.m.

Eric didn't know how long they'd been driving. It could have been twenty minutes or two hours. His perception of time was hopelessly skewed, with each second seeming to either drag on forever or zip by at sickening speed. When the van turned onto what felt like the world's most potholed dirt road, Eric had to put his head between his knees to keep from being sick.

He lifted his head long enough to watch the van pass a dilapidated house that would have fit right into the *Texas Chainsaw Massacre*. Dim lights illuminated some of the windows downstairs, but otherwise the place was a two-story wall of darkness outlined by the moonlight. The van rolled past this house and slowed in front of a building that Eric couldn't get a clear view of.

Les brought the van to a stop, and the interior was briefly illuminated as Terry's SUV, driven by Mark, pulled up alongside them. Les opened the door and slid out in one fluid movement, too fast for any of them to even consider taking advantage. He closed the door, but Eric could hear some of what Les was saying.

"Go on; get Nate and have him help ya put this one in the closet in the back room. Lay him down gentle, ya hear? Once you got that done, come round and help me bring the rest of these fuckers in too." Eric heard the gravel under Mark's feet as he hustled away.

Eric hadn't realized how uneasy the silence made him until he heard the sounds of movement outside. Julie held her breath as the doors of the SUV next to them were opened.

"What the hell is all this?" they heard someone ask.

"What's it look like?" Mark replied.

"This is what you woke me up in the middle of the night for? Clean this up yourself."

"Aw hell; you know I can't pick him up myself. 'Sides, Les is the one askin', not me."

"All right, but this is all I'm doing. You're on your own after that." The two men stopped talking. All Eric and the others heard were the grunts of exertion, footsteps on the gravel, then silence again.

Eric looked at Ricky, who was examining the stained white sheets.

"This isn't blood," Ricky whispered to Eric as he rubbed the stain between his fingers. "I don't know what it is. I don't think its food, either."

"There's some weird shit these guys are up to."

"Does anyone see anything sharp?" Julie asked in hushed tones. "Anything that maybe we can cut these ties with?"

"No. It's all just, well, junk really. I don't know what any of this stuff is being used for."

"You know," Terry said, "I saw this guy on TV once, he said if you ever get cuffed with these zip ties, you can break them over your knee."

"I don't think it would work with how they have our wrists tied together," Eric said. Terry scowled.

"Just trying to think of something, anything. I fuckin' hate sitting here waiting."

"I don't think we'll be waiting much longer," Julie said. "I just heard the door of that trailer open again." She was right. In a moment Les opened up the back of the van, letting in a cool blast of October air. Shock had kept Eric from noticing how warm and stuffy the van was.

"All right," Les said. "I want all of you to ease out. You're gonna follow Mark into our little guest home here." He motioned toward the trailer home with a nod. "Now, don't be gettin' any brave ideas in your head. We're about as far from other people as you can get in this state. I could empty three whole clips into you without anyone else noticing."

Julie was the first to move, sliding out awkwardly as her bound wrists threw her off balance. Eric and the rest followed suit, careful not to pull each other over. He saw an open field fenced in by thick woods. Eric was no stranger to mobile homes. The van was parked in front of a model very similar to the Fleetwood double-wide he'd shared with his wife and child not so long ago. He looked out past the trailer home and saw another structure. This one was a cargo container. Eric couldn't make out many details in the darkness, but he did notice what looked like an air-conditioning unit sitting on top of it.

They walked carefully up the stairs to the front door, which Mark was holding open. Les followed behind them. As they got to the threshold, Eric choked out a cough. It stank of trash, cigarettes, and sour laundry. The front door led to an entry room with two threadbare gray couches and a TV/VCR combo sitting on an ancient scuffed coffee table. Cassettes with pornographic images were scattered on the table around the TV. On the other side of the double-wide split was a kitchen. The yellowed linoleum peeled up in areas where chairs had torn holes in it. A rusted card table with four folding chairs was set up in the dining area. Several rolls of paper towels sat on the table. A refrigerator was pulled out halfway from its nook, the door hanging open.

Les motioned them down the narrow hallway toward a bedroom door. It was already open. Inside, the room was completely empty. A bare bulb burned in the light socket of a ceiling fan that was missing all of its blades. Eric saw Burt laid down in the closet, a large walk-in space with no shelving. Burt's bandages were still in place, but Ricky's shirt had more red on it than white at this point. The heavy bleeding may have stopped, but Eric thought Burt would definitely need a blood donor, if he even made it that far.

Les stepped into the room, gun out and pointing at them. Mark followed him. It was still just the two of them, but Eric knew there was at least another one. Probably a lot more than just one.

"Your friend is comfortable, for now," Les said. With his free hand, he pulled a seven-inch serrated blade out of the holster on his belt. He handed the knife to Mark, who quickly cut through the zip tie around Ricky's wrist. Ricky stared at Mark, wild-eyed, unsure of what was happening, and Eric saw him clench as if readying to strike.

"Calm down, tiny. Don't try anything. Just get over there and take care of your friend. Don't let him die on ya." Ricky moved toward Knox without taking his eyes off Les, crouching down next to Knox and putting a hand on his shoulder. Les turned to look at the rest of the wrestlers. "All of ya, take a seat on the floor." Les brought the muzzle of his gun up to the door and tapped it. A hollow clang sounded from it. "Ya'll ain't gonna break down this door, I promise you that. And if somehow you do, I'll shoot you fuckin' dead." He pointed toward the window on the back wall. "Those windows are boarded up tight too. Even if you could bust them open, we're the only one's who'll hear you. So I suggest you focus on taking care of your friend there."

"You're just going to kill us, aren't you?" Eric asked.

"Right now no one's dead. Focus on that." Les stepped out of the door and closed it behind him with a clang like a death knell.

Les secured the door from the outside with three padlocks and a deadbolt and then handed the gun, a Desert Eagle, to Mark.

"What are you giving this to me for?" Mark asked.

"You think I'm leavin' them alone in my house? You're gonna wait here while I go clean the diner. If anyone tries to get out, fucking shoot them."

"Wait, I thought *I* was cleaning the diner?"

"Changed my mind. I'd rather it not get fucked up."

"What the hell am I supposed to do? Just sit on my ass for the next five hours?"

"Read a book, watch porn; I don't give a shit. You got us into this, Mark, so you're gonna watch 'em for now."

"I dunno why we don't just shoot 'em all now." He scowled and looked toward the door. Les smacked him in the back of the head.

"I don't trust you to do the cleanup and everything else without me. When I get back, I'll decide what to do with them. Till then, just sit tight."

The door opened again, and Mark's father, Norm, walked in. He looked from Les to Mark and then the locked door. His scowl deepened at the sight.

In the time since Les had gotten out of Mount Olive, Norm's already precarious physical condition had deteriorated markedly. While Les had been motivated to whip himself back into shape, Norm had gone the opposite direction—fat, pasty, and constantly reeking of sour sweat. Les could barely stand to be in the same room as Norm these days.

"What the fuck is going on in here?" Norm growled. It was a lot harder to understand him these days—he had quite a few more teeth missing than just his incisor now. It was easier to follow along if you watched his mouth, but whenever Les saw Norm's lips wriggling around those black and yellow stragglers he called teeth, Les felt like getting out his toothbrush.

"Just a problem," Les said. "Not really one you need to be involved in."

"Like fuckin' hell. It's in my house, with my kid. I want to know what's going on."

Les sighed as he considered how to answer. It *was* Norm's house now. Louanne's death saw to that. Mama Goode wrote Les out of the will the day he was carted off to Mount Olive.

"There was a fight at the diner. Group of wrestlers. One of 'em's hurt pretty bad."

"Who hurt him?"

"I did," Mark said. He raised he chin defiantly.

"You?" Norm asked. He sneered. "Didn't think you had it in ya." He turned back to Les. "Why'd you bring 'em here, then?"

Les rolled his eyes. "I'm only doing all'a this 'cause you asked me to. I ain't excited about going back to Mount Olive." He glanced at Mark. "I don't wanna see him end up there, either." He turned back to Norm. "But that's what would happen if we just left everything at the diner. How long do you think it'd take for the cops to sort out what we got goin' on with Bud? Even the dumbass ones at Chimney Corner PD." He stared at Norm, who replied with an exaggerated shrug.

"So, get rid of 'em. It ain't like you don't know what to do."

"These aren't some Black dealers," Les said. "They're in Midwest American Wrestling. Someone will notice they're gone. Someone's gonna come looking, probably soon."

"Well, shit," Norm said. "So what you wanna do?"

"I'm still trying to work that out."

"Have you talked to Bud yet?

"No, but I'll call him as soon as the sun's up."

"Who else was there?"

"Just Mason."

"Fuckin' Mason." Norm shook his head. "How much does he know?"

"He don't know shit!" Mark said. "Les made sure of that."

"He knows they were at the diner, but that's all," Les said. Norm frowned.

"That's a lot more than nothing," he said. He pointed a finger at Mark. "Your buddy is a halfwit. He ain't gonna hold up if anyone asks him something."

Mark turned on Les. "You told me he'd be fine! Tell my dad, you tell him what you told me. We don't gotta do nothin' to Mason."

"We'll see," Les said. He put a hand on Mark's shoulder. "Just stay here for now. Your pa and I are gonna do some talkin' back in the farmhouse."

"What is there to talk about?" Norm said. "Seems pretty fucking open and shut to me." Les turned on him then, approaching fast. Norm backed up in surprise, almost tripping as he bumped into the wall. Les was glad to see that he could still put some fear in Norm—at least as long as Nate wasn't around.

"We talk alone," Les said in a low, agitated whisper. "He's your son, for Christ's sake. Try to be a little gentle when you're talking about killing his goddamn best friend, huh?"

"Fine," Norm said, trying to hold on to his composure. "Let's go to the farmhouse." He turned back to Mark. "Like Les said; you wait here, keep an eye on them." He walked out the door with a pseudo-strut, trying to regain the composure he'd come inside with. Les followed him, giving Mark one last nod of the head before closing the door.

Alone now, Mark sat heavily on the couch and stared at the gun in his hand, wondering how much longer it would be before he'd have to use it on someone.

5

Richmond, Virginia
9:00 a.m.

Jack Mayer was not particularly pleased as he waited outside the small community gym he'd rented out for tomorrow night's big event. He expected every member of MAW to pitch in with setting up the ring for the event. He wanted to walk through every match, rehearse every promo, before they performed in front of what would be their largest audience yet.

MAW was starting to get noticed by more than just the local wrestling fanatics. Jack had read in all the news zines that agents from both WWF *and* WCW were expected to be here. Normally Jack didn't like the idea of the Big Two coming to poach his wrestlers. He could spend hours complaining about how both Vince McMahon and Ted Turner didn't really know anything about wrestling, what it was *supposed* to be about. They'd rather trip over themselves trying to find the next Hulk Hogan before the original model was completely run into the ground.

But this time was different. He'd heard the rumors. He knew which way the wind was blowing. Paul Heyman over at Extreme Championship Wrestling had started a reaction. After a decade of dominance, it wasn't just going to be the Big Two anymore. McMahon was already using ECW as a training ground for some of his guys, but Jack knew he wanted something more than that. He'd heard McMahon and Turner both wanted to buy up old National Wrestling Alliance brands to use as training pipelines, just like the majors and minors in baseball. Jack had high hopes that MAW might fit the bill.

Which is why he was so pissed off that Terry's group hadn't even checked into the hotel last night. He'd been on the phone with the half-wit desk manager for twenty minutes trying to figure out if they'd checked in or not. All he'd gotten out of her was that their rooms were still available and that they'd called late last night to say they'd be running late.

"Fig!" he barked at a large wrestler standing by the entrance to the gym. "Where the fuck is Eric, eh?"

Donnie Figueroa lowered his gaze to Jack and shrugged. "No idea. Thought I'd see him at breakfast. Maybe he got delayed in that accident on I-64."

"Nah, I don't think so," John Coors said from behind Jack. Coors was the second-best Black wrestler in MAW. Of course, being second-best also made him last. "I was stuck in that accident myself. They got it cleared up pretty quick."

"Maybe they had an accident themselves?" Fig asked. "I mean, Terry's a pretty aggressive driver at the best of times."

"Well, they definitely got off the highway at some point," Jack said. "The manager at the hotel says they called last night to say they were running behind. I'm gonna see if I can get Ricky on his cell." Jack went to his truck to get the Motorola. He rarely used it, hated to use it in fact, but desperate times and all that. Ricky was one of the few guys in MAW who carried a cell phone, and he constantly yammered on about how essential they were for people on the road. That it was important to always be able to stay in touch. Just in case.

Just like now.

He scrolled to Ricky's number and pressed "Send." He waited with the phone held to his ear for what felt like an eternity. He pulled the phone away and saw it was still trying to dial Ricky. Jack had a strong signal in Richmond, so that must mean wherever Ricky was, he wasn't getting any service. It seemed ridiculous to Jack to have a cell phone if it wouldn't work in the remote places where you would most need one.

The call eventually failed and Jack threw the phone to the ground. "Piece of shit," he muttered. He grudgingly picked it back up and went to his truck. The map for the Virginia / West Virginia / Kentucky area was already unfolded in his passenger seat. He'd highlighted the best route to take from Lexington to Richmond and had expected everyone to follow it. Of course, Terry would take any excuse to deviate. He loved to demonstrate his knowledge of back roads and shortcuts. Always wanted to show off how much he knew. He had a chip on his shoulder bigger than Jack's truck.

"Brick!" he called out. Across the parking lot, an obsidian hulk of a man turned around. His hair was cut into a very short Mohawk, and he wore one of his own merch shirts. Most of the MAW merchandise sold in fits and starts, but so far all of Brick's items had moved like greased lightning. The one Brick sported had an image of his clenched hand on the front, colored to look like classic red bricks. On the back it read "Big Brick Fist." Jack was particularly proud of that one. It had, what do you call it, alliteration? Very fancy.

"What do you need, boss?" Brick asked as he approached Jack's truck. His real name was Richard, or Rick, but everyone just called him Brick.

"Your opponent for tomorrow night hasn't shown up yet."

"So?"

"So, he's your opponent. That makes it your problem, *capisce*?"

"Yeah, well, I don't know what you expect me to do about it." Brick crossed his arms. "Besides, Eric's never ghosted a gig his whole life. If he can be here, he will be."

"That's the problem, that whole 'if' part. I'm worried he's come across an unforeseen delay."

"Okay, so again, what does that have to do with me?" Brick was visibly annoyed now, feet shoulder-width apart.

"You still got friends from being a cop?"

"If I had that many friends, I would'a stayed a cop."

"Yeah, well, you got like a network or something? Like, you know, one trooper calling another trooper, see if there's been any accidents or some shit?"

Brick thought about this for a moment, his expression unchanging. It unnerved Jack the way Brick could put on a poker face so well.

"I'll call a friend back in Atlanta, see if he'll reach out to someone else for me. You got any idea at least where they might be?"

"Probably around I-64, near the Kentucky–West Virginia border."

"Okay. Still a big area, but I'll give it a shot."

Jack paced anxiously as he waited on Brick to get back to him. This was a disaster-in-waiting. If the zines were right, if there were scouts planning to attend tomorrow's event, a major change to the main event would be more than just an embarrassment. Not to mention the chaos all the way down the card. An entire match flushed down the toilet without Terry and Burt. The finish for the women's match in disarray without Julie doing her run-in at the end. A manager who couldn't keep track of his workers wasn't much of a manager, and certainly not one someone like Vince McMahon would trust.

Jack lost track of how much time he spent turning over these problems in his head, his frenzied reverie only broken by the approach of Brick Lamar.

"I've got nothing from the cops," he said.

"No crashes, no arrests? Nothing?"

"Not that anyone will tell me about, anyway. And they're not obligated to. But," he said as Jack began to pace once more, "I did talk to the front desk clerk at the hotel. Fort Knox called in last night, around one o'clock or so. He was worried they'd be late 'cause they were stopping to eat. Wanted to make sure they'd have a room."

"Did he say where he was?"

"No. But he called from a pay phone. Area code puts him in Fayette County; that gives you some place to start at least."

Jack scratched his head, ruing the thinness of his hair. This situation certainly wasn't helping.

"Did you call the cops there?"

"I did."

"And?"

"And I told you," Brick said. He sounded exasperated now. "Nobody says they saw anything."

"I need someone to go get them," Jack said, almost to himself.

"Excuse me?" Brick asked. "Look, I know it messes up the card for tomorrow, but we've dealt with stuff like this before. Why're you so stressed about it now?"

"I got a lot riding on tomorrow, is all."

"So what are you going to do?"

Jack pondered this. He'd been thinking it over ever since Eric and the rest no-showed. He hated to do it, but his options were limited and time was short.

"I need you to go find them, Brick."

"I'm sorry, what?" Even behind his aviator glasses, the surprise was written all over Brick's face.

"I got no way to reasonably track these guys down. You do. I don't like having you go, but I got no choice. I need you to go find them. I have this nightmare that they're all holed up in some scuzzy West Virginia jail cause Terry pissed someone off."

"Even if they are in a drunk tank or something, what then? You think I have some magic 'Get Out Of Jail Free' card? 'Cause I didn't exactly leave the force on the best of terms."

"Yeah, yeah, I know. But you got connections, more than anyone else here at least. You're the best chance I got." Jack prayed Brick would play ball. Jack couldn't afford to take off on his own to look, not with so much needing to be done to prep for the show. He had to make sure nothing else went off the rails. "Look, I'll even give ya my truck to use. So no miles on your Beemer there."

"And gas?"

Jack rolled his eyes. "Ugh, yeah, of course, gas, of course."

"Now, I haven't said yes yet. I want a little extra pay after tomorrow night too."

"What?" Jack tried to sound more surprised at Brick's request than he really was. "I'm already giving you my truck, and gas to boot!"

"And I'm missing the warm-ups for the promos and probably any downtime I'll have between now and Sunday."

"It isn't so bad as that."

"It is for me."

They stared at each other for a long hard minute. Jack hadn't told the other wrestlers about the rumored scouts coming by tomorrow, but most of them weren't stupid. They knew that it wasn't normal to rehearse like Jack was insisting on for this show. And Brick probably already had a good idea of why it was happening. He didn't know whether to call Brick's bluff or fold. He knew he didn't have a winning hand, though.

"Fine, fine. Extra two hundred right out of my share. Now, will you please go?"

"Not by myself."

"Well, I can't go."

"Nope. Wouldn't want you to." Brick cocked one eyebrow and shrugged. "No offense."

"None taken. So who is it you want to take?" Jack was genuinely intrigued. While he wasn't surly or impersonable, Brick also didn't go out of his way to make friends with the other guys. He was notoriously private. So who the hell would he want coming along?

"John Coors."

"Huh?" Jack wasn't sure he'd heard right. "John Coors? Is this, uh, some kind of Black thing or something?"

Brick snorted. "Yeah, that's it. Can't drive a White man's truck unless we got at least two brothers." Jack cringed.

"Jesus, I'm sorry. I just didn't know why you wanted Coors to come with you."

"It's nice to have someone to talk to, is all. Radio out there is crap. Just a bunch of country music and preachers. And since you don't have Coors doing anything tomorrow night but a run-in on me and Jiggolo, well . . ."

"Touché. Fine. I'll have him go too." Jack turned and began to walk away.

"Two hundred for him as well," Brick added. Jack stopped in his tracks.

"Now you're getting a little crazy." He turned toward Brick. "Two hundred's more than Coors will make for the whole event." Brick stared at him, saying nothing, waiting. He cocked an eyebrow expectantly.

So that was it. It *was* a Black thing. Jack calculated the risk and reward on the cost. If they found Jiggolo? Very worth it. If they didn't? Well, he could spin that somehow. Maybe put Coors in there instead. Make him earn that money. And he wouldn't have to pay Jiggolo, either.

"Okay, that's fine. Just hurry the fuck up, okay? Time is money. Literally."

"You want to go for a road trip?"

John Coors turned quickly at the unexpected greeting, almost spilling his coffee. He was stunned to see Brick Lamar standing there grinning. John had never seen the man smile like that before. He wasn't quite sure what to make of it.

"I just finished one last night," John said. "You trying to ask me to do a Dunkin' Donuts run for you or something?"

"Naw, nothing like that. The boss is wondering where Jiggolo's group is. The one he was traveling with. Had Ricky and Goth Girl and all them."

"Yeah, okay; but what's that got to do with us?"

"That's what I said," Brick replied. He gave John a knowing smile. "He wants me to go find them, though."

"You?" John couldn't hide his surprise. "Why would he want you to go?"

"He's got his reasons. And he's going to pay me two hundred to go find Jiggolo and the rest. Thinks the whole bunch of 'em ended up in some cracker-ass jail or something. And I want you to come along for the ride." He pulled out a map that had a chunk of West Virginia highlighted in yellow and grinned. "We just gotta go through this little county here and see what we can find." John was incensed. He knew that he was getting paid peanuts compared to Brick. He didn't need to see the checks to know that. But now Brick was getting two hundred dollars just to look for someone?

"Sounds nice," John said, "but I got work to do. Don't want Jack to have a reason to pay me even less."

"You don't understand. I'm not the only one walking away with an extra couple of Benjamins. I insisted on it for you too."

"Bullshit."

"No bullshit. I just got you a bigger payday than you've had at the last two shows."

"Jack must be desperate. But you and me, we've barely said five words to each other in months. Why do you want to help me out?" He looked at Brick closely, admiring the impressive straight white teeth in his grin.

"I think you've got a raw deal. But I also like you, kid. I think you've got potential." Somehow, his grin got even wider. "Plus, can you imagine the looks on those hillbilly faces when two big motherfuckers like us come marching in?" He laughed again, and it was contagious. John doubled over, imagining how those people would act at the sight of them both walking into some redneck dive with their best ass-kicking faces on.

Once they'd both calmed down, John put his hand out to shake Brick's. "Thanks, man. This is going to be a hell of a lot better than setting up a ring for fucking pennies."

"Oh, I know it." Brick grabbed John's hand and clapped him on the back. "Now come on; I got the boss's truck *and* his credit card."

"Oh, his 'magic cash flow generator'?" John said with a laugh. "Sure beats the hell out of staying here." He looked at Brick more closely. "So what do you think happened to them?"

"I dunno. You know how they are. They probably wanted to take a picture in front of the World's Largest Teapot or some shit."

They laughed together as they walked to Jack's truck.

6

Goode Farm, West Virginia
9:15 a.m.

"How's Burt doing?" Julie asked. Ricky was bent over the giant of a man in the closet, trying to make sure Knox was comfortable but visibly frustrated about his inability to do anything else.

"He's breathing, but that's about the extent of it. I'm no doctor, but I can tell he isn't doing so well. Skin's clammy . . . breathing shallow . . ." He spoke slowly, trying not to be overly emotional. "And he's nonresponsive to stimuli." Ricky's whole body was rigid. Julie could see the muscles tensed under his wiry frame. While the rest of them were preoccupied with getting themselves out of the trailer home, Ricky's only concern was Knox's well-being.

"We need to be thinking about what happens next," Terry said. "They only brought us here to kill us, and we all know it. We have to get out of here."

"We can't do much of anything until we get these zip ties off," Eric replied. He pulled futilely against the one connecting him to Julie.

"We need to keep trying to bite through it," Terry said. "Like I've been telling ya'll. Ricky, why don't you stop wasting time on Knox and help us get out of these ties."

Ricky glared over his shoulder at Terry. "You do whatever you want. I'm not going to just let Burt die."

"Neither are we," Julie reassured him. "But we can help him a lot more if we can get him to a hospital." Ricky considered, then stood up and walked to Terry, who was trying to gnaw at the tie connecting his wrist to Julie's.

"You're wasting your time," Ricky said. "You'll never break through these things with just your teeth." He looked around the empty room. "We need something to cut them with."

"Where the hell are we gonna get that?" Terry grumbled as he dropped the zip tie from his mouth. Julie wiped her wrist off on her pants leg. Ricky gave him a frustrated look then scanned the room again. He stopped and stared upward for a minute, shielding his eyes.

"The light bulb," he said. A large bare bulb burned in the housing unit of the broken ceiling fan. It was at least half a foot in diameter and looked thicker than a normal bulb. Eric considered it and nodded.

"You know, that could work. Better than chewing off our own arms, at least." He looked at Julie and raised both their arms. "Should we give Ricky a step up to reach it?" Julie nodded, pulling at Terry, who gave token resistance before standing up as well.

"Okay, Ricky," Eric said. "Hop up onto my shoulders and unscrew that light." Ricky did so, draping his legs over Eric's shoulders. He reached up to grab the light and quickly snatched his hand back with a small cry of pain.

"Are you okay?" Julie asked. Ricky nodded.

"The light's overheated. Should have expected that. Gotta cover my hand." He removed his shoe and peeled off one of his socks, stretching it over his hand.

"That ought to do it," Julie said then glanced at Eric. "You still okay with him up there?" Eric nodded.

"I could do this all day," he said. Ricky put his hand around the bulb and unscrewed it.

"This thing is still really hot," he said as the room was plunged into darkness. Thin scraps of light leaked through the edges of the window around the wooden shutter, but otherwise they were blind. Ricky climbed carefully down from Eric's shoulders and moved to the boarded-up window.

"You can't even see what you're doing," Terry said. Ricky ignored him and huddled by the window, using what little light there was to guide his hand. He set the sock on the floor with the bulb ensconced in it. He pressed down with his shoe over one hand. The glass cracked with a muffled sound. He opened the sock gingerly, taking out the largest of the jagged pieces.

"Somebody come over here," he whispered, and Julie obliged, holding up her wrist that was attached to Terry. Ricky lifted the bottom of Julie's shirt, motioning that he intended to wrap it around the glass. She nodded her permission. With the bottom half of the shard wrapped, Ricky began to saw away at the tie, trying to cut through it without breaking the glass or cutting anyone's skin.

He tried from multiple angles, coming at the zip tie from the top, attempting to cut into the locking mechanism from the side, and finally trying to pull up on it from underneath. The glass shattered suddenly, spraying shards wildly. Everyone cried out in surprise, and Ricky fell backward, hard. Within seconds Mark was swinging open the door, and all the wrestlers squinted at the sudden burst of light.

"What the hell are you all doing?" he demanded. "Why's it so damned dark in here?" He looked from Ricky to the other three hostages to the floor where Ricky's sock lay under the window. Pieces of glass glinted in the light from the hallway. "All o' ya, get the fuck back against the wall," Mark said, waving the Desert Eagle menacingly. They did as they were told and Mark came forward, picking up the sock and looking inside it.

"What is this, some kinda weapon?" No one answered him. He stared at Julie. "Is this your sock?" She said nothing. He walked up to her, examining her as she stood silently. Droplets of sweat had started to pool in the hollow spot at the base of her neck. Mark licked his lips unconsciously. "Or maybe you was trying to cut yourselves loose?" He glanced down at her wrist, where bits of blood were oozing from small cuts on her arm. "Yeah, I think that's it." He raised his gun hand up, grazing the front of her chest with the back of his hand. Julie shuddered, and he stepped back.

"Boy, you've got a real problem with guys touching your titties, huh?" Mark asked with a leer on his face. Eric opened his mouth to say something, but Julie squeezed his hand to stop him. Mark peered at Julie for what felt like an eternity before stepping back.

"Take off the bra," he said. He scratched the back of his head nervously.

"What?" Julie asked. She couldn't possibly have heard him right.

"Your, uh, your bra. Take it off and give it to me."

"No fuckin' way," Eric said, and Julie squeezed his hand once more, harder this time.

"Okay," she said. She looked at Eric, who was tense and ready to strike. "He has the gun," she said simply. "Sorry about this." She reached under her shirt with the hand tied to Eric, and he felt her fingers fumbling at the two clasps on the bra strap. Her skin was cool to the touch, her shoulder blades pronounced with the effort of undoing the bra. She unclipped the shoulder straps as well so that she could shrug it off and let it fall to the floor without lifting the front of her shirt. Mark eyed the black bra, a Walmart push-up, and then looked back at Julie. For a moment they worried that Mark would insist she pull up her shirt as well, but he just grinned instead, shaking his head in disbelief.

"Jesus Christ, I wasn't even grabbing your real tits back at Bud's." He shook his head with a smirk. "Bet ya wish now you'd just stayed quiet about it." He looked over at Ricky then.

"How's your friend doing? He still breathing?" When Ricky didn't move, Mark waved the gun at him. "Check 'im. Now!" Ricky moved toward Burt then, never taking his eyes off Mark. He leaned down and placed the back of his hand on Burt's cheek, which was clammy and cold. He gripped Burt's wrist with his other hand and felt a pulse that was too soft and fluttery for his liking.

"He isn't doing well. Obviously. He needs a doctor."

"He ain't gonna get one," Mark replied. "Maybe you should spend more time making sure he lives, instead of looking for dumbass ways to escape. I'm gonna get another light bulb for ya; stay put." He picked up the bra and exited the room, leaving the door open. They could all hear him rummaging in the hall closet just outside the door. He reemerged in less than a minute with another, smaller light bulb in his hand. The bra was nowhere to be seen. He tossed the bulb to Ricky.

"Go on then, champ. Put it in. If you break this one, I ain't gonna give you another." Ricky got to work, standing on his toes to screw it all the way in.

"Some kind of man you are," Terry said. "Grabbing on a woman and then stealing her undies. I bet the girls are just crazy about you." Mark stepped forward, holding the gun up to strike him with. As Terry tried to raise his hands in defense, Mark instead kicked him in the groin as hard as he could. Terry collapsed to the floor with a soft *whoof*, dragging Julie and Eric on top of him. Julie pulled herself up into a crouch as Terry moaned on his side.

"Are you okay?" she asked him. Mark let out a flat chuckle as Julie checked over Terry, backing up to the door as he eyed them all.

"Let's not get too mouthy," Mark said. "Ya'll keep yourselves quiet now. I don't wanna have to come in here again, ya hear?" He looked around at all of them, breathing heavily. "Too fucking bad. I loved watching you guys on TV. Guess you weren't as tough as ya'll looked." He left the room, closing and locking the door behind him. Terry blinked rapidly, involuntary tears starting to leak down his cheeks. Ricky went back to Burt, kneeling at his side and stroking his arm. Eric watched him for a minute before speaking.

"You and Burt . . . how long have you been together?" he asked. Ricky answered without turning around.

"About seven months now. Give or take a few days. We didn't exactly have a day we settled on as our first one together."

"Does anyone else know?"

"Not unless they figured it out and didn't tell me." He turned around now and looked at Eric. "It isn't exactly something that would help either of us get ahead in the business, after all."

"No, I guess not," Eric conceded. Julie sat down next to Terry.

"That's not fair for either one of you," she said. "I'm sorry."

"I guess that's why you hopped into Terry's car at the last minute," Eric said.

"Yeah," Ricky said. "Burt didn't think it was a good idea, but he also couldn't protest without making it look weird." He sighed, his voice shuddering. "I was willing to let him be mad for a few hours, you know? Just so I could ride with him."

"I don't fuckin' believe it," Terry said, still lying on his side. "I've been wrestling him for weeks now, letting him put his hands all over me."

"Jesus, Terry; it isn't like he's some kind of pervert," Eric said.

"Speak for yourself. Least he coulda done was tell me beforehand, am I right?"

"Well, lucky for you, it looks like you won't ever have to worry about him putting his dirty fag hands on you ever again," Ricky said. Tears welled in his eyes.

"Terry, just shut your fucking mouth," Eric said. Terry started to protest, but Eric spoke over him. "No, I said shut it, goddamn it. Or I'll do a whole lot worse than kick you in the balls." Terry surveyed the room, begrudgingly staying silent as he went back to nursing his injured testicles. Eric heard a bird outside, soon joined by a chorus of others in a sound that under other circumstances would have been soothing and enjoyable. Right now, though, it only meant that more time was passing. Morning was here, and they were running out of options.

Part Two

Breaking Kayfabe

7

US Highway 60, Near Victor, West Virginia
11:32 a.m.

"You're not much of a talker," Brick said, keeping his eyes on the road. Of course he could have been side-eyeing John behind those aviator glasses of his and John would have no idea. He drummed his finger on the doorframe.

"I don't know what you mean."

"I mean, we've been on this ride for almost an hour now and you've barely said one thing."

"I think that's a bit rich coming from you." After a moment, John corrected himself. "Sorry. Just still getting used to this, you and me, being social. Like I said before, you've barely spoken to me, or anyone in the crew for that matter. Doesn't seem like you were interested in making friends." John could see Brick's tight cotton tee strain as he kept the truck straight.

"People are usually intimidated by me." A smile now, those pearly teeth dazzling in contrast to his charcoal skin. "Can't imagine why. I got used to it. It came in handy when I was on patrol. Folk were less likely to try something stupid if they were scared shitless."

"Patrol?" John asked. He sat up now, giving Brick his full attention. He'd never spoken to the man beyond the perfunctory niceties, and like every other wrestler in MAW, he knew next to nothing about the private life of the man who was now at the top of the card. "You mean, like, in the army or something?"

"Naw, not army." Brick laughed. "Marine recon. Two years right outta high school. Got hurt, got discharged, and moved on to Georgia Highway Patrol."

"Really?" John could believe it. Now that he thought about it, Brick did carry himself like a cop. John had plenty of experience with them from various traffic stops in Chicago. He remembered the aggravation, pulled over just for driving down State Street in a Mercedes late at night. He wondered how differently some of that might have gone if he'd been pulled over by a Black cop like Brick. "How the hell did you end up at MAW then?"

Brick shifted in his seat, sucking air through his teeth as he readjusted position. "Felt like it was time for a change. Besides, big fucker like me, you don't think I seem like a natural? Honestly, I think it's more surprising to see you in MAW than me."

John cocked his head in surprise. He had a feeling he knew what Brick was referring to, but how? He waited for Brick to continue, but when he just sat there, John finally asked, "What do you mean?"

"Oh, you wanted everyone to think you were a badass Chicago street thug. It's your gimmick. And it works, sort of. You got the look to pull it off." Now he gave John a more direct glance. "But you don't sound like a gangster. You speak well. You're educated. Oh, you try to hide it, but it's your tone." He leaned back, drumming his fingers on the steering wheel. "I wondered what your story was, so I did some checking. It wasn't really hard, not for someone who still had friends in the GHP. No criminal record whatsoever, besides a couple of speeding tickets and moving violations." He gave John another sidelong glance. "But I'm betting those weren't exactly on the level."

John squirmed uncomfortably. He'd never spoken to anyone about his life. Had never really expected to. It infuriated him that Brick had dug into his life like that. He thought another Black man, even a cop, would understand. Maybe his original belief had been right though. Cops across the board were drunk on power. He'd heard about black-on-black crime all his life. Why should he think a Black cop would be any more likely to treat him fairly than a White one?

"You're pissed," Brick said. "I can tell. You're wound up tighter than a wet cat. I didn't tell anyone, if that's what you're worried about."

"How gracious of you," John said acidly.

"You know, you should be thanking me. If you were just some upstart gangbanger, I would've left ya back in Richmond to do ring duty."

"Why, because people who've made mistakes don't deserve a second chance?"

"Sure they do," Brick replied without missing a beat. "They've just gotta pay their dues."

"Spoken like a true cop."

"Okay, let's back on up before you say something you can't take back. I know you've had some rough shit with cops. I know you're pissed I was looking in on you. But you should know, I checked on everybody. At Jack's request."

"What?"

"Yeah. You remember that mess with the Vulture a month or so back?"

"Uh-huh," John said warily.

Brian "The Vulture" Stegall had been a workhorse mid-carder for MAW, just about to break through to main eventing. Jack had things in line for a feud with Jiggolo, but those got thrown out the window when Vulture was arrested for lewd and lascivious behavior with a minor. Jack defended his employee passionately, until it came to light that Vulture had a history of unsavory behavior with underage girls. The headlines were bad enough, but Jack was furious that he'd unknowingly been put in the position of defending a convicted pedophile.

"Yeah, well, that's part of what got me my job. Jack wanted me to do a very thorough background check on everyone else in MAW, make sure we didn't have any more surprises in the pipeline."

"I thought you had to get permission to do that kind of thing."

"Yeah, legally you do. But are you gonna file a complaint? Especially since it didn't really affect you?"

"So you didn't tell him about me," John said.

"Hell no; that was none of his business. And I'm not gonna try to force it out of you. But I am hoping you'll fill me in."

"What do you care?"

"I'm old for this business, John. They ain't never gonna put me in against Goldberg or Steve Austin. But you? Jack may not be able to give us a better gimmick than big, tough, and black, but I think you've got potential. I think you could be something. I want to see you make it, if you'll let me help."

John considered it. In all the years since he dropped out of the university, he hadn't ever spoken to anyone about it. As much as he loved being a wrestler, he couldn't shake the residual shame that clung to him like a stubborn odor. Nobody was happy with his choices. It tainted everything he did, sucking the joy from every triumph he achieved. He had no close friends anymore, no family to speak to, and it was lonely. John hadn't allowed himself to even consider that word, but now, sitting next to the first person in five years to really know who he was, the relief began to wash over him in a cooling wave that he had not expected.

"It starts with my dad," he began. "Fancy hotshot lawyer, corner office downtown. I grew up really respecting him, you know? I didn't realize there was anything unusual about us for the most part. It just seemed nice, stepping out of the apartment and onto Miracle Mile, taking the free summer trolley down to the Field Museum. Kids don't usually see the differences between being rich and poor, Black and White; there's just no frame of reference."

"Mm-hmm. When did you start to notice, then?"

"Fourth grade. I wanted to play with some kids during after-school care. They were making a fort with these cardboard bricks; I don't know if you ever saw any." Brick shook his head. "Yeah, okay; well, they made this fort. Or part of one, at least. So I came up to these kids and wanted to play too. The lead kid just looked at me, then his friends, and then back at me."

"'There's no more room,' he told me. So I said that's okay, we can just make it bigger. He looked like he was thinking for a few seconds, then said 'Well, this is a clubhouse.' When I asked if I could join, he said, 'No, it's only for White people.'"

"Huh." Brick didn't say anything else, but John saw the muscles in his jaw tighten.

"Yeah, I know. The kid claimed later he was just trying to find a reason to say no. I couldn't prove otherwise, but everyone else in their club was White, so . . ." John rubbed the back of his neck and looked out the window. "It seemed like a good, excusable reason to say no from his perspective, I guess."

"That sounds like cover-your-ass to me."

"It was. Little asshole just wanted an excuse to not look like an asshole."

"Yup." Brick glanced over at him once more. "So, what did you do then?"

"I told him I had white teeth, white eyes, wasn't that white enough? And he looks at his arm, rubs it a bit like he has a bugbite or something, and says, 'Yeah, but it isn't *pure* white, like this.' And that's when I realized that no matter what I said, I wasn't going to get to play fort with these kids." John shifted in his seat. It wasn't a memory he revisited often. He tried to actively avoid thinking of it.

He went on, telling Brick about how the teacher reacted when he ran up to her, crying that the boys wouldn't let him play with them because he wasn't white enough. He'd expected her to insist the boys include John in their game, maybe threaten them with a time out if they refused. Instead, she practically dragged the young man by the arm out of his makeshift fort and shuffled him out the door. John didn't see him again for the rest of the afternoon.

When John's father picked him up, the teacher had requested a private conference with him. John sat in the front office for what felt like an hour, wondering what was going on. When his father came out, he had such a fierce scowl that John became terrified he would be punished as well, banished to whatever twilight zone the other kid had disappeared to. His father didn't say a word until they had pulled out of the school's parking lot.

"I'm sorry you had to experience that," he said to John.

"Why are you sorry?" John asked. "I don't get any of this."

"He shouldn't have said that," John's father replied, like John hadn't even spoken. "I knew sending you here, with all these White kids, it was going to come up eventually. That's the world we live in. But you've got to be tough, Johnny. You've got to show them that a Black kid is just as smart as them, has just as much reason to be here as they do. Because you aren't going to get to Ivy League without schools like this on your record."

John realized then what was going on. There was retribution against all the boys who'd participated in building that fort. The entire school had to attend an assembly on racial sensitivity. Years later, John found out that the only reason they'd even done that was because his father had threatened to bring the full force of an

NAACP lawsuit on them if they didn't. Suddenly John was aware of what made him different in a far deeper way than just how brown his skin was. Everyone else knew it too.

"Seems like that would be a good thing," Brick said. "You can't just not know your history, your culture."

"Maybe. All I know is, I wanted it to be like it was. I didn't want to be aware of how different I was. My dad had always been really pushy about what activities I did, but after that, he got even more overbearing. He wanted to make sure I participated in every academic extracurricular we had. If they were doing a computer club or having a Jeopardy geography tournament, you'd better believe I was there."

John looked out the window, recalling the hours of time his father spent pouring over materials with him, trying to mold him into a model student.

"I was big, though. Bigger than my dad by the time I was thirteen. Must have been from my mother's side, I guess. By middle school I was pushing for sports. I wanted basketball, baseball, football. I had posters of Jackie Robinson, Bo Jackson, Michael Jordan, and Magic Johnson. You know, those guys."

"Ah, I bet your dad loved that."

"No. Not at all. He told me it was a waste of my talents, a waste of my brain. Said the whole country was full of Black athletes running around for White people to watch. I told him I wanted to play football. He asked me when was the last time I saw a Black quarterback; when was the last time I saw a bunch of inner-city kids with nice pads and a clean field to play on."

"Yeah, well, they'd probably have things like that if..."

Brick trailed off, exiting the highway without warning. He turned right toward a small town John hadn't caught the name of. "Why here?" he asked.

"Look at the sign," Brick replied. John saw a billboard just over the trees. "Twenty-four-hour diner. It's the most logical place to start.

Chances are, wherever they stopped would be a place like that, and this is the first one in the area code the call came from."

"How many all-night diners do you think there are in one zip code?" John anticipated they'd be stopping every five minutes at this rate.

"Not as many as you might think. This ain't Cincinnati. I'm guessing there's only about four or five between here and Kentucky." They pulled into a parking lot that had access to an overnight truck park behind a rustic gas station and diner. John spied about six or seven semis in the back, with only a couple of regular cars in the front lot. The parking spots were barely delineated with faded white lines that looked hand-painted on the potholed asphalt. They parked the truck, and Brick reached across John's lap to fish a black-holstered pistol out of the glove box.

"Whoa, what the fuck is that?" John demanded as Brick exited the truck. The former marine clipped the holster to his belt and pulled the shirt down over it.

"It's my pistol. Don't worry; I have a concealed carry permit."

"And you're taking it in the diner because?"

"Well, I'm sure as shit not leaving my baby in the car." He headed toward the entrance, with John rushing to catch up.

As John approached the doors, Brick handed him a pair of sunglasses. They weren't as nice as Brick's aviators, but John figured they would give him a similar intimidating presence.

"Keep these on inside until we start talking to the owner. Don't speak unless I motion for you to. Hands at your sides; don't cross them over your chest or put them in your pockets. Got it?" John nodded, putting on the shades. He thought it seemed a bit over the top, but he was also out of his element and willing to follow Brick's lead.

They entered the diner, which was quiet except for the background clink of flatware on porcelain. One man sat at the counter nursing a steaming mug of coffee. Three of the booths were taken by single burly men, two of whom were reading *USA Today* while the third read a well-worn copy of Steven King's *It*. All were White. Brick approached the cash register on the counter, behind which stood a matronly woman with gray-streaked black hair and an ample bosom. She barely glanced up from the receipts she was sorting as Brick waited.

"Grab a seat anywhere, hon. I'll get over to you in just a minute."

"I'd just like a coffee; black," Brick said as he eased into the closest stool to the register. "Are you the manager on duty right now, or is there someone else in the back?" John stayed on his feet until Brick motioned to the stool next to him. The woman turned toward Brick now, and John saw the name "Rita" spelled out on her name tag.

"Did I already do somethin' to piss you off?" she asked with arched eyebrows. Her eyes met Brick's with practiced indifference.

"No ma'am," Brick replied. "I just have a few questions I need to ask about last night."

"Are you a cop or something?"

"Why do you ask?"

"You sound like a cop, s'all." Rita waited, flicking her gaze between Brick and John.

"It's not *official* police business, ma'am, but I'd appreciate any help you can give me all the same."

"Mm-hm," Rita hummed through pursed lips. She considered Brick for a moment longer then disappeared into the back without another word.

"Isn't there some law about impersonating an officer?" John asked when she was out of earshot. Brick shrugged.

"Sure. But I'm not impersonating anything. I didn't tell her I was a cop, and I also very specifically told her this wasn't official police business."

John crossed his arms and cocked an eyebrow. "That seems like the very definition of splitting hairs."

"Someone with a father like yours ought to know that entire cases are made or fall apart on things like how someone said something and when it was said. Rita *can't* say I told her I was a cop, while I *can* say I told her I wasn't investigating anything for the police."

Before John could say anything more a barrel-chested man with a salt-and-pepper moustache barged through the swinging door of the kitchen. He made a beeline for Brick at the end of the counter and leaned over in a conspiratorial fashion.

"Rita told me you had some questions about last night?" he began. Brick nodded. "Well, I don't know what it could be about. Things were real quiet here all night." Rita squeezed between them, setting down a mug and saucer with Brick's coffee. She glanced over at John.

"How about you, sweetheart? You want anything?" John started to speak, but Brick cut him off.

"Just coffee for him too, Rita, thanks." He turned back to the manager. "I'm looking for five people that might have come through last night. Four men and a woman? One big as a house?" The manager leaned even closer now, eyes narrowed with suspicion.

"Listen, son, I don't know what this is about, but I ain't in the habit of answering questions like that. Who comes here and when is private business, if you catch my drift."

"Yeah?" Brick sipped his coffee, glancing around the diner. "Anyone else around last night that might tell me?"

The manager paused and shook his head.

"Nope. I ain't gonna tell any of my employees to cooperate unless I know why. But a man like you comes in, packing, with a big bastard like that in tow, I believe he's got nothing good going on." He turned to Rita as she poured a cup of coffee for John. "Rita, why don't you check on Mr. Stephen King there, hon?" She nodded and made her way to the table of the man with the novel. The manager, Jim, turned back to Brick.

"Now, son, Rita thought you were police, but lookin' at ya, I'm pretty sure you're not. I don't want trouble. If you came here looking for some, I will kindly ask you to please leave." John tensed up at this,

his coffee halfway to his lips. Brick gave a small smile, no teeth, and cocked his head.

"Jim, if you don't want trouble, you may want to do a better job clearing out the riffraff from this here truck stop. I saw at least two lot lizards making their way into the trucks that are parked in your back lot area. Who knows how many others might be there already. And I imagine this is not a onetime occurrence. It would be a real shame, I think, if some of my friends in the West Virginia Highway Patrol decided to stop by here in, say, the next hour and give this place a once-over." He sipped his coffee. "Don't you think so?" Jim stared at him with hard eyes, but Brick was unflappable.

"Now, you mentioned my firearm. You should also know I have a license to conceal carry. Of course you can tell me not to bring a gun on your premises, but are you gonna tell him that too?" Brick motioned to one of the customers reading a newspaper. John couldn't help but stare, trying to see what Brick must have, but nothing looked amiss to him. "So, Jim, you haven't got much ground on that. Think hard now. If you want to make any of this a pissing match, I promise you I will win." Jim dropped his shoulders in resignation, looked back at the patron Brick had pointed out, then leaned in closer to Brick once more.

"Okay, you win, but I dunno if there's much to tell. I only came in this morning."

Brick smiled as he finished his coffee.

"Okay, well that's better. I'm really not looking for any trouble."

Jim considered for a minute before answering.

"If they came in last night, Rita may have seen them." He motioned to the waitress, who had come back behind the counter once more. She approached quickly, and Jim leaned in to confer with her. She shook her head slowly but firmly as he spoke, confirming what Brick had begun to suspect.

"No one said anything to Rita, either. I guess we don't have what you're looking for."

"Mmm. And no word of any accidents, along the highway or Route 60 maybe?"

Jim shook his head slowly. "Nope. At least nothin' big enough to make the news over here." Brick nodded, considering. Finally he pushed the coffee cup away from himself and shrugged.

"Well, I guess that's that, then. Thanks anyway for the help."

Jim looked Brick over once more, crossing his arms over his chest. "So are we good here? I don't imagine you boys want any food." Now it was Brick's turn to shake his head.

"No, we're fine with the coffee, thanks." He took out a ten and laid it on the counter. "I hope that's enough to cover our bill. Make sure Rita gets the change." He clapped John on the back. "Come on, Coors, we gotta hit the road again." John looked up from his half-finished coffee, motioning toward it disappointingly.

"I haven't even finished—" he began, but Brick cut him off before he could say anything.

"We gotta get goin'." He grinned that same shit-eating grin John had seen when Brick invited him on this venture. "Next time drink faster, my man. And thanks for your help, sir." He waved to the manager as he ushered John out the door.

When they were back on the highway, Brick patted John's shoulder in solidarity. "You did good back there, Coors, thanks."

"I don't know what you mean. All I did was sit there while you asked all the questions."

"It's about presence. Two big beefy guys is more legit than one, right? So you did good."

"Well, thanks, I guess."

"You guess?" Brick snorted a laugh. "Isn't there anything that makes you happy, Johnny?"

John shrugged. "Plenty. But it's harder to be happy when you always get the shit work. Even here, I'm just the bodyguard to the star."

"Some people call that paying your dues."

"Yeah, like you? You come in, and suddenly you're champ in just a few months."

"I'm sorry if I took your spot. I didn't realize there was room for only one Black wrestler at the top."

John looked at him, smirking in disbelief. It was uncommon enough to even have *one* Black wrestler at the top. Two was unheard of. "What, you never actually watched wrestling growing up?" That wouldn't surprise John. There were plenty of people in the business now with no wrestling knowledge, just a good look that pushes them to the top. Lex Luger instantly came to mind.

"Oh, I watched plenty. You better believe I was all about that Junkyard Dog. I was watchin' when Michael Hayes blinded him. I watched the dog collar match with the Freebirds. I watched his feud with DiBiase. I loved the Dog, man."

"Yeah, so did I, but I mostly knew him from WWF," John said.

"Aw, man, that's a damn shame. First Black man to win a world championship. First Black man to take the top spot in a company. He didn't have anything like that in WWF."

"No, but he was national at least."

"I suppose," Brick said. "But we'll see how long it takes before McMahon makes a brother the **champ."**

"Well, they just brought in Ron Simmons."

Brick laughed so hard John was worried he might veer off the road.

"You mean 'Farooq Asad'? With that stupid silver helmet? The only good thing about that is he gets to parade around with that fine-ass girl Sunny. But I promise you, he will never get close to the WWF championship. Especially not coming from down south. Look what they did to Harley Race, for instance."

"They gave it to Ric Flair, though."

Brick laughed at this, and John couldn't help but look wounded. "What? What'd I say?"

"Let me tell you a story. When I was a kid, I loved Dusty Rhodes. I'd watch him fight Flair, and I'd get so pissed when he lost. I'd bitch to my dad about how Flair cheated, about how he was a crook and couldn't beat Dusty fair and square. And you know what my dad told me?"

"What's that?" John asked, genuinely intrigued.

"He told me not to waste time cheering for a fat slob like Dusty Rhodes. Told me he was a disgusting blob of a man, and that birthmark looked like a big old shit stain on his belly. He says to me, 'Son, you can cheer for the common man—the son of a plumber and all that horseshit—or you can cheer for Ric Flair, the guy who has all the money, all the women, all the style. Why the hell would you not want to be like Ric Flair?' And that's fuckin' true. People bought his feud with Randy Savage because you could really believe a guy like that could get Miss Elizabeth, or whomever the hell else he wanted. And that's a man to be admired."

"I never really thought of it like that."

"Yeah, well, good thing you have me to educate you. You wanna be at the top of the card? You stick with me; I'll show you how to get there."

John thought about that for a minute then turned back toward Brick. "Something else I wanted to ask you about," he said.

"Oh yeah? What's that?"

"Back at that truck stop. How'd you know that guy was carrying? I couldn't see anything on him, and I saw *Get Shorty*. I 'savvy bulge,' if you know what I mean." Brick laughed and laughed at that, his deep voice shaking the cabin of the truck.

"Johnny, I have no damned idea if he was carrying or not. But our friend Jim didn't know either."

"You mean you lied?"

Brick shrugged. “I made a bet. This time it paid off; next time it might not. Just like I didn’t actually see any special ladies out in that truck yard, either.”

“What?” John could hardly wrap his head around all of this. “Then why would you say that?”

“That was just an educated deduction. Anyone on the highway patrol knows what goes on in those truck stops. If any of the owners tried to crack down, they’d just be cutting off their own customer base. So I knew, and Jim knew, and he didn’t want to rock the boat.” Brick leaned back and smirked. “Easier to just answer my questions, even if he didn’t like the look of us.”

They pulled off the interstate at that point, heading for the next all-night diner. John checked his watch to see that it was about 10:05 and estimated that, at this rate, they’d get through this stretch of highway by 1:00 p.m. John settled in comfortably, abuzz with the possibilities of what he might learn at Brick’s side.

8

Goode Farm
10:22 a.m.

Julie sat as comfortably as she could between Eric and the still-groaning Terry. Ricky continued to kneel at Burt's side in the closet, having stayed there ever since Mark left the room. She watched Eric pick at the zip tie on his wrist, trying to wedge the fingers of his free hand underneath it. The only effect it had was to jerk Julie's hand at intermittent moments as he rearranged his grip over and over.

"Can you maybe give it a rest for a bit?" she said finally. Eric looked up in surprise. "It's just that I don't think you're going to get anywhere, and I'm tired of you yanking my arm around." Eric stopped what he was doing immediately, then lowered his eyes and looked away. Like a chastised child. Julie closed her eyes. She knew Eric wouldn't be so meek if Terry had scolded him. She was so tired of men acting differently around her just because she was a woman. It was exhausting.

"Sorry," Eric muttered. "It feels better than just sitting here doing nothing."

"Don't be sorry," Terry said, finally making the effort to sit upright. "So far as I can see, we're the only ones actually trying to do something to get out of here." He glanced at Julie as he said this, and for the first time she noticed the dull, mean glaze to his eyes that so many other people claimed was his default expression.

"If you have something you want to say," Julie told him, "go ahead and say it." Terry shook his head as if he was clearing out cobwebs, leaning hard on his right arm.

"I think you know," he said. "The little dickwad was right when he said we wouldn't even be here if you hadn't acted so fucking nuts at the diner."

A disquieting silence came over the room. By now, Ricky was turned toward them, his gaze fixed on Terry.

"And you think what, exactly?" Eric asked. "She should just take it? Let someone grab her like that and let bygones be bygones?" Julie held up her hand to stop him from going on.

"I reacted on instinct," she said. "You would've done the same thing if someone grabbed your cock."

She was willing to make appeasements to calm the situation down, but she hated doing it for someone like Terry. She doubted he'd even care she was making the effort, and she was quickly proven right.

"I think that's bullshit. Everything you put up with from the marks, almost every fucking night, and this is the one time you snap?" He shook his head. "I mean, Jesus, I'm surprised you even felt anything under all that padding."

"Shut up, Terry," Ricky said. He stood up and walked toward the other three. "You want to bitch about Burt touching you during your matches? Think about how it must feel for Julie."

"That's different," Terry said defensively. "At least those are men touching women. It's natural."

Julie felt color rising to her own cheeks now, but not in embarrassment.

"You're just as bad, Terry," she said. "You might tell yourself otherwise, but you think just like him and all those other men who thought I was only good for one thing all these years. That perv who stole my bra thinks just like you. He grabs me, and he's probably thinking about doing a lot more than that, but it isn't a whole lot different from the way you think. You're so sure I'll eventually have to fuck you just because you let me ride in your truck for free. And now that it's looking like you'll never get to, all your fake kindness toward me is out the window." Julie held Terry's hard stare. She wondered if he truly hadn't expected her to know why she was the only person who didn't have to pony up for gas.

Julie had known men like Terry all her life. She'd spent years training to wrestle, but Terry only saw value in what was between her legs. She knew she was swimming against the tide when it came to women's wrestling, but she had always wanted nothing more than a chance to prove to men like Terry and Jack Mayer that women could do more than just the bathroom-break match.

From her first day in high school, Julie had balked at the traditionally "female" sports. She hated soccer, had no aptitude for basketball, and found the entire idea of softball degrading. State athletic rules kept her off the football team, but thanks to the weight classes, there were no such restrictions on joining the wrestling team.

"Of all the sports, wrestling's the only one that's co-ed?" her father had asked. It was something Julie had a hard time explaining to him. As long as she trained hard, bulked up, and knew the fundamentals, she'd be able to go toe to toe with any boy within a ten-pound range of her own weight.

"I don't know," her father had replied. "I love you, and I want you to do what makes you happy, but this just seems like a bad idea." He was nervous, but he'd never denied his precious only girl what she'd wanted. Julie wondered if it was his way of making up for her mom skipping out. Things might have been different with another woman in the house. As it was, though, two weeks later she was in the gym after school for tryouts, wearing the new wrestling shoes her father bought for her at Dick's.

"You've got a high opinion of yourself, sweetheart," Terry said to her. He was about to say more, but Eric interrupted him.

"Stop it; just stop it, for God's sake. How will we ever get out of here if you're picking fights with everyone?" He looked toward Ricky. "How's Burt doing?"

Ricky shook his head slowly, wringing his hands as he spoke. "Not good. I don't know much about this sort of thing, but if I had to guess, he's got a cerebral hemorrhage." When no one reacted, he explained, "He's bleeding in the brain, I think. It's putting pressure on his skull, and eventually it's going to . . . to . . ." He couldn't quite get the words out, but they all understood.

"If we don't get out of here soon, Burt's not going to make it," Julie said. She hated to put it so bluntly with Ricky, but the time for delicacy was long past.

"If you have any ideas, I'm all ears," Terry said. His attitude had soured considerably after that kick to the balls, and Julie's blunt answer to his unspoken offer hadn't helped matters. Regardless, Julie was determined to find a way out of this, and that meant keeping Terry on board.

"We need a distraction," she said, a plan starting to form in her head.

Les stared across the cluttered kitchen table at Norm, not bothering to hide his disdain for the man. He'd grown up in this house, had spent countless hours at this very table enjoying fried eggs, biscuits, gravy, and all kinds of other farmhouse dishes prepared as only

Mama Goode could do. It broke his heart every time he saw what a disgusting shithole Norm had allowed the place to become since Louanne's death.

Dishes were constantly piled in the sink, only washed as needed. Flies buzzed back and forth from them to whatever stray plates were left abandoned around the house, often with hardened bits of food and congealed grease on them. Every room was cluttered nearly to the point of unusability. If Les dared to sit down in the living room, he had to move piles of fast-food bags, dirty clothes, and unopened mail to make space on the couch.

Les's own room was in the Fleetwood trailer, where all the wrestlers were being held. It was his own trailer, moved there as a favor from a friend before he'd gone to prison. Technically it belonged to Norm as well now, since he'd passed it to Louanne and she'd left everything to Norm after her death. He wondered, for perhaps the millionth time, why it couldn't have been Norm who was blown to pieces in the family's Tahoe instead of his cousin. At least then Mark would have gotten some actual parenting.

If Norm noticed Les's poisonous stare he didn't acknowledge it. He'd gotten a lot more confident since realizing Les was completely dependent on him, not only for housing and employment but also to make sure Mark, the last real family Les had, didn't end up a felon like Les. Power had gone to Norm's head, and he was becoming harder and harder to deal with as time passed. It wouldn't be long, Les knew, before this whole enterprise he'd built for them fell down around their ears. He just hoped he could get Mark clear of it before that happened.

"I can't believe you've left them alive this long," Norm said, breaking the silence. "What are you getting out of it?"

"Ask your son," Les responded. "Soon as he found out who we had in the van, he insisted we keep them alive as long as possible."

"Nate . . . ," Norm began, trying to find the right words. He attempted to hide it, but Norm was just as scared of Nathan as Les was. As the whole damn town was, truth be told. People saw Nathan and were scared of how big he was. Then they spoke to him, and somehow that was even scarier.

"Nate's bored," Norm finally said. "I think he's getting tired of playing around with pigs."

"What you're suggesting is pretty fucking sick," Les said. "Have you seen what he does to them? The look on his face when he's dressing them out? Christ, I think that's the only time I've ever seen him smile. I don't even want to know what he's doing with the ones he takes to the basement."

"That's just, like, science stuff or something."

"I heard that sow he took down there screaming!" Les shouted. He composed himself, trying to keep the conversation private. "Have you ever heard a pig scream?"

"Of course I have," Norm said, waving his hand dismissively. "They always do when you slit their necks."

"No, not squealing. Screaming. Like a fucking human." Les leaned across the table, getting as close to Norm as he could stand. "Maybe you couldn't hear, up in your bedroom, but I was right here. You pretend there isn't something wrong with him, but you and I, we both know he is *not* right in the head."

Norm sighed, turning his head to avoid looking Les straight in the eyes. "We're all fucked up. How many men have you killed, Les? How many men's teeth do we have buried in the woods back there?"

"That's different and you know it. I don't *like* killing people. I don't *enjoy* hearing anybody beg. I don't think that's the case with Nate."

Norm picked up a lukewarm Hot Pocket, nibbling at the cheese leaking out the sides. "Okay, so don't kill them yet," he said, trying to change to subject. "I mean, that big guy's not gonna last much longer anyway, so there's that." He put the Hot Pocket down and finally looked at Les straight on. "But do you really think it's safe to just leave Mark in there with them?"

"Mark's gotta learn responsibility some time," Les replied. "And those guys aren't going to try to run as long as their friend is still breathing."

"Sure, but they got that chick with 'em."

"Yeah? So?"

"So how long do you think it is before Mark starts getting his own ideas? Dante stopped lettin' us use his girls a few months ago. I bet Mark's getting real tired of jerkin' it every night."

"You really think your own son could just do something like that?"

"You and I both know what Mark's like. He thinks with everything except his brain. That's how we ended up in this mess tonight." Norm looked on calmly as Les scowled at him. "I mean, I don't really care what he does with her, but those other guys . . . well . . . they might be thinking to do something stupid if the girl's in trouble."

"Fine," Les said. "Why don't you go to the trailer and take over for a while?"

Norm shook his head. "Uh-uh, cuz. This is yours and Mark's mess to clean up. You can go check on him, and I will go upstairs and get wasted." He stood up from the table, leaving his half-eaten Hot Pocket on the table. As he walked by, Les grabbed him by the arm.

"You're gonna get wasted? Right now?"

Norm shook Les's arm off disdainfully. "You're forgetting your place, Les. Unless you want me to kick your ass out. I'm sure Officer Jerrold would love to hear you ain't got a permanent address anymore." Les's fists tightened on the table. He had a lot to lose if Norm kicked him out, it was true, but he also knew that Norm would lose a lot if he didn't have Les's inside knowledge, connections, and skills to run their business. He wondered if things were set up well enough now that Norm could run it without him. The answer was, they might be; and as much as Les wanted to find a way out, right now, over this particular argument, was not the way he wanted to handle it.

Truthfully, Les didn't give a shit if Norm wanted to smoke meth until his brains melted. Mark had quickly picked up his habit, though, and no matter how hard Les tried, he couldn't get Mark to drop it. Mark had picked up every terrible choice Norm stumbled into, and rather than try to steer Mark away from it, Norm seemed to encourage his slide into the wastelands. It was a constant sore spot between him and Norm, a large weeping pustule of rage that never scabbed over. He stood up as well, keeping a hard gaze on Norm.

"You can't keep me here forever, you know. I've got less than a year on my parole."

"Yeah, and I bet you got plenty of cash stashed away for then too. You never buy anything nice, never treat yourself to anything. You have to be doing something with all the money we've made you."

"There'd be more of it if you and Mark weren't using up over half the shit we cook. We could be clearing fifty thousand a year if you'd actually sell all we're making."

Norm sidled around Les, waving him off dismissively with his right hand. "You just don't know how to enjoy life any more's the problem. Thank God I ain't like that."

"You can do whatever you want," Les said to Norm. "I'll let you know if anything changes." He headed out the kitchen side door to the yard as Norm stomped heavily up the stairs to his second-floor bedroom. Les was certain Norm was trying to push him into a reaction, but he let it go. He'd worked too long and too hard to let it all be undone now. Gritting his teeth, he trudged through the dewy Kentucky bluegrass toward the double-wide.

Mark sat on the couch across from the TV, the Desert Eagle on the coffee table in front of him. One hand held Julie's bra to the side of his acne-scarred face, the other rested between his legs, slowly moving back and forth across his hardening crotch. He'd put on his favorite of Les's porn collection, a point-of-view anal extravaganza. He'd never actually engaged in any anal intercourse, but he'd heard it felt even better than getting a woman from the front. None of the women he'd been with would consider it, not even Dante's girls, no matter how much he offered them. Things were looking like that might change, though.

Goth Girl was far from his favorite girl wrestler, even just from MAW. That honor went to Kristy, the cheerleader, Goth Girl's ongoing nemesis. Now that was a hottie he could fantasize about, with the basketball-sized tits, long blonde hair, and a face like Jenna Jameson. Goth Girl wasn't anywhere near that. Mark hated her short hair, with those spiky bangs coming down over her eyes. He couldn't get himself worked up at all over her flat-chested body, although he'd never seen her from behind very well until tonight. Her ass was tight and firm under those athletic shorts she was wearing, and though Mark was holding her bra, his mind kept wandering back to the shape of her bottom underneath that Lycra.

Goth Girl would never be his top choice, no, but she was here. And Mark had never been with anyone even close to being a celebrity. The more he thought about it, the more appealing she became. He hadn't been with a woman in months, the longest since he'd first met Dante. He'd gotten far too used to having girls on call whenever he wanted, but thanks to Nate, that was all a thing of the past. Mark had gone out to the bars several times since then, sometimes with Mason, but he wasn't ever able to close the deal. Uncle Les told him it was because he was such an obvious meth head, but Mark thought it probably had more to do with the acne scars he'd sported since his junior year.

Mark was starting to really enjoy himself, about to unzip the crotch of his Dickies, when he was interrupted by repeated knocking on the door of the back room. It was impossible to miss because of the steel reinforced door, normally meant for exteriors. Zipping back up with an angry curse on his lips, Mark grabbed the pistol and walked to the door.

"What the fuck is it?" he shouted. He was on high alert, anticipating this would be some kind of attempt to rush the door. To his surprise, it was Goth Girl he heard replying.

"I, uh, I need to use the restroom," she said. It was muffled by the thick door, and Mark could barely understand her. He pressed his ear against the door.

"What'd you say? The bathroom?"

"Yeah," she said more loudly. "None of us have gone since you brought us here. I really need to, though."

Mark considered what she was saying. He was finding it hard to focus. He was tired, agitated, and hungry. He hadn't had a hit since the afternoon, which was a pretty damn long time for him these days. It was on Les's orders, though. He never wanted Mark using when they did deliveries. Said it was a bad look for all of them. Mark didn't really care what people thought, but Les had beaten him pretty badly one time for getting high with a customer; since then, Mark did his best to follow Les's orders.

Normally he'd have gotten high the second he got home from Bud's, but this mess had thrown everything to hell. He had some crystal in his wallet, though. He pulled the tiny baggie out now and sprinkled it in his hand before snorting it quickly. Now he could think straight as he struggled to decide how best to handle the situation Goth Girl had just thrown at his feet. He had a gun, sure, but he'd never actually shot anyone. He'd practiced with the Desert Eagle, but the recoil damn near broke his wrist most of the time. He was counting on the size and presence of it to keep the wrestlers calm, but what if it didn't? What if they rushed him as soon as he opened the door? Even tied up, they could probably put a hell of a hurt on him.

"Mark?" Goth Girl called out again. "Please?" He pursed his lips to keep from groaning in frustration. The prospect of getting to see her pull those shorts down, even for something like taking a piss, was exciting to Mark. He knew he'd have to cut her free to do it, but . . . but dammit, he had the gun. He. Had. The. *Fucking.* Gun. He was the one in control. He just had to believe that, to show it on the outside, like Les had told him, and everyone would believe it.

"Okay, just back away from the fucking door first," he said, making his voice as commanding as he could. Taking a deep breath to steady his nerves, he unlatched the three deadbolts, unlocked the doorknob, and swung open the door, gun pointed in front. He eyed the room carefully.

The three wrestlers had done as he'd asked and were against the far wall. The manager, Ricky, was still huddled over Fort Knox. He barely even glanced toward Mark. In between the two men Goth Girl stood defiant, her body straight, her eyes boring directly into Mark. Somehow, in the glow of the ceiling fan light, she looked absolutely radiant. Mark could see the beads of sweat twinkling on her skin like a sky full of stars. The long bangs he'd found so unsavory were slicked back behind her ears, showing off a face he found unsettlingly attractive. As he looked at her toned arms and legs, all he could think about was how good it would feel to have them wrapped around his body, squeezing him tight as he did the same to her, the both of them exerting so much force it felt like they might explode.

He gave a quick shake of his head to focus his thoughts and fished his pocketknife from his side pocket. As he looked between Jiggolo and TJ Azz, he had second thoughts about doing this, but one more glance at Goth Girl made up his mind. He dropped the knife on the floor and kicked it toward her. She stared at it for only a second before lifting her gaze back to Mark. He motioned toward it with a nod of his head.

"Pick it up," he said. "Cut yourself free, then drop it and kick it past me, out of the room. I see you make any move to do anything else, and I shoot him first." He pointed the gun at Jiggolo as he spoke, who looked like he might fall over as the barrel leveled with his chest. "This is a Desert Eagle. One shot from this will blow out his fuckin' heart, so don't take any chances."

Goth Girl nodded slowly, and all three of them crouched down so she could grab the knife. Slowly she cut the tie connecting her to Jiggolo and then the one between her and TJ.

"Drop it and kick it," Mark said. "Now!" Startled, Goth Girl dropped the knife, which bounced in front of TJ. He looked at it and tensed. "Hey, hey! Don't fucking move! I am one second from killing this guy right here!" TJ relaxed, and Goth Girl slid the knife in front of her with her foot and gave it a strong kick. It went skittering past Mark, bouncing off the hallway walls and into the living room. Mark nodded.

"Good, good. Okay, Goth Girl, come forward, nice and slow, and I'll escort you to the bathroom. You two, stay right the fuck there." Goth Girl stepped forward slowly, and Mark backed up to give her room.

"It's Julie," she said as she came closer. Mark raised his eyebrows in surprise. He'd never bothered to learn their real names, but she was telling it to him. Why? Was she starting to like him? He'd heard that sometimes hostages, women hostages, fell for the people holding them prisoner, but he hadn't really believed it. And yet, had she smiled a bit as she told him her name? His heart pounded as he considered it.

She exited the room and he held up his other hand to stop her. "Now close the door," he said. "Lock the doorknob and all the deadbolts." He watched carefully as she did so. When she was done he nodded his head and inclined it toward the open door next to him.

"There's the toilet," he said. He stepped back so she could enter. As she walked past he smiled at her, but she didn't return the favor. Instead, she tried to close the door to the bathroom, but he put his foot out to stop it. "Uh-uh," he said; "gotta leave it open."

"Why?" she said. "Did you want to watch?" Mark gritted his teeth in embarrassment.

"I'm not getting off on it," he lied, desperately hoping she couldn't see his erection.

"Sure you're not. And I guess you just took my bra so you could wash it for me." She stared at him.

Mark felt heat rising up his cheeks, a feeling he wasn't used to or even understood. He almost responded with a comment about her not even needing a bra, but thought back to his fantasy about them entwined with each other and tried a different track.

"Listen, I'm sorry you were upset back at the diner. I really didn't mean anything by that." He waited anxiously to see how she'd respond. The last time he'd actually apologized to a woman was when his girlfriend found out he'd been using Dante's girls behind her back. It hadn't helped much then, but Julie seemed like a much more mature, much more understanding woman.

Julie's eyes grew wide with surprise, and Mark felt a moment of soaring hope. Julie looked for a moment like she might say something, then caught herself.

"You're sorry?" she asked. Mark nodded quickly. She gave him a smile, one that Mark would have noticed didn't quite reach her eyes if he'd been more attentive. "I guess I'm sorry too," she said. "I shouldn't have reacted the way I did." As she spoke, Mark felt the burning in his cheeks intensify. She looked at Mark sheepishly as she went on, all vestiges of what Mark found unappealing disappearing into her conciliatory tone. "If you really are sorry, Mark, maybe we can, I don't know, find a way to be friends." She raised her hand slowly to his cheek. He unconsciously jerked away, then stopped and let her touch him. Her hand was cool and soft, not at all what he had expected. He smiled at the smoothness of her palm against his stubbled cheek, anticipating more to come.

I hate you with every bit of me. You disgust me. If you want anything from me, you're going to have to take it by force, but I will fight you with all the strength I have. Julie kept these thoughts to herself as she put her hand on his stubbly, sweaty, scarred cheek. It made her nauseous to touch him like this, but Mark had made a fatal error, and she intended to capitalize on it. He's sorry he upset her? Of course. Not sorry for what he did, but sorry for how she felt about it. Just like so many men. But she could use that. She stepped back, consciously avoiding the conspicuous bulge in his grime-streaked slacks. "But please, I feel . . . shy. Can I please close the door? I promise I won't do anything bad." Mark blinked, unsure of what to say now. He was so overcome with desire he almost felt dizzy. Numbly he nodded and backed away, allowing her to close the door in his face.

Mark stared at the door, wishing he had X-ray vision. Maybe it was too soon to hope for anything more yet between Julie and him. That made sense, he supposed. Mark sighed and walked toward the couch, where Julie's bra lay in a tangled heap. He picked it up, looking it over, but it was no longer quite as alluring. He inhaled the scent of fabric, but the gentle feminine odors that had gotten him so enticed seemed mildly unpleasant now. He only noticed the sour sweat in the armbands. After her touch, this was just a cheap bit of fabric, a pale imitation of what he could have, and it made him even hungrier for more of what Julie seemed to be offering.

He was about to return to the bathroom door when the front door swung open and Uncle Les stormed in. He was scowling, probably from another fight with Dad, and Mark immediately realized that maybe he hadn't handled things the way Les would have expected.

Les took a look around the room, seeing Mark standing by the couch, gun in one hand, bra in another, and a noticeable hard-on poking at his pants. He saw the TV, paused on a particularly graphic shot of a man's penis entering a woman's ass to its full length. He rolled his eyes and saw the closed door to the bathroom.

"Jesus fuckin' Christ," he said. "What the hell are you doing in here? Is someone in the goddamn bathroom?"

Mark dropped the bra to the floor, scratching at the back of his head with his now-free hand. "Well, yeah. The girl, uh, she needed to pee, and I thought, you know, I have the gun and everything, so—"

"Stop," Les said. He brought his hand to his face as he lowered his head. "This is . . . this is . . . God, this is actually worse than I was worried about."

"What, uh, what were you worried about?" Mark was terrified to say anything, but he genuinely wondered how this could be worse than what Les had imagined.

"I thought you might be fucking her. On my bed, even." Les shook his head sadly. "I mean, I guess I'm glad you didn't, but holy hell, Mark, this is fucking stupid."

Inside the bathroom, Julie heard two men's voices talking, and not softly. She swore under her breath. Mark was one thing. She was pretty sure they could overpower Mark without much trouble. The other one though, Les, was a lot more dangerous. He was smarter. Julie knew she wouldn't be able to fool him like she did Mark.

She stood above the toilet contemplating her next move. She had long forced out the urine she'd been holding in for hours. It stank in there, like the worst gas station restroom she'd ever been in. Fortunately she was an expert at the "crouch" method, as she didn't even want to use the toilet paper to cover the seat. She could have held that position, hovering over the seat with her shorts bunched around her knees, for probably half an hour, but what would that solve? No one was going to believe it took her this long to pee. She stood and pulled her shorts up, using her foot to flush the toilet. It barely bubbled as the yellowed water trickled down the drain. The stench was so thick she felt like she could cut it with a knife, but she didn't dare leave just yet. She had to think, had to reformulate their grand escape plan.

If it had just been Mark, she'd have gone ahead with the plan to ambush him when he brought her back to the others. But Les's presence screwed all of that up. She doubted they could overpower Les on his own, let alone with Mark there as backup. Right now, Terry and Eric were braced and ready, waiting to spring on Mark as soon as the door opened. She'd have to find some way to warn them, a way without tipping off the others to what they'd been planning. She prayed the wrestlers could hear Mark and Les arguing as well, but she doubted they would hear anything through that door.

Julie knew she was quickly running out of time. Les and Mark were probably arguing about her, and any second now she expected Les to throw open the door and demand she finish up. Unlike Mark, he wasn't going to be sidetracked by the idea of her on the toilet. He'd barely paid any attention to her either before or after the fight at the diner. Les didn't see any of them as anything but a problem to be solved, and that was more frightening to Julie than the nauseating specter of Mark trying to force himself on her.

Julie had defended herself from plenty of Marks in her life. Of the few dates she'd had in high school, most ended badly, and she wasn't afraid to lay a hand on the boy if she didn't like where they laid theirs. More than once the guys she'd gone out with had to explain away black eyes, swollen lips, and crooked noses as anything other than their feisty date putting them in their place.

Les didn't care about her gender, though. That much she could tell from his attitude. If she did attack him, he would clock her in the jaw the same as he would any of the guys. Given what she saw at from Les at the diner, she was in no hurry to feel the force of his fist. No, she needed to find a way to stop their escape attempt before it turned into a bloodbath.

—

"You're letting that woman get in your head," Les said. "I know you're hard up, but for God's sake, I made it eight years without a place to dip my stick. Find someone to fuck, or find another pimp besides Dante."

"You're sayin' if you had, like, the hottest chick ever right here, you wouldn't?" Mark looked at Les with hopeful eyes, a look that made Les's heart sink. He wondered, not for the first time, if the boy was just too far gone.

"Mark, no, for fuck's sake, no." He sighed and sat down heavily on the couch. "Did anyone ever tell you why I went to prison?"

Mark shook his head no. "I asked, but Dad and Mom wouldn't ever tell me. Mamma Goode wouldn't even talk about you at all. She was real pissed about it."

"Yeah, I know," Les said with a chuckle. "Believe me, I know." He got serious then as he stared at Mark, whose eyes shone with reverence. "But what you don't know is, I killed three men at Mount Olive over the years. I did it fast and quiet; no one ever knew it was me. Not the ones that could do something about it, at least. But you know how I did it?"

Mark shook his head, and Les stood up, walking toward him. Whenever Les got this close, Mark felt uncomfortable, but he tried not to show it.

"I kept a shiv I made out of a toothbrush and razor shoved all the way up my ass almost the whole time I was at Mount Olive. Eight fucking years I had a razor up my goddamn ass!" He grabbed Mark's own ass then, jamming his fingers between the cheeks. Mark cried out and squirmed away. Les nodded.

"Jesus, Uncles Les, what the fuck?" Mark asked.

"Uncomfortable, ain't it? Imagine having that shiv up there. Eating with it. Sleeping with it. The only time I took it out was to shit, or to kill someone." He walked closer to Mark once more, and this time Mark openly squirmed. "I can still feel it with every step. Every time I take a crap, I feel sore where it used to be. Tell me, Mark, would you do that? Could you do that?" Mark didn't reply. "No, I don't think you could. And I wish I didn't. I'd rather be a giant fucking pussy than have to go through that. So for Christ's sake, listen to me, and get ahold of yourself before you end up at Mount Olive too." He stopped speaking then, looking over his shoulder at the closed bathroom door.

"How long you think she's gonna be taking a piss?" Les asked.

Mark shrugged. Les walked to the door and without any warning gripped the handle and twisted, throwing open the bathroom door.

Julie cowered in faux surprise as the door swung open. She was dismayed to see Les standing in the doorway, hands on his hips as he stared at her.

"Can't imagine you're enjoying yourself in here," he said. "Were you hoping one of us might leave and make it easier for you and your buddies to run?" Julie said nothing, trying to make a show preparing to wash her hands. "Don't bother, honey, I know you were just stalling for time. Come on, then, come on out." She stood staring at him, not moving at all. "Don't be shy. I promise I'm not gonna touch you."

Julie started forward, taking care to appear as meek as possible. As she stood up something hit her in the face, and she winced in surprise as it dropped to the floor. Her bra.

"Go ahead and put that back on. Ain't no one out here gonna need it." The last thing Julie wanted was to put the bra back on. She tried and failed to block out images of Mark pleasuring himself into her undergarments, but as she picked it up and looked in the cups, she was relieved to see they appeared to be dry. She turned around and slipped the straps back on the hooks and slid it under her shirt, working to get the bra on as quickly as she could. She didn't think Mark would be watching with Les standing there, but she didn't want to make that assumption.

When she turned back toward them, Les was standing in front of Mark, blocking his view of Julie. *Thank God for small favors,* she thought as she exited the bathroom. She willed herself to keep her eyes away from the door to the back room, where she knew Eric and Terry were waiting to pounce. She hadn't heard all of the conversation between Les and Mark, but she'd heard Les talking about the men he'd murdered. Three people stabbed to death in a prison, and Les had gotten clean away with it. What scared Julie more than the act itself was the casual, flippant way Les seemed to regard it. It wasn't something he enjoyed, but it wasn't something he seemed troubled about either. If it needed to be done, it would be done. Julie didn't even try to tell herself that Les would hesitate to put them down if he needed to. She wasn't sure why he hadn't already.

"What are you waiting for?" Les asked. She started at the sound of his voice, looking everywhere but the door.

"I'm not really excited about going back in there," she finally said. Les nodded.

"Yeah, well, it ain't a choice. You're staying in there till we get all this sorted out." He pushed her, gently but firmly, by the shoulder. "Come on then."

Julie stared at the doorknob, trying to move her hand up, but it remained stubbornly at her side. She could feel a cold sweat trickling down the valley of her spine as she strained to hear anything on the other side of the door.

"We have a show tomorrow night," she said. Her voice sounded like it came from the other side of the trailer. "People are going to be looking for us if you don't let us go."

Mark, agitated now, pushed past Les and reached up to grab the door.

"Would you just shut up and get back in there?" he asked as he swung the door open. Julie blocked some of their view and she saw Terry first, crouched and ready to pounce. She splayed herself against the door as flat as possible to give Terry room to move.

Terry launched himself. He tackled Mark by the waist, knocking him down. The impact pressed Julie hard against the door, but as she was falling she felt a firm hand seize her by the upper arm and yank her back up.

"We have to go," Eric hissed in her ear, pushing her past an unsettlingly calm Les. "Fucking *run*!" Julie stopped as she stumbled into the living room, looking over her shoulder long enough to see Les brutally connect to the side of Eric's skull with a right hook. Eric's head bounced off the wall and he took a few faltering steps backward, falling over Terry as Terry reared his fist back to strike Mark in the face. Julie didn't have to think. Her legs did what they needed to, propelling her toward the door even as she struggled to look away from the hallway. She felt sick leaving Eric like that, but if she could get away, maybe she could bring help. In seconds she was out the door, almost tripping as she sprang down the steps and onto the cold, wet grass.

Terry continued to drive his fist into Mark's face until Les grabbed Terry's forearm in mid-strike, wrenching it backward. "Get up," Les snarled at Mark. "Go after the girl." As Mark stood up, nose bloodied, Les thrust the pistol into his hands. "Fucking shoot her this time."

Terry tried to take advantage of the distraction and pull free, but Les's grip was like a vice on his wrist. Instead, Terry brought his knee up, catching Les with a glancing blow to the inner thigh. Les released Terry just long enough to take hold of his shirtfront in both fists, and rammed his forehead into Terry's face. Terry felt an explosion of pain spread to the back of his skull as his vision flickered, but before he could even process what had happened Les struck him again and again, breaking Terry's nose as a torrent of blood poured down his face. He struck out blindly through the pain, connecting solidly with Les's Adam's apple. Les gagged and dropped to one knee, then brought his right arm up in a hard arc to Terry's groin. Gasping, Terry crumpled to the floor.

"You keep this up, you ain't never gonna shoot a load again," Les said. He heard several shots ring out, and couldn't help but be disappointed that it took Mark more than one shot to kill Julie.

Eric struggled to get to his feet, bracing his hand against the wall for support. As a wrestler, he'd had his bell rung more times than he cared to count, and while he could finish a match in that state, he wasn't sure he could have a knockdown, drag-out brawl with an opponent like Les. He had to try, though. Those gunshots, he knew, were meant for Julie, and he had to find a way to get out to her. He stared glassy-eyed at his captor and took a step forward, working on muscle memory at this point.

His first punch missed the mark as Les dodged, clipping the ear rather than belting the eye, but it made a satisfying smack against his fist. Eric's best hope was to keep Les off his feet, so he struck again, two quick left jabs that caught Les on the forehead and a roundhouse right that knocked Les onto his back, spilling into the narrow hallway. He moved forward and raised his right foot to bring it down on Les's head, but Les surprised Eric by leaning forward, seizing him by the ankle and sinking his teeth into the meat of Eric's thigh. Eric howled in surprise, jerking his leg backward and bracing himself against the door to keep from falling over.

Les shook his head and kicked Eric in the left kneecap, sending him to the floor as well. Les stood up, swinging the tips of his boots into Eric's ribs. He did it again and again, satisfied when he heard the crunch his steel toes made against the bones of Eric's ribs. Eric rolled over as he wheezed desperately for air. He let out a weak whimper of a scream as he laid on the floor. Les looked at Ricky, still huddled over the motionless Burt in the closet. "You want to take a shot too?" He walked to the closet, looking over the still form of Burt. "Move," he said to Ricky. Ricky stared back, unwilling to relinquish his guard over Burt. Les kneeled, coming face-to-face with Ricky. "You need to move so's I can see if your big-ass pal is still with us." Slowly, Ricky backed away, taking a seat at Burt's feet as Les looked him over.

Despite all outward evidence, Burt still had some shallow awareness of what was happening. He could feel a pressure in his head, but couldn't make his hands move to touch it. He knew, vaguely, that he wasn't in the diner, but he couldn't understand where he was or how he'd gotten there. All he knew, all he could understand, was Ricky's hand in his, Ricky's soothing voice in his ear telling him things would be okay, that he loved Burt. Burt took comfort in this, understanding that he probably should be afraid, but really he was just too tired to feel much of anything. He wanted to open his eyes, look at Ricky and thank him, tell Ricky he loved him too. But his eyelids were just so damned heavy. Easier to just rest for a bit. Ricky wasn't going anywhere.

But then he was gone, though Burt wasn't sure if he'd just fallen asleep. Could he even be awake if he couldn't open his eyes? Awake or not, Ricky suddenly wasn't there. Instead he heard someone else's voice, felt someone else's hands on his body, at his neck. (Or was it his face? Too hard to tell.) A new feeling crept into him then. His heartbeat accelerated as he began to panic. He wanted to cry out for Ricky but found he couldn't move a single part of his body. He couldn't even twitch his lips. It was getting harder and harder just to make his body breathe, and as his panic worsened he found his lungs were burning through oxygen faster than he could provide it.

On one level Burt understood he was dying, but that wasn't what scared him. He wanted Ricky, he was scared to die without Ricky, and no matter how hard he tried, he couldn't make his mouth move, couldn't force out the words. All he wanted was to ask for Ricky. He wept, or at least felt like he was weeping. He wondered, as the last synapses fired in his brain, whether tears were actually seeping from his steel-lidded eyes.

"He's gone," Les said, sighing as he stood back up. "I mean, I kind of expected it, but still, that's some shit luck." He was considering what the immediate next step should be when a screech like a wounded animal caused him to glance toward his left. He saw the blurred form of Ricky literally launching himself off his feet at Les, colliding hard with Les and knocking them both to the floor. That sound continued to come out of Ricky's mouth, not a wail or a scream but just a high-pitched noise, almost like a whistling teakettle, and it was driving Les nuts. Ricky peppered him with surprisingly effective stiff shots to the face, and Les felt a cut open over his left eye as Ricky's knuckle connected with it. Finally he'd had enough, and he shoved Ricky to the side as his temper flared. There was only so much bullshit a man like him could be expected to take.

He was on Ricky in an instant, punching him repeatedly in the face as he tried to stop that awful screeching. He was aware, primally, that he had to stop or he'd kill Ricky. He also knew that if he gave Terry and Eric enough time, they'd recover and make it a two-on-one—even three if Ricky's adrenaline kept up. He stopped and stood back up, leaving Ricky bruised and bloody on the floor. Behind Les, Eric was on his hands and knees, dry heaving. Terry was tentatively touching his ruined nose as he laid curled up on his side. Les was disappointed but not surprised. They were tough, sure, but nothing hardens you like Mount Olive. That's why they called it "hard time." A shame for them. He'd have Mark scrub down the room later, something he'd hoped would be unnecessary until Terry bled all over the carpet. They were lucky he'd given his gun back to Mark, or Les would have shot them all right there on the spot. He decided he should probably take them out to the pigpen to do that anyway. No sense making more work by having to dig bullets out of the walls. It occurred to him then that Mark should have already come back inside. The fact that he hadn't made Les uneasy. It was quiet outside, a type of quiet that, in Les's experience, meant something was wrong. He stood up, stepping over the prone bodies of the wrestlers as he walked out, closing and locking the door behind him. As he walked outside the trailer, he braced himself for bad news, but as he stepped into the early-morning sunlight, his stomach lurched at just how bad things were.

9

Halfway between Ansted and Chimney Corner, West Virginia
12:15 p.m.

Brick scowled as he held his Motorola flip phone to his ear. John thought it looked like a toy in Brick's massive fist, and he wondered how Brick could even dial the numbers on it. Brick still wore his aviators, but John could almost see his eyes narrowed to slits as he tried to make himself clear to Jack Meyer back in Richmond.

"Yeah, look, I'm just trying to explain what I can while we've still got a signal here. We're between the mountains right now it looks like, so try to pay attention."

"I'm listening," Jack said. He was loud enough that John could hear him clear across the cabin. "But it sounds like you're almost all the way outta West Virginia and haven't found anything yet."

"I wouldn't say we're empty-handed. I've at least established that it looks like they didn't make it too far last night, wherever they ended up."

"Have you talked to anyone? Any cop buddies who might have access to, I don't know, incident reports or something?"

"I'll tell you what, Jack. How about you let me, the former cop, do the cop stuff? I just called you so you didn't have a stroke wondering where we were."

The road twisted through another mountainous area, with gray rock faces rising up on their right and a steep downhill fall on their left. Signs warning of falling rock zones and semi runoff ramps dotted the area.

"Jack, can you still hear me?" Brick asked.

"Wh . . . I . . . you need . . . back!" was all Brick could make out. He cracked his neck with a twist of the head and flipped the phone shut.

"Well," he said, "what's coming up next on the map?"

John scanned through the roadways with his finger.

"It looks like a little place called Chimney Corner," John said. "One of the first towns Terry would have come across, if he took this road to avoid I-64."

"So either they're around here somewhere," Brick replied, "or we're back at square one." They traveled in silence for a few minutes as the road wound through heavily wooded areas dotted with churches every couple of miles. John noticed access roads that were unnamed, mostly dirt, leading off the road at various places toward what he assumed were farms of some sort. After a bit they exited the woods onto a bridge that carried them over a mud-colored river toward the center of a small town. Across the bridge the road continued to follow the riverbank westward, with shops on the north side and small, single-family homes on the south side along the water. To the right was the main business area of town, with shops and restaurants and a small inn overlooking the river. Brick pulled into a Marathon gas station even though they still had half a tank left. John looked at him, puzzled, but said nothing.

"Gonna get some gas," Brick replied to his unasked question, "and ask that attendant if this little place has an all-night diner."

"You don't think he's going to wonder why you're looking for an all-night diner in the middle of the afternoon?"

"Maybe I just like the atmosphere," Brick said with a grin. "Come on in with me, learn a little something about how to get what you want." John obliged, having planned to anyway, and exited the truck as Brick was rounding the front of it. Together they walked into the tiny storefront, where a pimply-faced teen with a John Deere hat sat behind the counter. He gave a cursory glance over the *Spider-Man* comic he was reading and started to return to it when he did a double take, setting the magazine down and staring at Brick with eyes that John imagined were wide, but still looked only half-lidded to him.

"Hey there," Brick said in his most charming tone. "I wanted to get ten on pump two, if that's all right." He pulled out Jack's American Express, which the teenager shook his head at.

"Cash only, mister, sorry." Brick raised both eyebrows in what John now recognized in him as mock surprise.

"Mmm, I guess we really are off the beaten path, huh? All right, hang on then." Brick slid the card back into his wallet and brought out a ten-dollar bill instead, setting it on the counter in front of the teen. "Here you go." The teen took it almost gingerly, ringing up an ancient push-button cash register that chimed loudly as the drawer popped open. "Oh, and I was wondering," Brick said as the teen put the ten in the correct slot. "Do you guys have any diners nearby?"

The teen finished putting the ten away and looked first at Brick, then John. "We got a few places," he said. "There ain't much here, but we do got some."

John was suddenly very aware of how small the space they were in was. There were two refrigerated cases—one full of beer, the other sodas. A solitary rack held boxes of Slim Jims, potato chips, beef jerky, and a modest assortment of candy bars. Near the door, about two feet from where they stood, was one more display rack with automotive supplies: oil, ice scrapers, and washer fluid.

"The Chimney Corner Café's up on Main Street about five minutes that way, and oh!" he exclaimed with sudden remembrance, "we got a Burger King on Franklin Street, but, I guess you probably seen the sign on the way into town."

"Anyplace open twenty-four hours?" John asked. The teen adjusted his hat.

"I dunno. My ma don't really let me go out that late. She says ain't nothin' good ever happens after midnight." He thought for a minute. "There's one place, up Riverside a bit, that I think's open all night. I don't rightly know for sure; I don't really go up that far usually, but I heard, you know, truckers like to stop there and stuff."

Brick leaned over the counter a bit, bringing himself eye to eye with the teen. He smiled and removed his sunglasses. His eyes were a warm hazel color. "Do you know the name of this place, son?"

"Uh, yeah," the teen said, meeting Brick's gaze. "It's Bud's. Bud's Diner."

"Bud's," Brick repeated. He nodded as he stood up. "Thank you, Jerry." The teen blinked at the sound of his name, and John looked at Brick, wondering how the man knew the kid's name. Brick pointed at the nametag sitting on top of a set of car keys behind the teen. The name "Jerry" was written out in faded blue ink on it. "Hey listen, one more thing. You know if anyone came through last night, big athletic dudes like us? Maybe they stopped for gas, maybe they had a flat tire or something? Woulda been after midnight."

Jerry shook his head. "Naw. We ain't open that late. Don't know many places that are around here. Well, beside's Bud's."

"Okay, well thank you again. You have a good day, okay?" He gave Jerry a small salute as he turned and squeezed out the door.

John watched as Brick's shoulders nearly touched both sides of the doorframe as he passed through. He moved quickly to catch up, coming round to the pump side as Brick inserted the nozzle into the truck's gas tank.

"I didn't know anyone actually still calls themselves 'Bud,'" John said as Brick watched the white numbers on the pump clack along cent by cent. "But honestly, it sounds like the type of place someone like Terry would stop at."

"You never bothered to stop off along any of these places between towns, I take it?"

"No, not really," John replied. "It never seemed like a good idea. Plus, I mean, what would I stop for? I dunno if you noticed, but we kinda stand out everywhere we go here."

Brick laughed, shaking his head as he pulled the nozzle back out. Behind him, the number on the pump read "7.63." "You talk like any minute now the Klan's gonna come riding up to drag us away," he said. "You're in more danger on State Street in Chicago than you are here. Jerry in there, he's more scared'a you than you are of him, I guarantee it."

"That's what I'm afraid of," John said. "Scared people do stupid shit. That kid in there could have had a pistol under the counter."

"Oh, he did," Brick said, opening the driver's door and getting in. John followed suit on the passenger side. "I noticed it sticking out."

"Is that a normal thing round here?"

"Normal enough not to be scared of it just being there. Around these places, most everyone knows how to shoot. It's like learning to drive." They pulled out onto the road and headed west, toward Bud's. The sky was a dull gray overhead, and a light bit of slushy rain started to fall. Brick turned on the wipers, and the water began to sluice in chunks down the sides of the windshield.

"What makes you so sure this is the place, and not any of the other towns where we stopped?"

Brick shrugged. John was starting to think that was his go-to response. "Call it a hunch. A feeling. Something about this place, it just feels right, in a wrong kind of way."

"A feeling? That doesn't seem like a strong thing to go on."

"Your whole life, I bet you had it drilled into you that you gotta go only by what's right in front of you. And that's fine. Lotta the time, that's exactly what you should be doing. But . . ." Brick took a deep breath and let it out slowly. "But I learned a different way. Sometimes, out in the jungle, you gotta be aware of your environment in a way that really don't make no sense. Sometimes you can feel it, that a place is just off. If I'd listened to that feeling, I might still be a marine."

"You ever miss it?" John asked. He couldn't imagine a life like that for himself, but Brick seemed positively wistful about rucking through the jungles.

"I do. They recruited me right outta high school, so it's where I really grew up. I was tight with my unit too. We were lean, mean killing machines. But I didn't pay attention when I should have, and only three years outta basic, I took a bullet to the knee. So long, jumping jacks, after that shit."

"But you wrestle," John said. "How the hell do you manage that if your knee is all shot to shit?"

"Bitch, please," Brick said with a laugh. "Ric Flair survived *two* fuckin' plane crashes, and he's still going strong."

"He did?"

"Yeah. Why do you think he's always rolling onto his right when he falls? Cause his back's all shot to shit."

John nodded, taking it in as they drove past several more neighborhoods overlooking the river. The shops to the right had disappeared, replaced by more trees.

"So," he said after a minute, "a feeling."

"Uh-huh."

"And, uh, if you're wrong?"

Another shrug. "Then I'm wrong."

They pulled into Bud's, a run-down diner in desperate need of fresh paint that sat on the north end of the road. Despite its distance from the center of town, its parking lot was half-full, including two semis with trailers pulled in along the back. Brick parked next to an Oldsmobile Cutlass Ciera that had so much trash in the back, John couldn't see the seats or the floor. Brick took out his Motorola and flipped it open, looking at it for a few seconds before pursing his lips and tossing it in the center console.

"What's wrong?" John asked.

"No signal. Not that I'm surprised. I just was hoping to call Jack before we went inside."

They stepped out of the truck. The drizzle had already stopped, but the vehicles still glittered in the light. The parking lot was overrun with weeds and potholes, which had been filled in with gravel. By the far corner of the building was a pay phone, battered and leaning to the left. Brick nudged John and motioned toward the phone.

"Betcha that's where Knox called from, if they stopped here." He looked over the pay phone, but the number for it had long been scratched off.

Brick and John walked across the lot and through the doors. It was only mildly warmer inside than out, so most of the customers still wore light coats or sweaters. The dull rumble of overlapping conversations was punctuated with the sounds of silverware clinking against plates. John noticed a distinct drop in the noise level when they walked in. It wasn't quite like in the old Westerns, where the whole place goes quiet, but it was enough to catch John's attention. He was glad that, unlike Brick's merch shirt, he was only wearing a black tee and jeans. No need to feel even more conspicuous.

Brick, for his part, either didn't notice or didn't care that their entrance had caused a stir. He walked straight toward the counter, where one young man sat eating a ham steak with eggs while talking to a striking woman with red hair and breasts that strained against a purposely too-tight shirt. He sat two stools down from the young man, and John joined him. The waitress behind the bar extricated herself from the conversation with the young man and sidled up to Brick.

"*Oof*, look at you," she said as she leaned on her elbows toward Brick. "Let me guess: You'll have one of everything, right, big guy?" Brick nodded and took off his sunglasses, meeting and holding her gaze. He turned away only to look at the menu, pretending to study it with gusto.

"You know, I bet a woman like you would know exactly what I want," he said. He put down the menu and looked into her eyes once more. "What would you recommend, honey?"

The waitress leaned in closer, almost touching her forehead to Brick's, and started scanning through the menu with one long, expertly manicured finger. John could smell the enticing mixture of her perfume and bacon from his own seat. She tapped her candy-pink nail against the menu Brick was holding.

"I think that's a good choice for you, sugar. Plenty filling." Brick raised his head, barely an inch from hers, and grinned.

"Can you believe I have never had a country fried steak?" Brick asked.

"Well, you're in luck, 'cause I make some of the best ones in the state," she said. "How you want the eggs with that?"

"Oh, over easy for sure. I like 'em nice and soft."

"I like mine over hard," she said with a wink.

"We'll have to share breakfast some time then," he replied with a smile.

She grinned, stood up, and looked toward John. Her tone was still friendly, flirtatious even, but the heat he could feel from her and Brick was gone like it was never there.

"How about you, sweety? Got an idea of what you want?" John smirked and shook his head. He'd heard stories, everyone in MAW had, of Brick's way with the ladies. The few women that came to the shows would go insane every time Brick took off his shirt, and he always made sure to toss it to the best-looking lady in the crowd, often with his hotel room number written inside. Whether they were married, dating, or single, it never seemed to matter. There was rarely a night that Brick spent alone.

John shook his head, amazed at the assuredness, the well-earned confidence Brick had. No women had ever been so overt in their flirtations with John. As he watched Brick in action at the diner, he felt a twinge of jealousy tweak at his guts. John wouldn't have been surprised to see those two start pawing each other right over the menu.

John ordered something called a pepperoni roll and some soup beans. The waitress smiled and disappeared into the kitchen.

"It's like you have magical powers or something," John said when she was out of earshot. "I mean, seriously, what the hell? She was all over you before you even said a word."

"Well," Brick said, leaning back and replacing his sunglasses, "I imagine the competition isn't exactly fierce around here either." John squinted at him. "Present company excluded, of course."

John took a look around the diner and saw that most of the customers were White men who looked like extras from *Deliverance*. There were a couple of families scattered about, but the majority of the clientele were men with missing teeth, missing hair, and missing manners. At the end of the counter was the youngest man in the place, but he had a distant, simple look to him that wouldn't light anyone's world on fire.

"Yeah," John said. "I wonder how she ended up here, then."

"Lot of people just stay where they're born," Brick replied. "This is a nice way to make a living in a place like this. Good tips."

"She's not just angling for a tip with you, though."

Brick took a sip of water before replying. "Yeah, well, sometimes it's charm, sometimes it's chemistry. But it's always 100 percent Brick."

John raised his eyebrow to that, making Brick choke a little on his water.

"Okay, okay," he acknowledged. "No more promo shit. What can I say? It's a pain in the ass to keep myself in this shape, but it's worth it every time a lady like that gives me the eye."

"It's just too bad we don't have time to do anything about it," John said, taking a long gulp of his own water.

"Never say never." Brick grinned as the waitress came back out with John's soup beans. She set the bowl down in front of John, but before she could go back in the kitchen, Brick waved for her attention. She stopped immediately and turned toward him, smiling. "I never did get your name."

"Marcy," she said, turning toward Brick with one hand on her hip. "You gonna tell me yours, stranger?"

"Well, I kind of like being a man of mystery." The waitress cocked her eyebrow at this, examining more closely the front of Brick's shirt, with his fist punching through a brick wall.

"You're not exactly dressed like James Bond," she said. Brick grinned.

"Well, sometimes you gotta try to blend."

"Honey, you ain't never gonna blend here.

Brick burst out laughing, an unexpected sound to John. He'd heard a few guffaws and plenty of chuckles, but had yet to hear an uncontrollable burst like that from Brick. If it was faked, John would never be able to tell.

"You're probably right, Marcy." He shrugged. "You can call me Rick."

"Okay then, Rick. So what are you in town for? Business or pleasure?"

"Well, business, but I think I can try to squeeze in a little pleasure."

"Is that so? I'd love to help you out with that." She looked down the counter at the other patron, who'd been sitting there since John and Brick walked in and showed no signs of leaving anytime soon. "But first, I'm gonna need to take care of poor Mason over there. Be back in a jiff, Rick." She winked as she sashayed to the end of the counter.

"So, how is Rick better than Brick?" John asked.

"No one's called me Rick since I was in middle school. I think we'll be fine." He watched Marcy talking to Mason, who kept giving Brick a withering sidelong glance. "I don't think that guy likes us very much," he said softly.

"You're really surprised that a White dude in a place like this wouldn't take kindly to having us around?" John asked. He took a spoonful of beans and shoveled it in. They were good, a little salty, but warm and filling on a chilly October afternoon. He heard a voice from the back announce an order was up, and Marcy hurried to the back.

"With any luck, that's our food," Brick said. "I'm starving." Marcy emerged from the kitchen carrying two steaming white plates and set them down in front of Brick and John.

"Oh, that looks delicious," Brick said, seizing the steak knife and fork as he greedily eyed the fried disc of beef on his plate. Two runny eggs oozed yolk that ran under the steak, mixing with the grayish gravy dripping down its sides. John's plate had a long roll cut in half with sticks of thick pepperoni and melted mozzarella inside. John assumed he was meant to eat it like a sandwich, but he was self-conscious enough to not want to just dig in with his hands without being certain. Brick showed no such compunctions, scooping the leaky eggs onto the top of the steak before starting to cut into it.

"So, Marcy," Brick began, "this place is open all night too, right?"

"It is," she said. "I'm not night shift, though."

"I'm glad to hear it," Brick replied. He ate the grayish-yellow chunk on his fork, swallowing after only a few chews. "It'd be pretty awful if you'd already been here all night."

"Are you boys staying in town a few days? Because we do have other restaurants here in Chimney Corner. We've even got a Burger King now."

"Yeah, so we heard," Brick said. He and John both chuckled. Marcy peered at them, but didn't ask what was so funny. Brick smiled and held up his hand. "No, it's just that we were already told about the BK, but, well, me and John get enough fast food on the road. I can't imagine it's really better than here, with your . . ." Brick paused a moment as he looked over the menu again. "Your authentic West Virginia ham. If I'm still around later, I think I'll try some of that."

"Well, you won't be seein' me then. My shift ends at five."

"Now that's a pity," Brick said. He leaned in closer. "I don't imagine you'd be interested in joining us for dinner here, then?"

Marcy grinned as she shook her head. "Nope. I get enough of this place as is. Mason there's the only one who comes in for food right after his shift."

"That guy at the end?" John asked. Brick gave him a look, but nodded subtly for him to go on.

"Yup. Works all night here, then comes in for a late breakfast. Some people, I guess they just like routine." She glanced over their heads at a customer who was loudly slurping up the last of his soda through a straw. "Excuse me, boys, I need to make my rounds for a bit." Marcy slipped from behind the counter and made her way to the slurper. As she engaged with him, Brick stood as casually as a man his size could and moved toward Mason at the end of the counter. John watched from his seat with interest.

"Afternoon," Brick said, sidling up to the end of the counter. Mason eyed him suspiciously as he dug into a pancake soggy with butter and syrup. He had an air of agitation to him that Brick chalked up to basic racism. It wasn't anything he hadn't handled before. When Mason didn't reply, Brick went on. "I hear you were the guy working here last night." Still no reply. "I just wanted to know if there was a group that came in last night. Four guys and a girl. One guy big as a house. You see anyone like that last night?"

Mason looked up from his plate then, still suspicious, still withdrawn, but with something else too. He seemed *scared* to Brick, and Brick wasn't sure if that was from the question or his physical stature. He sat down on the chair next to Mason in an attempt to alleviate any of those concerns.

"I'm not trying to stir up trouble. I'm just looking for my friends. We were supposed to meet up this morning, but they never showed. Did you see them last night?"

Mason swallowed and turned back to his plate. He replied without looking up. "Nope. Sorry. We don't get a whole lot of business overnight, ya know. Usually just truckers and shit."

Brick nodded and stood up. Looking down, he noticed the floor around Mason's stool was visibly cleaner than the grimier linoleum around it. Someone had cleaned it recently, and only that particular spot. He bent down and made a show of tightening his boot laces, glancing around the area as he did so.

"Well, I'm sorry to have bothered ya then," Brick said as he turned to walk away.

"No problem," Mason said, still not looking up from his plate.

Brick sat back in his spot, digging into the steak in a much more hurried fashion. John prodded him with his elbow, leaning in to whisper.

"Anything interesting?" John asked.

"Not now," Brick replied. "Just finish your food like normal. I'll talk to you in the truck." Marcy made her way back over to them then, refilling their mugs with coffee.

"How's that steak treatin' you?" she asked. "Is it everything you ever dreamed of?"

Brick grinned, but his attitude was stiffer now. "It's pretty damned good, yeah." He swallowed another bite, then put his hand out gently on Marcy's arm as she began to move on. "It looks like we're gonna need to stay here in town overnight," Brick said. "Is there a hotel or something nearby?" She grinned now, because even with the change in his attitude, Brick still had a clear interest in her.

"There's a little motel back up the road a bit, just on the outskirts of downtown. Cheap rooms, only forty bucks a night." Cheap enough for them to each have one, in other words. Brick didn't think Jack would agree, but he was willing to spend a little out of his own wallet, if need be.

"Thank you," Brick said. "So since we're gonna be here and you're off at five, maybe we can meet up again later."

Marcy took a slip of paper out of her order pad and scribbled something on it. "Why don't you give me a call when you get a room," she said, sliding the paper into Brick's hand. "We can make the plans from there." Marcy looked like she might actually wink, but she didn't, instead turning away and heading back into the kitchen with just the slightest exaggeration of her swaying hips. To their right, Mason drilled them with a gaze that could level buildings. Brick realized that Marcy, not the food, brought Mason here after his shift.

Brick pulled out a few bills and left them on the counter, standing up and motioning for John to follow. John quickly gulped down the rest of his coffee, burning his tongue, before rushing to catch up to Brick. They got out to the truck, and as soon as the doors were closed, John was talking.

"Okay, so what's going on? Why are we renting a room? Jack's gonna be pissed if we skip out on a whole second day of prep."

"Because," Brick said as he pulled out of the diner's parking lot and headed back toward town. "That Mason fellow's shifty as hell. I think something happened last night, and I get the feeling he knows something about it."

"That's a big leap. You ever think maybe he just doesn't like you? I mean, he seems like he has a thing for Marcy too. He's probably just jealous."

"He probably is," Brick said. "But that doesn't explain the counter he was sitting at."

"What about it?"

"There was blood on it. Under the lip. Looked fresh. And I'm pretty sure our Mr. Mason knows exactly where it came from."

10

Goode Farm
12:22 p.m.

Julie burst out of the front door of the trailer like a greyhound hitting the track from the chute. She vaulted over the flimsy wooden steps leading up to the door and came down hard on the grass, still slick with morning dew. She almost went sprawling face-first but managed to keep her balance and took off running, her long athletic legs pumping hard as she raced for what she hoped was the entrance to the property. The farmhouse approached on her left as she ran, but she paid no attention to it. Behind her she heard Mark slamming the door open and clambering down the stairs. He bellowed for her to stop, but no way in hell would she do *that*.

Part of her felt guilty about leaving everyone else back there, even Terry. She felt certain they'd be killed for this, but that knowledge pushed her onward. Her entire body buzzed with adrenaline as she ran, and she reassured herself that this is what they wanted. Or what Eric had wanted, at least. He'd sacrificed himself for her and that knowledge softened her attitude toward him considerably. She'd never known a man, besides her father, whom she could say unequivocally would do that.

A shot rang out, though at first she didn't register it. Julie didn't have much of any experience with firearms, so the sound of it wasn't immediately recognizable. When the second one came, realization hit her and she thought, *My God, they really are shooting everyone.* Then the ground exploded a few feet to her right and she knew then that *she* was being shot at, and of course it would be her. Why would they kill everyone else and let her get away? She spared a moment to glance behind her and saw Mark, feet planted, aiming that gigantic pistol at her, and her stomach somersaulted at the sight. She whipped her head around and willed herself to run even faster, trying to zigzag now, but her feet struggled to find traction on the wet grass. She looked down to avoid any dips in the ground, and when she looked up she saw another man, a huge man, one at least as large as Burt Knox, hurtling across the grass from the farmhouse to intercept her. As she tried to zag once more, Mark fired again and she felt something strike her leg. It was a burning sensation, accompanied by a feeling like her thigh had been smacked with a baseball bat. She lost her balance and stumbled just as the huge man from the farmhouse reached her. She screamed as she fell into his arms and he enveloped her in a bear hug that pressed her face uncomfortably into his chest.

"Stop shooting!" he screamed. "I have her; stop shooting!" His voice was higher pitched than Julie would have expected but carried an air of authority to it. She struggled against his grip but had no hope of breaking free. He squeezed tighter in response, forcing the air from her already-taxed lungs. She heard panting as Mark approached at a jog.

"Good timing," he gasped out between lungfuls of air. "Help me get her back to the trailer." Julie felt dizzy with fear. Their best shot, probably their only chance of getting away, had evaporated in seconds. Once back in the trailer, it was only a matter of time until they were burying her in a shallow grave somewhere out here. She held her breath and struggled again, trying in vain to wiggle out of the man's grip. He readjusted himself and refused to loosen his grip, continuing to talk as if she wasn't even there.

"No." His reply was short and invited no argument. "She's coming with me." Behind her, Julie felt the tension oozing from Mark.

"What do you mean, no?" he asked in shock.

"I mean I'm not handing her over for you to kill. I'm taking her. I'll keep her in the basement."

Julie started twisting even more when she heard him say that. The basement. Nothing good ever happened in somebody's basement.

Les groaned as he looked out from the stairs at the scene unfolding before him. The girl was being held by Nate in a bear hug while Nate and Mark argued over her. Les didn't know what the argument was about, but he could guess. It had been Nate who had insisted on waiting to kill the wrestlers. If it had been up to Les, they would have been dragged out and shot almost immediately, just like all those damned gangbangers they'd dealt with before. But no, Nate wanted to wait. Les had tried to argue, had wanted to just overrule Nate and shoot the wrestlers, but then Nate gave him that look. The one that made all of them nervous. The one that even Norm knew meant that to argue the point would be very dangerous. So Les caved again. It seemed to Les like he was doing that more and more these days. It was another sign that it was time to cut his losses and get the hell out of here. Soon.

For now, he had to deal with Nate and the girl. He'd had a feeling Nate would eventually come looking to take one of them for himself, because why else leave them alive? Now he'd had one dumped in his lap. If it had been one of the others, Jiggolo or TJ Azz maybe, Les wouldn't have cared as much. But the fact that it was the girl bothered Les in a way he couldn't quite identify. Les didn't think Nate wasn't the type to rape anyone. But Nate did like to experiment.

"What's going on?" Les asked once he got within earshot. He could see Julie's right leg was covered in blood, already sticky in the cold air. She struggled uselessly against Nate, and Les found himself admiring her moxie. It was pointless to fight, but she still did.

"Nate's sayin' he wants to take Goth Girl to the basement," Mark said, hoping that Les could set things straight.

"Yup. I figured it might be that." He looked at Nate, who was impassively restraining the girl with barely an effort. "What is it you're looking to do exactly?"

"Does it matter?" Nate asked. In terms of the final result, no. Dead was dead, and all of these people were going to end up dead very soon anyway. Something in Les's head couldn't let it go, however. He looked at the girl twisting in Nate's arms and felt something inside him turn like a sharpened stick.

"It's risky. Like I tried to tell you, they have people who are probably already looking for them. The longer they're here, the more likely someone will find them."

"Uncle Les's right, Nate," Mark said. He rubbed his cheek, already swollen from Terry's punches. "Come on, let's take her back and finish this up."

"Yeah. We're gonna need your help anyway. The big one's finally gone." Hearing this, Julie froze in Nate's arms. Was he talking about Burt? Julie felt weak, and suddenly her legs couldn't stay straight. Her right one throbbed like someone had been kicking it for hours, and she began to slip on her own blood coating the grass beneath her feet.

"Quit that," Nate said, rearranging himself to properly brace Julie. "I have to get her to the basement. Clean up this bullet wound before she goes into shock."

"How badly is she hurt?" Les asked.

"It just grazed her."

"What's the point?" Mark protested. "She's gonna be dead soon anyway!"

"No, she's not," Nate said, giving Mark as hard a stare as he ever had. Mark, having always felt inferior to his older brother anyway, quickly shrank away from that gaze. Les stepped in, trying to salvage a situation he saw rapidly spinning out of control.

"Nate, come on. Just bring her back. We'll take them all out to the pens. This, whatever this is? It's a huge risk. Trust me, okay? Isn't that why you guys keep me around?" If anything Les was saying had an impact, Nate didn't show it.

"No. I'm taking her. I'll fix her up downstairs, and then I'll come help move the others. But no one dies. Not yet at least." He glanced down at Julie, who looked to Nate like she was barely conscious at this point. "I'll let you know when."

"Nate," Les began, then stopped himself. This was new territory for them all. Nate had never taken an interest in the business before, besides in the most hands-off way possible. No deliveries, no manufacturing, and, most tellingly, no killing. Nate never showed any interest in the times Les had to eliminate some of the competition. He never requested any of those men for his basement experiments, either. He slaughtered and dressed the pigs, and he disposed of the bodies, but he'd made it clear that was the full extent of what he'd do. Norm was furious, of course. Someone Nate's size was a hell of an asset when it came to intimidation, but they all quickly learned that Nate only did what Nate wanted to do. And since Les was the only other person who knew how to properly dress a pig, he was more than happy to let Nate handle that chore.

This interest in Julie, however, was a new and disturbing development. Les had heard all the stories about psychopaths who started with animals and moved on to people. Like that fucking Dahmer sicko in Milwaukee. Was that what they were dealing with concerning Nate? If it was, would it be smarter for Les to let it go or stand in the way?

Les decided on the former.

"Okay," he said finally. "You take the girl. Fix her up or whatever the fuck, but then get back up here to help with the others." Les phrased it as an order, but it was a request. No one ordered Nate to do anything, but Les never asked for anything. Nate understood this and let things stand without objection.

By now Julie had completely passed out. Nate pressed his hand to her forehead.

"I need to take care of her. Now."

Les nodded in reply, and Nate scooped her up like a small child, carrying her with hardly any indication of her 133-pound weight. As Nate walked back into the farmhouse, Mark handed the Desert Eagle back to Les.

"Shit, she's lucky Nate was here," Mark said as Les holstered the gun in his waistband.

"I don't think so," Les replied.

"Huh? But he just saved her life."

"No. When the fox hears the rabbit scream, he comes running." Les stopped for a minute as they watched the door to the house slam shut. "But not to help."

Mason finished eating his food, never lifting his head up to gaze around. This bothered Marcy because Mason was always a bright, talkative, bubbly presence in the diner. It always helped ease her into the day when she got to serve him breakfast. She loved to talk with him, even if it felt strange since she used to babysit him not so long ago. Mason carried a torch for her—hell it was a whole bonfire apparently—and that made Marcy feel guilty about possibly leading him on. But then again, she figured he'd rather at least talk to her than have her just ignore him completely.

This morning, though, he'd been withdrawn. Barely smiled. Bud had been the only one working when Marcy came in, opening up the diner, but he wouldn't tell her why it had been closed to begin with. Neither would Mason when he finally came round. All he'd say was he'd just been told to close up early for the night. And after that tall hunk of prime beef Brick spoke to Mason, he wouldn't even look up anymore.

Marcy slid over to Mason, pushing his plate out from under his nose. He looked up in confused annoyance until he saw her standing an inch away from him, and then his expression actually darkened. That was unexpected.

"Whatcha need, Marcy?" Mason asked. "I actually wasn't ready for the check just yet."

"I know, hon; I just wanted to see what's got you so beside yourself today. You just ain't being you, you know?" She put a hand over Mason's, and he moved like he was about to pull away then stopped. His face softened a bit.

"Aw, hell, I can't stay mad at you. It ain't right anyway, it's not like you and me's a thing or nothin'." Color darkened his cheeks as he said that, and Marcy felt a swell of sympathy balloon in her chest.

"Oh Mason, what would you want with an someone like me anyhow? I mean, I'm old enough to be your momma."

"Only technically," Mason said, and Marcy was honestly surprised he knew that word.

"It's very flattering, sweety, but you've gotta find someone your own age, you know? Someone you can actually grow old with, not someone who beat ya to the punch." She gave a quick look around the diner. None of her tables looked like they needed anything, but that wouldn't last long.

"So," she went on, "Are you gonna tell me what happened last night, or do I gotta beat it out of ya?" Mason looked at her with rheumy eyes. He looked for all the world like he'd just watched someone shoot his dog.

"I really can't, Marcy, okay? Bud already made me swear, and I can't risk losing this job. No one else in town's gonna pay me as much as Bud does."

Marcy pursed her lips, tapping her manicured nails on the counter. This was even more outside the norm than she thought. And with Brick and John here the next morning, she wondered what the hell Mason had gotten himself mixed up in.

"Does this have something to do with Mark and Les?" she asked. She knew they had something going on with Bud, but like most people in town, whatever the Goodes were up to these days was mostly rumor.

"Marcy, I can't," Mason said, pleadingly this time. She felt the counter rattling as Mason's shaking leg thumped against it.

"Okay, okay, I won't press it," Marcy said, shushing Mason as she stroked his arm. "But I've said it before, Mason, and I'll say it again: You need to stay away from those people. I know Mark's been your friend since you was a boy, but that family is nothin' but trouble these days, you get me?"

Mason only stared.

"Look, I known Les a long time. There ain't no one he really cares about 'cept maybe blood. If they got you wrapped up in some crap they're doing, you're the first one they gonna throw to the wolves when shit goes bad. I don't wanna see that happen to you, hon. You're a good boy, and I want to see you get married and grow old and shit."

Mason smiled, finally, and met her eyes. He still looked like he hadn't slept in days, but his mood had brightened at least. "You ain't gotta worry about me, Marcy," Mason said. "Like you said, I known Mark practically my whole life. He couldn't never even hurt a fly."

Terry twisted his shirt around, looking for a dry spot to press against his still-bleeding nose. His crotch throbbed, causing him to sink back every time he tried to flex his calves to stand up. He sat uselessly against the wall, shirt pulled up and pressed to his face, nursing his bruised ego as well as his nose. To his left, Eric lay sprawled against the opposite wall, one arm wrapped around his ribs and the other pressed to the side of his head where Les had walloped him. At least, Terry thought, Les had given all of them a licking, not just him. Terry could only assume that Julie was dead, which meant time was even shorter for the three of them. *Well, I won't go out without a fight,* Terry said to himself. Les had rushed out fast, not bothering to bind their hands again. Terry planned to take full advantage of that mistake. He wasn't going to take this sitting down, even if that was all he was capable of doing at that moment. He glanced to his left, where Ricky sat motionless. Terry had seen men lose fights before, but he'd never seen someone he could say had been beaten to within an inch of his life. He'd be able to now, though.

Terry couldn't make out Ricky's eyes anymore. The glasses that had always been present over them were a mangled wreck on the floor. His bare chest and abdomen were already distended and discolored from the beating Les had given him, and Terry could hear Ricky's breath wheezing as it passed in and out of his battered rib cage. Ricky, a former lifeguard, had been the closest thing they had to a doctor. He at least had been certified in CPR. Terry had no clue what the extent of Ricky's injuries might be. There wasn't much blood, but Terry thought that might be a bad thing rather than good.

Eric pulled himself up slowly, using the wall as leverage and grunting with exertion. Terry figured Eric was concussed and probably had at least one broken rib to go with it. Those steel-toed boots Les wore were real shitkickers. Eric swayed slightly, and for a moment Terry thought he might faint or throw up. He prayed it wasn't the latter. Terry didn't think he could stand being trapped in a room with fresh vomit. When it became clear that Eric wasn't going to do either, Terry spoke to him.

"I guess we're pretty fucked, huh?"

"You sure . . . you sh . . . you sure know how to brighten the mood," Eric said. He squinted as if he was having trouble focusing on Terry.

"Double vision?"

"Yeah. I got my bell rung for sure."

"Too bad we don't have any dirt to rub on it," Terry said.

"How's Ricky?"

"Not responding. If I couldn't hear him wheezing, I'd think he was dead."

Eric frowned and lowered his head. "Really wish we could turn that light off right now."

"I'd get up to turn it off, but that asshole did a number on me after you pushed your girlfriend out the door." He steadied himself against the door. "Nice job with that, by the way."

Eric brought his head up again and stared at Terry through slitted eyes. "What are you trying to say?"

"Well," Terry said, repositioning himself to sit straighter against the wall. "We were all supposed to run, yeah? Overpower the one asshole and we all run. But you pushed Julie ahead right before Les coldcocked you. If you had been more focused on Les, he might not've coldcocked ya."

"There were two of them," Eric said. "We were never going to overpower two guys with a gun. We were stupid to try."

"Maybe we could have if Julie had stuck around to help. Now she's dead, and we're next."

"You know," Eric said, leaning forward in anger, "I actually used to think you were tough. Like Harley Race tough, you know? Hardest man in MAW and all that shit. But it looks like you're less Harley Race and more Shawn Michaels."

Terry bristled at the comparison. While Harley Race was a legendary tough bastard of a wrestler, Shawn Michaels—WWF champion Shawn Michaels, WrestleMania headliner Shawn Michaels—had earned a reputation as someone with more bark than bite, especially after stories passed around about his ass-whipping in a local bar fight. Posing for the cover of *Playgirl* hadn't helped, either.

"Fuck you," Terry said. "It ain't like you did any better."

"Yeah, well, I never tried to overcompensate for being a giant pussy either." It was harsh and unnecessary, but Eric needed to vent. Burt was dead, Julie might be too (though Eric hoped not), and it looked like they'd be next. Who cared if he torched his professional relationships on the way out?

Neither man was willing to acknowledge they'd each done what they could. To do so would be to acknowledge that they'd been bested, and neither Eric nor Terry was willing to consider what that said about them.

Both men were silent for a long few minutes. If Terry had been able to get to his feet without hobbling around like an idiot, he'd have been on Eric in an instant, fists swinging. As it was, he had to consider what to say instead, and words weren't really his specialty. He sat and silently fumed instead.

Terry wasn't ready to die. Inasmuch as most people didn't want to, though, Terry felt he was even more unwilling. Even if others didn't understand this desire, Terry had a lot he still wanted to live for. He knew what people thought about him, even if he didn't give them the dignity of acknowledging it. He might not have ever been the champion, but he was the man who made the man. Not everyone was a Hulk Hogan, after all. Most people were a Paul Orndorff, the ones who made the Hogans, the grit that helped the oyster make the pearl. It was a thankless job, but Terry felt a certain sense of righteousness knowing that he had an important place in the company. People like Eric might be the face of the company as Jiggolo, but Terry's TJ Azz was the backbone that held everything up.

The throbbing pain in his groin began to subside, prompting him to scoot on his ass toward Ricky, who continued to wheeze softly against the wall. Terry pushed aside his new knowledge of Ricky's sexual proclivities. Despite what Terry thought of it, Ricky was in this with them, and Terry didn't see a way out without at least some help from the man.

Still, a part of him, a part he didn't even want to acknowledge to himself, feared what would happen if Ricky survived this. He'd jobbed out multiple times to Burt Knox, had looked at the lights in front of some of MAW's biggest crowds while the ref counted 1-2-3. If Ricky made it out of here, if people found out that Terry had been pinned by a gay man? Terry might as well call his career over. You couldn't be a gay man in wrestling and be the face. Going all the way back to Gorgeous George, gay men in wrestling were there to be mocked and beaten on a nightly basis. No one would ever buy that a gay man, even one as big as Burt, could defeat an all-American hard-ass like TJ Azz. Not unless there was something wrong with Terry too.

As Terry wrestled with those conflicting emotions, he peered at Ricky, trying to examine him without touching him. It occurred to Terry that he'd been touched by Burt almost nightly for weeks now, had been bled on by Burt after they'd both bladed in cage matches. Did Burt have AIDS? Did *he* have AIDS now? Who do you even go to for a test? No, that was ridiculous, Terry thought. He had to focus on surviving right now.

He wasn't going to make things worse by touching Ricky. But just visually he could tell that Ricky was in no shape to fight, to do much of anything really. He tried to get Ricky's attention by saying his name, each time getting louder and louder. Ricky stirred a bit but didn't show any reaction beyond that. With his eyes swollen the way they were, Terry couldn't even tell if Ricky was passed out or not. He leaned back, not caring to do anything more.

"Why don't you check his pulse?" Eric asked Terry from across the room.

"What for? He's definitely alive."

"What if his heartbeat's too fast? Or too slow? We need to get an idea of how he's doing." Eric stood unsteadily, swaying back and forth a few times before stumbling in Terry's direction. "Come on, move; I'll check him." Terry didn't protest, scooting back as Eric plopped down heavily in front of Ricky. Eric didn't have to say anything. He knew why Terry didn't want to touch Ricky, and it stoked his contempt even more. They didn't have time for Terry's gay-bashing bullshit.

Eric pressed two fingers into Ricky's neck, looking for the artery. He had almost no experience with this type of thing, but he knew how to check his own pulse at least. After probing a bit, he felt something pumping against his fingers and held them there. The pulse was there, but nothing like he expected. It was erratic, going quickly for a few beats and then softening, slowing down, then speeding up again. Eric had no idea what that meant, but he assumed it wasn't anything good. He raised his hand and gave Ricky an open-handed pat on each cheek to try and rouse him.

"Hey," he said softly. "Hey, Ricky, are you with us?" Ricky shifted his head away from the palm of Eric's hand, which seemed to be a good sign. He turned to Terry.

"He's alive and responding, sort of. I don't know how bad a shape he's really in, though." Eric looked around the room as he thought of what their next move should be. "I wonder why they haven't come back yet to finish us off."

"It's probably got something to do with Julie," Terry said. Eric thought he was probably right, but what that something was continued to elude them.

"I wish we knew. It's hard to make a plan when you've got no idea what the other person even wants. Why are they keeping us here?"

Terry shrugged. "They're criminals. What other reason could they need?"

"Yeah, but they're pros at this," Eric said. He looked slowly around the room. "I mean, look at this place." The door was steel, stormproof, impossible to break down. The windows were boarded up tight. Eric hadn't checked, but he was betting the walls probably were reinforced as well, judging from how it felt to be thrown against them. "This is a fucking prison. But why? Who do they usually bring here?"

"I don't know. Maybe they're like some kind of cannibal serial killer family, like in *Texas Chainsaw Massacre* or something. It don't take much to keep people prisoner like that. Look at John Wayne Gacy."

Eric considered this. He wasn't sure he bought into that explanation, especially with the way Les had reacted to the whole situation. He seemed pissed that they were still here. So why were they?

"I wonder," Eric said, "what Jack's doing about us being gone. By now it's almost noon, I think. He'd have realized by eight or nine that we weren't showing up."

"Maybe he called the cops," Terry said.

"And what? Told them some of his employees skipped out on him? Not exactly a reason for an APB. Besides, what cops would he even call? Richmond PD? Louisville?"

"Can they track Ricky's cell?"

"I don't know. I don't think so, not if it's turned off, and definitely not if it isn't getting a signal. It's gotta, like, ping off the towers or something to track it." Eric shrugged. Who even knew where Ricky's cell was right now anyway?

"So we're on our own," Terry said. He looked deflated as he slumped against the wall. Eric nodded in agreement with that grim assessment.

"Let's count ourselves lucky that we've been left alone this long. Every second we're alive is another chance to keep living." Eric's head swam as he concentrated. He tried to formulate ideas on what to do, but the words kept slipping out of his grasp like little minnows in a stream. He grimaced with the effort.

"You can barely speak, let alone fight," Terry said. "And you need to get Julie out of your head too. Even if she is alive, what are you going to do? Go save her? Be the knight in shining armor while you trip over your own feet?" Terry snorted derisively. "Don't make the same mistake I did, thinking being nice to her is going to soften her up. You heard what she said to me in front of everyone else. That's a cold hard bitch, and she ain't never gonna take a shine to you."

Eric considered how to respond, with words or fists, and decided words were probably the better option. "Unlike you, Terry, my goodwill is motivated by more than whether or not someone will fuck me for it." Terry laughed, an unexpected response to Eric.

"Are you kidding me? The guy who named himself after all the tail he chased is lecturing me about chivalry?"

"Fuck you," Eric said quietly. He didn't really have the energy for anything else.

"Shit, I was just trying to make a point," Terry said as he watched Eric hunch over limply. "Come on, man up. You gotta get angry if we're gonna live." Eric glanced up, raising an eyebrow at Terry's statement. "We can either sit here and give up, or we can fight our asses off and go down swinging." He grinned, which highlighted the asymmetry of his face due to his smashed nose. Blood smears outlined his mouth, giving him a maniacal clown appearance that conjured the image of the previously-mentioned John Wayne Gacy. That didn't bother Eric. Right now, crazy could be good. Crazy could work.

"What are you thinking, exactly?"

"We can run our asses off," Terry said. "In the open, one of us can get away at least."

"That's not really a plan."

"Look, do you want to just let us all die here? 'Cause that's where this is headed so far."

"You said yourself I can barely walk straight." Eric crossed his arms and leaned back against the wall next to Ricky. "Have any other ideas?" Eric asked this rhetorically. He could see the logic in what Terry proposed. He also knew that Terry was more mobile than him at the moment. If they ran, Eric would likely get taken down while Terry escaped. He didn't like the idea of being a sacrificial lamb.

Terry shook his head in response to Eric and shrugged his shoulders. "We try to fight, and maybe die on our feet, or we just lay here and die on our knees."

Eric was about to respond when he heard the front door of the trailer open. He exchanged a frantic look with Terry and tried to brace himself in case the chance to attack was now. They weren't tied up, they'd had some time to recuperate, so it might be now or never.

Footsteps approached the door to their room, and they both waited on the balls of their feet as the latches on the door were thrown open. A pregnant pause hung in the air as they waited for the door to swing open, but nothing happened. Finally, just as Eric thought his legs would give out, the door opened and he lunged forward at the figure entering the room.

Eric anticipated Mark or, at the worst, Les, but instead he crashed into the unyielding bulk of a man as thick as Burt had been and crashed to the floor. The force rattled his already fragile stability, and he struggled to stand himself up. The man, Nate, readjusted his stance and stepped over Eric, crossing the room in two quick steps to Terry. The wrestler came out swinging and connected with a meaty right hook to the man's jaw. His head jerked to the side momentarily, but he otherwise seemed unfazed. With a speed that seemed unnatural for someone that large Nate reached out with his left hand and seized Terry by the shirtfront, pinning him to the wall. He brought his right hand up, holding a pistol by the barrel, and walloped Terry with the butt of it two times in quick succession. Nate let go and Terry crumpled bonelessly to the floor with a sickening thud. Nate turned to Eric as he was starting to get to his feet.

"Get on this one, Mark," Nate ordered. Mark was already entering the room, zip ties at the ready, and Eric started to move away. "Stay put," the big man said. "Or else I'll make you watch while I kill Goth Girl slowly."

Eric stayed where he was, on his hands and knees. Julie was alive. Was it true? Was this new guy full of shit? Eric didn't know the answer, but being alive now meant he still had a chance to do something later. Mark knelt down and shoved Eric roughly onto his chest, securing his hands behind his back with another zip tie. "You got any more ties, Nate?" Mark asked. Nate nodded and handed him a few more from his back pocket. Mark moved to Terry and secured his wrists, then finished up with Ricky. As he finished tightening the tie on Ricky's slack wrists, Eric objected.

"Is that really necessary? He's barely alive."

Neither man said anything. Nate scooped up Ricky and put him over his shoulder like a bag of sand, looking down at Eric as he did so. "Follow me," he said as he carried Ricky out of the room. Out of options, Eric scrambled to his feet and followed. Terry stirred listlessly on the floor. Eric tried to take in everything he could as he walked after the large man, who'd stopped in the living room to talk with Les.

"The other one's in the back out cold. He'll be up soon."

"What did you do?" Les asked.

"Pistol-whipped him. He got me on the chin, but I'm fine."

"I'm not surprised," Les said, peering at Nate's chin. "Take them out to the pen first. I wanna talk to Jiggolo for a minute."

Eric's stomach lurched, and he nearly fell on his ass. Les steadied him with one steely hand and directed Eric to the dining table, a circular, scratched-up Goodwill special.

Mark came out of the room, shoving a groggy Terry ahead of him.

"Move your ass," Mark said. Terry grimaced, a new rivulet of blood streaming down the side of his head. Les shook his head.

"I gotta say, you boys got more balls than I expected from fake fighters." Eric bristled at this but said nothing.

"Okay, let's go," Nate said. He walked out the door, ducking to make sure his head didn't hit the frame. Eric stared impotently as he watched them leave. Les grabbed a cold beer out of the fridge, sat heavily in the chair opposite Eric, and waited. Finally, Eric turned to look at his captor.

"What do you want?" Eric asked.

"That's a loaded question. Do you mean right now? Or with all your friends? Or just in general?"

"Let's start with me, right now. Why am I sitting here?" Eric shifted uncomfortably against the zip tie. Having his hands behind his back made sitting like this uncomfortable. Instead of responding, Les popped open the beer and took a long swig. After he finished, he looked at Eric as he wiped his mouth with the back of his free hand.

"Have you ever been to prison?" Les asked. It took Eric off guard, and he answered without thinking.

"I spent a long weekend there," he said.

"Mmm. So you know what it's like. You know, you actually know more about it than anyone else at this farm, except me." Les looked out the window and took another slow sip from his beer. Eric saw a nasty white scar twisted around the back of his hand and wrist.

"Is there anything you wouldn't do to keep from spending another minute there?"

"So that's what this is about? You don't want to get put away?" Eric leaned forward, trying to alleviate the growing cramp in his back. "Yeah, I'd do anything to stay out of there. So I stayed straight."

"Uh-huh. And what did someone like you go in for? Poppin' uppers and downers for all those long nights and days?" Les's words dripped with contempt. Eric knew why. Most of the wrestlers he knew used some kind of drug to keep themselves going, or had experimented with it at any rate. Coke if you could get it, meth if you couldn't. Sometimes sleeping pills to get yourself down at night. Probably Les had met at least one or two other people in the business, and it was not a good look.

"I'm not telling you shit," Eric said. And he had no intention of doing so, either. If Les wanted to lift some kind of weight off his conscience, Eric had no intention of helping.

"Suit yourself," Les said. "To be honest, I don't even know why I've got ya here. I should've just shot ya'll hours ago and been done with it."

Eric knew what the plan must be, what the endgame was, but hearing Les put it so bluntly made his blood run cold. He tried to respond, thought about asking why, but his mouth was so dry now that he could barely move his tongue from side to side.

"You had a chance to just walk away, back at the diner, but you wanted to play hero. You had to take that camera, huh? You thought you could just walk into our town, disrespect us, and not have anything happen to you?"

There was so much Eric could say. He thought back to the look on Julie's face and how, in that moment, she reminded him of his own wife, Cynthia, eyes wide with shock after he'd exploded. Oh, there'd been times before, of course, times when arguments about possible infidelities or a lack of funds had led to broken lamps, cracked countertops, and holes in walls. But this time, Eric had finally gone too far.

Cynthia wasn't a small woman, but she was hardly a match for MAW heavyweight champion Jiggolo. After she accused him, for the last time, of wasting extra funds on poppers, Eric had lost it and struck out blindly, backhanding her across the cheek. Cynthia had stumbled in shock, braced against the wall of their kitchen, and almost fallen to floor. But instead she had lunged up and off her feet, barely over a hundred pounds, a furious cloud of nails and hair and teeth. She'd knocked Eric to the floor, clawing at his eyes, screaming epithets and raining spittle on him.

It had only stopped when Eric wrapped his hands around her throat. The screaming had stopped. The flailing had stopped. He'd looked into Cynthia's face, not comprehending, just wanting her to shut up for once. His hands, so huge on her they laid over each other, had constricted across her neck, and he could feel the pulse in the pad of his thumb.

Eric didn't know if he would have stopped on his own. He'd only let go when Lillian, all of three years old, came into the room and screamed. Eric had let go, and Cynthia had fallen to his side, coughing roughly. He'd stood on shaking legs, staring into the wide saucer eyes of first his daughter and then his wife. They were scared of him. Eric had bolted from the kitchen and into the bathroom, where he kept his prescriptions: Xanax, Ritalin, and others he couldn't even remember the name of. He collected them all and poured them down the toilet, flushing multiple times to make sure they were all gone.

"I'm not going to take any blame. If that's all I'm here for, you might as well drag me outside with Terry and Ricky."

Les's lips thinned to the point of near-invisibility. "I don't need anything from you. I just was curious, is all. Curious if you was anything like I thought you were."

"And?" Eric asked.

"And, I realized it don't matter. You're gonna be dead all's the same. I guess I'm just sentimental." He polished off his beer, slamming it flat onto the table. "Come on, get your ass up. It's time to go."

Mark marched Terry around the side of the Fleetwood trailer, where a dilapidated stable of some kind sat on the other side of a pen, mostly mud with perhaps half a dozen troughs along the far fence wall. As they got closer, Terry could hear muffled snorts and grunts from the stable.

They reached the fence, the height of which only came to Terry's chest and just above Nate's waist. Nate roughly dropped Ricky into the cold mud on the other side of the fence. Even that didn't elicit much more than a grunt of discomfort from Ricky. The large man turned back to Mark.

"Hurry up with that one. I don't want to be out here all day."

"Then why don't you help me out with this one. He's the biggest pain in the ass."

In spite of the situation, Terry felt a stab of pride. He'd have that etched on his tombstone.

Nate cut the ties and forced Terry's hands against the fence posts. He held out his other hand to Nate. When Nate only handed him one tie Mark looked back in annoyance.

"What the hell's this? I need two."

"This is all we have left," Nate said.

"Well, we need more. Two for each of these assholes. You can't just leave 'em out here with one hand free, for Chrissakes."

Nate shrugged. "Well, I'll go get some more then."

Les came toward them then, pushing Eric forward with a hand on his shoulder. He stood face-to-chest with Nate. "This whole clusterfuck is your idea, Nate. What we ought to do is shoot all of them right now and be done with it."

Eric's heart dropped like a rock. Their lives were on a razor's edge, teetering apparently between Les and Nate, and Eric couldn't imagine why Nate would want them alive still.

Nate didn't bother responding to Les's complaints. "You get the ties while we deal with the body."

"If I'd known you didn't have enough on ya, I wouldn't have brought them out here to begin with," Les muttered. Nate only shrugged. Disgusted, Les shook his head and marched off. "This whole thing is already fucked!" he shouted. "Ya'll are gonna have it blow up in your goddamn faces, I guarantee."

"Okay, now let's get the last one," Nate said to Mark. Mark raised his hands in protest.

"I thought you could handle that on your own."

"You want me to drag 250 plus pounds of dead weight myself? No." Nate, who rarely made eye contact with anyone for more than a few seconds, glanced back at the trailer. "After we get him into the slaughter room, you can go on."

The two walked away then toward the trailer, leaving the three wrestlers in the mud. Eric turned toward Ricky, who had finally raised his head.

"How are you doing?" he asked. Ricky contemplated his answer before replying.

"I'm not sure." His words sounded slurred and thick. He spoke slowly and softly, so much so, Eric had to strain to understand him. "How . . . how should I feel? Burt's dead . . . it hurts bad." He looked at Eric. Or at least seemed to. Eric had a hard time determining that through Ricky's swollen eyes.

"We're gonna get out of here," Eric said, hoping to reassure him. He knew it was hollow, but what the hell was he supposed to say?

"No, we're not," Ricky said. He raised his head, as if he was looking at the clouds.

"Speak for yourself," Terry replied. "I'm getting out of here with or without you guys."

"What about Julie?" Eric asked.

"What about her? I think at this point it's every man and woman for themself."

"You can't really believe that."

"I do." Terry stared at Ricky and Eric. "Julie had her chance. We might still have ours. Someone has to get out of here. At least one of us, for God's sake."

"It was different when I thought she was dead," Eric said.

"Well, okay," said Terry, shaking his head. "You keep thinking like that. We'll see who gets out of here first."

All three of them turned at the sound of the front door to the trailer slamming shut. They saw Nate and Mark carrying Burt's body, Nate at the head and Mark at the feet. Ricky turned his head toward the ground, putting his free hand to his face.

"I'm sorry, Ricky," Eric said. He watched as they brought the body to the fence, swinging open the gate and moving past them. Mark was walking backward, breathing heavily and trying not to drop Burt's feet. On the other end Nate walked as if Burt weighed hardly anything at all. They reached an open room at the end of the third stable building. From their angle, they couldn't see anything except a large metal trash can at the entrance to the pen. They could hear the dull thud of Burt's body, though, followed by Nate's voice.

"Okay, Mark, you can go back to the house now," Nate said. Mark came back through the pen, glanced down at the three wrestlers, and turned back to Nate, who followed after with Ricky's bloody shirt bunched in his fist.

"You sure you don't need me for anything else?" Mark asked.

"No. Go ahead and go on now," Nate replied. He tossed Ricky's shirt into the metal trash can by the entrance to the pen then returned to Burt's body. Eric could hear the sound of scissors cutting fabric as Mark left without another glance their way.

In less than a minute more clothing, Burt's this time, was being thrown into the trash can: Shorts, underwear, socks, shoes, shirt.

"Jesus Christ," Eric whispered as he heard the dull wet thunk of a hatchet striking a body. He could close his eyes but not his ears, and his stomach churned as he listened to the sounds coming from that pen. He kept his eyes closed as more items landed wetly in the trash can.

Ricky wanted to pass out. He felt like he was on the verge of it, but his cursed brain betrayed him and kept him awake. *This must be what it feels like to go insane*, he thought.

After what felt like an eternity, Nate emerged from the building pushing a wheelbarrow to a smaller fenced area by the first building. He tipped it, emptying the gruesome contents into the muddy pen. The soft snorts and snuffling that Ricky had heard earlier became louder, more insistent, and Ricky could hear the groaning of a fence being pressed upon.

The gate swung open hard, smacking into the opposite wall, and a stream of pigs poured out, at least two dozen from what Ricky could tell. None of the wrestlers could watch as the animals went to their grisly work. Ricky found himself unable to continue looking away, however, and almost involuntarily opened his eyes to see what had become of the first man he'd ever loved.

A scream came from Ricky's throat then, a wail of primal, bottomless sorrow echoing until he began to cough in ugly desperate hitches. Eric shivered at the sound of it. Nate poked his head out from the pen to peer curiously at Ricky, then ducked away once more. Ricky heard water running from a hose as Nate cleaned out the pen, the smell of bleach piercing his nose as it drifted by. Seconds later came a dull *fwump* as flames flickered from the battered trash can; then Nate walked silently by, wiping his hands on his jeans.

Eric choked back his own urge to vomit as Nate closed the gate to the pen and walked back to the house. He readjusted himself enough to look at Ricky, who sat slumped against the fence. He looked almost catatonic. It occurred to Eric that, outside of his daughter, he'd never loved anyone enough to react like that.

"Are you—" Eric started, then stopped himself. How the hell could he ask if Ricky was okay as they listened to pigs snort and whine in their pen?

He looked at Eric, eyes wide and unseeing. "He almost made it. I wish . . . I . . ." His mouth moved, but nothing came out. Another tear rolled down Ricky's face. Eric scooted closer, leaving a trail in the mud, and reached out with his free hand to grip Ricky's shoulder.

"This isn't the end," Eric said. "It's not."

Ricky just stared, his gaze piercing the lie.

Nate unlocked the door to the basement and walked down the stairs. It was cool down here, almost always a pleasant 70-something degrees no matter what season. Right now, even though it was a crisp 43 degrees outside, here in his basement Nathan Goode felt comfortable. He always did; it was his retreat from the outside world. Technically his bedroom was upstairs, in one of the first-floor guest rooms, but he only went there to sleep and change his clothes. His books, his computer, his every treasured possession was down here. And now, he thought as he rounded the corner at the base of the stairs, *she* was here too.

Julie Sandusky, Goth Girl to her few but dedicated fans, sat in a worn leather office chair, high-backed, with her arms handcuffed to the armrests and her feet tied to the wheeled base. Nate had been exceedingly careful not to tighten the handcuffs too much, a concern he hadn't shown for her friends in the pen with the zip ties. He'd stitched up the flesh wound where the bullet from Mark's Desert Eagle had winged her and given her an IV of fluids. He had no idea what her blood type was or he may have tried to give her a transfusion. He'd never actually done one before, but he was curious to try it out.

Les assumed that he knew what Nate wanted with Julie and objected to it, but he didn't understand. Les thought he knew a lot of things, but he really didn't know Nate very well at all. Not that this did much to change Nate's opinion of the man. Les was the only person in this house Nate had any true respect for. It's why he'd changed his name to Goode, even though Les had strenuously objected. His father hadn't liked it either, but Nate's estimation of *that* man couldn't possibly be any lower. Nate was just awaiting the day that Norm would bungle into an early grave.

Nate pulled up an old plastic patio chair that sagged under his weight and sat down, watching Julie intently. He wasn't sure how much longer she would sleep, but he wanted to make sure he was down here when she awoke. Now that Burt had been taken care of, Nate saw no need to leave the basement until that happened. He waited for several minutes, watching the slow rise and fall of her chest as color returned to her cheeks.

To Nate, Goth Girl was the perfect catch. He always indulged Mark, watched MAW when he wasn't absolutely preoccupied with other interests, but that was only out of a sense of filial affection for his half-brother. Mark watched wrestling because he wanted to believe, and at times really did, that these men and women were truly beating the shit out of each other. Nate watched because he was enthralled with what these men and women were willing to do to make it *look* like they were really beating the shit out of each other. The men would do anything. They'd cut themselves with razor blades; they'd throw themselves onto concrete floors and do flying headbutts into steel chairs. It was a fascinating spectacle.

The women were different. Disappointingly so, Nate thought. Their currency was in their looks, and they jealously guarded it. Women didn't bleed. They never used weapons; they didn't perform gruesome moves that made people wince. They were happy to simply roll around in the ring pulling hair and screeching while most in the audience were barely entertained. Goth Girl was different, though. Her opponents wouldn't let her hit them with a chair or make them bleed, but she wasn't afraid to take it. She would threaten, she'd act like she was about to smash in her cheerleader opponent's pretty face with a steel chair, then react in shock as she was reversed and DDT'd headfirst onto that same chair. Because of this she usually ended up losing, but fans like Nate knew the truth. They called Goth Girl the Queen of Hardcore. It wasn't about whether you could swing the chair or not. It was whether you were hard enough to take the chair shot to the head. In a world of fake punches and worked matches, real blood was the most valuable currency some wrestlers had.

Mark hadn't told Nate about the woman. He'd mentioned Jiggolo, he'd mentioned Fort Knox, but his interest in Goth Girl seemed like an afterthought. Nate was glad he'd heard the commotion when he did and come running. He'd had a hunch he should keep the wrestlers alive when Mark first told him about them, and now that feeling was rewarded with the woman in his basement. Nate wasn't yet sure what to do with this prize, but for now he was content to consider the possibilities as he watched Goth Girl dozing quietly.

When he heard Nate return to the house and go to the basement, Les stood up from the couch and left the living room. He knocked on Mark's door, then hollered up the staircase that led to Norm's loft on the second floor of the old farmhouse. He wanted to avoid going up there and hoped Norm was willing to acknowledge the summons. Mark came out of his room, and Les motioned with his head to have Mark join him in the dining room. Heavy footsteps on the old wooden stairs let Les know that Norm was coming as well. All three sat down at the antique dining table that had been Les's great-grandfather's but now could barely be seen under the piles of old mail and kitchenware that had accumulated on it like wreckage at the dump.

"I thought you needed to see Bud today," Mark said.

"I wanted to talk to you and your dad first," Les replied.

"What the hell are you callin' me in for?" Norm groused. His hair was greasy and tousled and his eyes were bloodshot. He was high all right, but at least he was coherent. Mark may have been getting ready to shoot up or snort or smoke or however the hell he ingested his meth these days, but it looked like Les had interrupted him. Thank God for small favors, he thought.

"We have a serious problem," Les began. "The big guy, Knox, he's dead."

"Yeah? So what?" Norm replied. "We were expecting that. Have Nate take care of it."

"He already did," Mark said. "I helped carry him out."

Les nodded. "Yeah, and that's the problem. We keep the pigs running hungry most of the time, just in case. But that's 250 plus pounds of meat we just fed them. You've got probably close to 550 or even 600 pounds more between the others."

Norm squinted as he tried to work out the math in his head. "Uh-huh . . . and again, so what?"

"So," Les continued, "we ain't never tried to get rid of more'n one body at a time before. The pigs ain't gonna eat the rest unless you give 'em a good three or four days of starving between each meal." Mark and Norm considered this. While Norm, in his foggy-headed state, struggled to work out the math on that, Mark was able to understand more quickly.

"We ain't got two weeks of time, though," Mark said. His gut sank as he began to worry for the first time that this might be an unfixable problem.

"No, we don't," Les said. "I don't know how long it'll be before cops are looking for those guys, but it surely won't be more than another day or so."

"Yeah, well, that's why we pay off the cops here for," Norm said, waving dismissively.

"Two half-retired cops manning a two-room police station aren't going to keep a federal investigation at bay," Les said. His head was beginning to throb. Until now he'd avoided thinking about where this was all going to lead, but he had to confront it, and he had to convince Norm of the seriousness as well.

"There's lotsa ways to get rid of a body. Why don't we just pop 'em and bury 'em? We got twenty acres out here, and God knows how much more woods beyond that. Plenty of places. Just do it now, before you go into town. Hell, I dunno why you ain't done so already." To emphasize the problem was solved, Norm started to stand.

"Well, Nate doesn't want to do that," Mark said, and Norm stopped halfway out of his seat.

"What?" he asked. It was almost a whisper.

"Nate said not to kill 'em yet. He has them tied up out in the hog pen. All except Goth Girl; she's in the basement."

Norm fell backward into his chair. "She's in the fucking house?" he asked. Les nodded.

"Yep." Les cocked an eyebrow and waited.

"Well, that's . . . that's not gonna work. Let me talk to him." Norm stood up once more. "Where is he right now?"

"Where do you think?" barked Les.

"The basement," Mark said.

Norm adjusted his athletic shorts and walked out of the dining room toward the entrance to the basement. "Are you sure you want to do that, Norm?" Les called. "You know he hates being interrupted." It wasn't often Les got to dig into Norm these days, but he seized every opportunity with relish.

Norm paused at the door to the basement, his sweaty palm inches away from the doorknob. He decided against trying to open it—even if it had been left unlocked, he didn't want to interrupt whatever might be going on down there. None of them did. He decided instead to simply knock and hope Nate would come up. He rapped the door with his knuckles, perhaps a touch too lightly to be considered assertive, then quickly dropped his hand and stood back.

Heavy footsteps could be heard coming up the stairs, and Norm took another reflexive step back when the door opened. Nate appeared at the open door, staring at his father, saying nothing, waiting for Norm to speak.

"Look," Norm said haltingly, "we can't keep that girl forever you know. Or the others. Sooner or later, someone's going to come looking around, asking questions at least, and they can't be here when that happens."

"I know," Nate said. He looked at the other three people with cold reptilian eyes as he considered how to respond. He hadn't decided yet how he wanted to handle things, but in the end, the wrestlers in the pen weren't the ones that mattered to him. He could give his father what he wanted. Some of it, at least.

"I'll take care of it today."

Julie came to consciousness. She felt strange. It reminded her of when her dentist had anesthetized her to remove wisdom teeth. Abruptly she became aware of pain in her leg and remembered being shot. She felt pressure on her neck from the way her head was inclined and straightened it, causing spasms to race up her neck and down her shoulders. She winced and moved to put a hand there but found it restrained. Alarmed, she opened her eyes fully, squinting against the light. Only a few lamps were lit around the room, but they made traces in her sight as she looked around. As her vision cleared, it was just bright enough to see what looked like a basement with no windows. She was strapped to what seemed to be a desk chair but couldn't move her feet enough to slide it anywhere.

In front of her was a desk with TV and a VCR. The VHS box next to the VCR said "Faces of Death 3" in dripping red letters. A stack of medical reference books lay neatly on the floor. Along the wall was a metal storage shelf unit, filled with glass jars containing animal parts of some kind. Julie could make out organs, entrails, and even what looked like an unborn piglet still attached to its umbilical cord. A wooden table sat next to the shelf with a large tool box on it. Julie felt her pulse quicken as she imagined what might be in that tool box. Then she looked down; the sight of an IV tube running into her hand terrified her, and she let out an uncontrolled wail. Her leg had a rough but competent stitching job on the wound. It was clear her captor had medical skill.

What the hell, she thought.

Julie mentally chastised herself. *I shouldn't have made a fuss at the diner. Maybe Terry was right. Maybe this is all my fault. I should have let it all go.*

Of course she *did* have the right not to be grabbed like that, but was it worth all of this?

Julie had never been one to accept being looked at as the weaker sex. She'd forced herself onto the high school wrestling team in spite the leering looks of the coach and his varsity team. She worked her ass off, hitting the gym every day, running five laps after school, never missing a minute of practice. She spent more time training than at home. Her father, tired of driving Julie back and forth for practices and workouts, finally gave in and bought her a car. She competed, and her father came, cheering her on with gusto. She lost a few matches, but more often she won, to the eternal burning shame of her opponents.

Toward the end of that year, she'd been promoted to the varsity squad, attending a tourney for state semis qualification. The boy she was facing was handsome, stringy but muscular, a kid called "Gumby" for the way he made it impossible to pin him. Her team captain, Mac Steele, warned her to watch out for the three-quarter nelson, urging Julie to "wing it" if Gumby locked it in. If locked in properly, a three-quarter nelson would feel like someone was wrenching your head off your shoulders. The only recourse was to quickly clamp the arm in your own and whip the opponent over your hips. Julie was ready for that, for anything really.

She faced off with Gumby, who licked his lips in what at the time Julie thought was a case of nerves. They locked up when the whistle blew, and just like his namesake, Gumby was able to slip under her arms and slide behind her. She anticipated he'd grab her waist to throw her down, but his hands went higher than that. He put one arm around her waist, yes, but the other went around her chest, with one hand firmly cupped around her left breast. Shocked, Julie tried to pull away, but Gumby pivoted on his feet and drove her facedown to the mat. One point to Gumby, but Julie hardly noticed, as he'd refused to take his hand off her breast. With his hand between her and the mat, out of everyone's view, he squeezed it harder, causing Julie to gasp with pain, and she realized with a sickening shock that she could feel his erection pressing between her legs through his singlet. Recoiling with fury, she bucked Gumby off, flipped on her back, and kicked him as hard as she could in the crotch.

Gumby howled in pain and fell over as Julie scrambled to her feet, furious tears leaking from her eyes. The ref blew his whistle, disqualifying Julie immediately as the whole gymnasium stared in stunned silence. Feeling the hot shame of embarrassment coloring her cheeks, Julie rushed from the mat and out of the gymnasium, straight to the women's locker room, where she was completely alone. Her father found Julie there about five minutes later, changed into her normal clothes and muffling her scream into the bunched spandex of her singlet. Quietly he gathered his daughter up, arm around her comfortingly, and they drove home together.

Julie never spoke to Mac Steele again. Or the coach for that matter. She never told anyone why she had kicked Gumby in the balls, though Julie imagined most wouldn't care or believe her anyway. Two weeks later Julie officially dropped out of school over her father's heated objections. She traveled north to Canada and learned professional wrestling in Stu Hart's Dungeon in Calgary. It toughened her up like a two-dollar steak.

Julie took pride in knowing that at least two of the holes in the Dungeon's wall were from her own body. When she graduated from the school, she found a place immediately with MAW, run by Jack Meyer, an old friend of Stu's. She'd been happy there in spite of the rampant sexism. She made a decent living. Julie always believed you don't make things better by being on the sidelines. You have to be in the thick of it.

Well, I'm in the thick of it now, Julie thought, tears running down her face. *A decade's worth of trying to prove myself in a man's world, leading to here. Have I proven anything? Am I going to die here like this? Are Eric and the others still alive? Did they escape? No. If they'd escaped, I wouldn't be sitting here right now.*

I have to survive. I have to. They'll make a mistake I can take advantage of.

Julie tested her arms, finding that although she wasn't uncomfortable, she was securely confined to the chair. She considered trying to rock it—maybe knock it over, break something, and get loose—but quickly dismissed the idea. This wasn't some cheap wooden chair like villains in movies tied damsels to. This was a good-quality leather office recliner, probably the one her captor normally used himself. It was heavy and sturdy. Even if Julie could get the leverage, what would she accomplish? They would find her on the floor, still restrained, pissed off she'd made things harder for them.

No, I'd better wait. I need to be patient. Careful. Calculated.

She'd gotten away before and knew she could do it again.

"Nate, I want to talk to you for a minute," Les said as the big man moved to open the basement door. Nate stood for a minute, not responding, and Les wondered if he'd just ignore what was said and go on anyway.

"What do you need?" Nate asked finally.

Les glanced over his shoulder at the dining room where Mark and Norm still sat, then motioned down the hall to Nate's bedroom. Nate nodded in acknowledgment.

Les hardly ever set foot in Nate's bedroom, but he wondered if Nate spent much of any time in there either. In contrast to the rest of the house, it was nearly spotless, with only a book lying out of place on the bed. Les assumed Nate slept there, but he wasn't sure just how much time Nate spent outside of that damned basement anymore. To sleep, probably. Unless he'd bought a cot or something.

"So?" Nate asked, impatiently. Les looked up at him and put on his most authoritative face.

"So, I want to know what's the deal with you. Every minute those people are alive is a minute everything could be yanked out from under us. Why are you making everyone wait?"

"There are opportunities here that don't normally come around."

"Oh, yeah? Opportunities like what? The girl? Her I get, but what about the others?"

Nate shrugged. "She likes them. They're her friends."

"Don't be stupid," Les chastised. "She ain't never gonna think you're anything more'n an asshole that kidnapped her. It don't matter how many bullet holes you sew up in her."

"You think you know what I'm thinking. You think I look at things the same way you do. I don't."

"Yeah, I got that idea a long time ago." Les looked Nate up and down slowly. "I'm still not convinced that Louanne's death was an accident, you know."

"That makes one of you." Nate's tone was dangerously neutral.

"I figure, if you could do something like that, what else goes on in that head of yours? I don't trust you. I don't think you want those wrestlers alive for any reason that's good for the rest of us. Maybe I'll just go out and take care of them myself right now."

Nate's face clouded with anger. Now looming over Les like a storm, Nate's eyes narrowed and his jaw stiffened. He warned Les in a gravelly tone: "You don't touch any of them. I'm the one that does it, got it? Anyone kills them before I do, they're gonna wish they'd put a bullet in their own head before I'm through." Nate's accent, so carefully masked in normal conversation, seeped out as he spoke. Les backed up cautiously and nodded. He decided it was better to wait, at least for a little while.

Nate turned, looking back once with that cold, reptilian gaze as he walked back down the hall. Les felt a twinge of fear, wondering what exactly it was that Nate had planned.

11

Chimney Corner, West Virginia
3:45 p.m.

Brick tossed John the key to their room as they left the front office of the motel Marcy had recommended.

"You really think we're going to need the room?" John asked. He had a knot in his stomach. Things were starting to seem a lot more serious.

"Always be prepared," Brick replied. "I've got a feeling, Johnny. Gimme a few hours to dig something up."

"Okay, you're the boss."

Brick smiled at John. "That's the spirit! Now let's do some sightseeing."

"What kind?"

"We're going to take a look at the world's smallest police station," Brick said.

They drove through the town. It was buffeted between sheer mountainsides to the left and a fast-running creek to the right. The road was shaped like a snake, and more than once John gripped the handle of the door as Brick zipped around blind corners and barreled into dips. John's lips pursed together with unease at the occasional signs on the trees warning, "Danger!" and "Get out of the water quickly if the depths change!" There weren't many places to turn off the main road, unless you wanted to plow almost vertically through treacherous-looking gravel streets. It didn't take long to find what they were looking for.

It was silent except for a bit of loose gravel under the heavy truck tires as the two men pulled into the weather-beaten parking lot. They faced a small brick building with a nondescript sign that read "Chimney Corner WV Police Dept." One aging black-and-white police sedan sat out front in a marked space. Two spots over sat a flashy, well-polished Cadillac with vibrant purple metal flake paint, pitch-black tinted windows, huge rims with thin golden spokes, and gold bumpers, handles, and trim. Brick raised one eyebrow appreciatively as they passed it. John elbowed him to get his attention.

"Who the hell you think drives something like that around here?" John asked.

"Someone looking to be seen," Brick said.

They walked into the station, where a young man with a lighter brown complexion stood at the counter speaking animatedly. He wore a long coat covering his pin-striped suit with matching hat. A large sheet of protective glass separated the young man from the bored police officer behind it. Brick nodded toward the cop as they walked in and took a seat on one of the chairs by the door with John. The young man in the coat turned to look at them, his eyes widening a bit with surprise, then turned back to the cop. He leaned in closer and whispered something then removed a thick gold chain from his neck and slid it through the opening in the counter's window.

The cop quickly slid the jewelry to the side behind a stack of papers and gave the man a terse nod.

"Okay, Dante; we'll have them out here soon enough."

The cop was older, at least in his mid-fifties, with heavy jowls and a paunch to match. His hair was buzz-cut to hide how much it had receded across the top of his head. He scowled slightly at the man as he turned to leave. On the way out, the young man pulled sunglasses from his shirt pocket, leaving them down on his nose enough to eye Brick over them as he was leaving.

"Sup?" he said. Brick nodded in reply. Brick and John stood up to approach the window. The other man sat down a seat away from John. The cop let out a long breath through slightly flapping lips and furrowed his brow.

"Can I help you?" he asked in a rough tone. He sat up straighter in his chair so that "Burton" was clearly visible on his nametag. Brick smiled, removing his sunglasses and hanging them neatly from the neck of his shirt.

"My name's Richard Lamar, GSP, retired. I was wondering if anyone had been brought in last night, like a group of rowdy drunks or something."

"Sorry, no," Burton said. "My partner was on duty until eleven last night. If we'd had someone here, he would have either had me come in or called in one of the staties to keep an eye on them."

"Okay," Brick said. John could hear an edge of agitation to his voice. Brick continued: "See, I haven't been able to locate my associates since yesterday. And my boss is real concerned, 'cause we have a show tomorrow night in Richmond."

"Mm-hmm. What kind of show?"

"Wrasslin'," Brick said, accentuating the accent.

"Oh, you're wrestlers, huh?" Burton said. "Thought you said you was GSP?"

"Retired. Anyway, I hope you understand, we're pretty concerned about these people."

"Yeah, I get that." Burton leaned back, folding his hands over his considerable belly. "But I told ya; we didn't get anyone brought in last night. All we've got is a couple of streetwalkers from a few hours ago. No wrestlers. I think I'd remember seein' more people like you in town."

"Well, I was thinking maybe we could file a missing person's report, then. Since they ain't shown up for work an' all."

At this Burton leaned forward again, trying not to look disinterested. "I don't know why you'd want to file the report here."

"This is the last place we think they might've been. They called from a pay phone in this county."

Burton considered this, drumming his fingers on the counter. "Okay, well, this isn't a huge county, but there are other police stations around besides this one." He paused, rubbing the bridge of his nose. "Look, I know you were a statie back in Georgia. So maybe you can understand. We got limited resources here. Unless you give me something more to go on, there isn't much I can do."

John slowly stood from his chair.

"If we're trying to make a legitimate report, aren't you legally obligated to at least make note of it?" John asked.

"Legally, huh?" Now Burton looked agitated again. "Look, we've got about fourteen hundred residents, and anything more serious than a traffic ticket we usually have to call in people from Ansted or the state patrol. How's it gonna look if I call 'em up to go on a wild goose chase for some wrestlers that maybe came through here last night?"

"So you're not even going to take a report?" John was getting more heated, and when Brick moved to wave him down, John brushed him off. "Because I'll tell you something; if it turns out these people did run into trouble here and your department didn't lift a finger to help, that's on you guys."

Burton leaned forward, a fire in his eyes. "I don't like your tone. Ya ain't from 'round here, and you ain't gonna come in bullyin' us, either. We don't put up with the likes of you."

"The likes of us?" Brick asked.

Burton nodded. "Yeah. Take it how you like." He stared at the two stone-faced wrestlers, and after a moment his demeanor softened. The door opened and closed behind them. "Ah, shit," he said. "I'll check some things out if it'll make you feel better. Ain't got nothing else going on today anyway."

Brick gave a curt nod. "Huh. Okay. Call me at the Cozy Inn if you find out something." Brick grabbed his sunglasses from his shirt and made for the door with John right behind him.

"I don't think we can count on the police here doing much legwork," Brick said. "We'll have to do most of that ourselves."

"Ain't surprised about that," said a new voice, and both men turned to see the young Black man from the station, Dante, leaning against the driver side door of the tricked-out Cadillac they had admired on their way in. "No police in this town gonna take a brother seriously. Even a brother *cop*."

"Were you spying on us?" John asked.

"Shit yeah. You know how many times I see a negro walk into that station on they own? Ain't never seen nothin' like it here."

"You were in there," Brick said. "I'm guessing for those two ladies Burton said he had locked up."

"Just a misunderstanding," the man said, standing up and walking toward them. "Happens every once in a while."

"I see," John said.

"Yeah, man, no worries."

"There a reason you're so interested in us?" Brick asked.

"Just curious, just curious. Got nothin' better to do while I wait for that cracker to let my friends out." He gave Brick a long once-over. "So, you still a cop? Both of you cops? Not from around here, that's for damn sure. I know every Black cop between here and Charleston, but I ain't never seen you before."

"We're not from around here, no," Brick said. "And we aren't cops, either."

"Maybe not no more, but you was. You got 'cop' written all over yo ass." Dante smiled again, showing off a sparkling gold front tooth with a black dollar sign. "My name's Dante, by the way." He did an overly flourished bow, catching his hat as it fell from his head. He stood up and replaced it carefully. "So you got some friends went missing?" John nodded. "Yeah, okay, why you think they was here, then?"

"We think they called from a pay phone at Bud's," John said before Brick could stop him.

"Bud's, huh? Yeah, they might'a stepped in some shit, then."

"Why do you say that?" Brick asked.

"Let's just say some of the people that go round Bud's, they ain't the type that honest folk wanna associate with."

"What kind of people would that be?" John asked.

"Dealers, probably," Brick replied.

"You said it, not me," said Dante.

"Seems like a small customer base. There a lot of business out here?" Brick asked.

"Sure there is. Nothing better to do, you know? Certain people round here, they got the market cornered real hard." Dante looked past them as the door to the station opened and two women came out, one Black and one White. They wore outfits that John had a hard time taking his eyes off of, showing skin in places you don't normally see in bright sunlight. They looked bedraggled, their hair tangled and their makeup unkempt, and neither seemed very happy to see Dante. He opened his arms wide as if to embrace them both.

"Ladies!" he called. "I been waitin' out here for, like, an hour." The White woman scowled as they approached, while the Black one raised her hand as if to slap Dante across the face.

"You fuckin' prick!" she said. "We been in there for hours. Where the hell were you?"

"I had business down in Ansted, Monica, you know that. I got over here as soon as I got your page." He looked at the White woman. "Holly, you girls get any business last night?" Holly gave a skeptical sideways glance at Brick and John. "Naw, baby, they cool, they cool. Ain't that right?" He looked at Brick for acknowledgement. Brick nodded, smirking slightly.

"Just one guy. That cop kept the cash in our purses, though." She grimaced, looking back at the station. Dante looked up as well, his mouth twisting in righteous fury.

"That fuckin' cracker-ass cop! I just gave him three hundred in gold chain too!" Dante shook his head. "I'm thinkin' it's getting too expensive to be working this town anymore."

Brick shrugged to John and started to walk toward Jack's truck. Dante called out after them.

"Hold on!" he cried, running after them. He pulled out a business card and handed it to Brick. "I'm gonna be in town for the rest of the day. You guys get bored or if you, ah, need a guide around town . . ." He grinned, showing two more gold teeth on the bottom. "You just give me a holler."

Brick stared at the card, which said "Dante's Classy Escorts" on it in gold-embossed letters. A pager number was listed beneath it. He looked back at Dante. "I'm not sure you're gonna have what we're looking for."

"Aww, baby, Dante's got something for everyone," he said with a wide grin. "You just gotta ask."

"We'll think about it," Brick said, putting the card in his pocket. He got into the truck, and John joined him on the passenger side. They pulled out of the parking lot, leaving Dante behind as he argued with Monica and Holly. John turned to Brick after they'd turned a corner and Dante was out of sight.

"You really think that guy has anything useful to tell us?"

Brick shrugged. "You never know. Probably not, though. Dealers 'disappear' all the time, whether because they're dead or because things got too hot and they took off. I seriously doubt it has anything to do with our guys."

"That cop just flat out took a bribe in front of us, though," John said. "That doesn't bother you?"

"I'm not surprised to see a small-town cop shaking down a pimp over letting his girls out. It's not like anyone's getting hurt, except the pimp's pockets."

"So what do we do now?"

"This whole trip was always going to be a long shot, so don't expect miracles. We'll head back to the diner, maybe see if the owner, Bud, shows up."

"I'm not sure what good that's going to do," John said.

"Right now, Bud's is our only lead. I'd like to talk to Mason again too. Maybe see if something shakes loose."

"And I suppose Marcy's got nothing to do with it?"

Brick grinned as they wound through the town on the way back to Bud's. "Don't be jealous, son. You get lonely, just give our new friend Dante a call."

12

Goode Farm
3:50 p.m.

"Mark, come here," Les said as he entered the kitchen. Nate had already gone back down to the basement, and Norm was upstairs doing who knew what. Now was the time to talk to Mark. Les wanted to make sure their privacy was secure.

"Yeah?" Mark asked. Les put a fatherly arm around the boy (the *man*, he reminded himself) and led him out the kitchen door to the side yard. The detached garage was over here, where Nate used to work on the locals' vehicles for extra cash. It bothered Les to see so many decent tools just sitting useless, rusting and collecting dust. Stopping at a metal mechanic's cabinet that was canted to the side on three wheels, Les turned to face Mark and put his hands on Mark's shoulders.

"I'm thinking things could get bad really quick around here," Les began. Mark's face, already creased with concern, contorted to one of barely-contained panic.

"Uncle Les, I'm sorry. I didn't mean to cause all'a this, honest!"

"I know, I know," Les said, unable to hide his impatience. "That ain't what I'm getting at. Things could go up shit creek for this whole operation. One warrant, one excuse for the law to take a look at the shop trailer, and we are good and truly fucked."

"So, should I try and clean up the shop? Move all the stuff somewhere else? I mean, we got a batch ready to go right now. I think I can sell it pretty quick to a guy I was talkin' to up in Moundsville—"

"No, no, no," Les said. "Once cops come here, it's all done. We have survived all this time because we had a good system going. But we ain't got no loyalty from anyone. You think Bud's gonna cover our ass if the cops start asking why he's been buying so much pork from us? You think he ain't gonna tell 'em that the people selling him the pork are usually the same ones buying it back?" Les shook his head.

"No, son, everyone's gonna save their own asses. Take it from me; it's something I learned at Mount Olive: Everyone snitches. All those movies about guys taking a rap for their homies or some shit is a bunch of bull. Everyone will sell out their own mother for a few years off their sentence." Les paused, unsure of how to proceed. He dropped his hands from Mark's shoulders and put them on his waist, staring at the ground as he thought.

"So, uh, what are you trying to say then?" Mark asked.

"What I'm trying to say . . ." Les sighed heavily. "I'm trying to say that you and me, we need to plan on gettin' the hell outta here while the gettin's good."

"I dunno, Uncle Les," Mark said. "I hardly got any cash of my own, and you're still on parole for another couple years yet."

"Yeah, I know," Les replied. "I wanted to wait till my parole was up, but we may not get that choice." He looked around then leaned in closely and whispered with a conspiratorial tone. "I got a fair amount of money stashed near here. Buried. We can take off, make a new life, go to Mexico or Costa Rica or some shit."

"I don't speak any Spanish, Uncle Les."

"Neither do I. You don't need to! Look at how many people live here and speak all kinds'a gibberish. And it's better than sitting in a cell at Mount Olive, or worse places." He seized Mark by the arm, gripping it tightly to hold his attention. "Mark, you're the only kin I have left. I loved your momma like a sister, and you're her only boy. You're the only thing I got to live for. You *have* to come with me."

Mark looked at Les. He'd never seen the man so wild-eyed before. He'd always thought of Les as the unflappable, totally cool backbone of this whole family. But now he was talking about ditching everything and running off?

"Mark?" Les asked. He was feeling nervous now. Mark didn't usually think this much about anything. Les was used to Mark just going along with whatever Les suggested. He had counted on the bond he'd made with Mark over the years being strong enough to pull him away from the rest of his loser family.

"I dunno, Uncle Les," Mark said. "I think, well, maybe we should tell Nate too, ask him to come with us."

"No!" Les shouted, then immediately lowered his voice. "Nate's the problem. Can't you see that?" He shook his head sadly. "There's something wrong with him. You have to know that. It's him that's made the situation more complicated than it needs to be."

"Oh, okay," Mark said, not wanting to argue with Les. He never wanted to argue with Les. "Okay, I'll go with ya."

"Great," Les said, grinning widely. He released Mark's arm and patted it congenially. "You go on and pack a bag, then. A small one. Just in case."

—

Mark looked over his shoulder at Les as he walked back toward the house. He walked into the kitchen, but as soon as he turned the corner into the hallway, he almost ran right into Nate.

"Oh shit!" Mark exclaimed. Nate looked down at him.

"Hey, Mark," he said. "What did Les want to talk to you about?"

"Huh?" Mark asked. He was caught off guard, but part of his reptilian brain knew enough self-preservation to at least start out acting dumb.

"I had a feeling Les was up to something," Nate said. "So I pretend to walk away, and the next thing I know Les is telling you he needs to talk privately." Nate shook his head. "Les didn't used to make mistakes like that. He always double-checked himself." Nate leaned over now to look Mark in the eyes. "So what did he want to talk about? Does he have plans for our guests?"

Mark hemmed and hawed, trying to avoid answering, but in the end he couldn't say no to his brother. Part of him was still hoping he could get Nate to come with them too, leaving their worthless dad to take the fall.

"He's plannin' to leave," Mark said. "He wants me to go too. Said he's scared this whole thing's gonna blow up in our faces."

"Hmm," Nate said, standing back up. "He wants to cut and run." He brought a hand to his face, rubbing the sides of his chin in thought. "I have to say, I'm disappointed. I told him I'd take care of those guys by evening."

"He thinks people are gonna come here, that they'll be lookin' for the wrestlers."

"Did he say when he wanted to leave? Where you were going to go, or anything like that?"

Now Mark started to worry. Inviting Nate to come with them was one thing. Talking about the actual plan was another. One of the few things of worth he'd learned from his father was that secrets are a man's greatest treasure.

"He didn't say much," Mark replied.

"No, I bet he didn't," Nate said derisively. Mark winced. When Nate started to get angry, Mark's usual response was to leave the room. It was hard not to do that now. "Les isn't going to leave without some kind of a plan. And I bet that plan involves leaving me and Dad to take the fall." Nate's agitation was starting to show now.

"I don't know," Mark wailed, embarrassed with how pathetic he sounded. "He didn't tell me much; he just wanted me to pack a bag!"

Nate looked down at his brother and smiled. It didn't look right on Nate's face, like putting human teeth in a fish's mouth. "Don't worry about it," Nate said. "I'm certain Les didn't tell you. Why would he?" Mark felt like he'd just been insulted, but he wasn't sure how. Nate looked down the hall toward the kitchen. Les still hadn't come back inside.

"I'll just have to talk to Les about it myself." Mark's eyes grew wide at the suggestion. Surely Les would blame *him* if Nate asked about Les's plan. Nate saw this and shook his head. "Not yet; calm down. I bet the girl's awake by now anyway. I need to check on her." He walked back to the basement entrance, with one last look back at Mark. "You just go pack your bag, baby brother. I'll come get you later on." He walked into the basement, leaving Mark alone in the hallway, shivering and feeling like he really needed to take a piss.

—

Julie heard the door to the basement open a second time, and the heavy footfalls on the concrete steps made her heart flutter a bit with anxiety. She had no idea what to expect.

Nate came around the corner and stepped into the soft light of the lamps, standing in full view of Julie. He was tall, probably taller and wider than anyone she knew, even Burt. Nate was more presentable than anyone else she'd seen of this group so far, clean-shaven with a neat and parted hairstyle. He wore a clean collared shirt tucked into dark blue jeans with a tan belt. He was handsome in a conventional sense, with a strong jawline and well-balanced features. His eyes were intelligent, but cold and menacing.

Nate grabbed a chair and placed it down with steady hands. He sat facing Julie, leaving some distance between them. "You're awake," he said in a smooth baritone. "Name's Nathan. Goth Girl, right?"

His voice hardly carried any of the accent she'd heard from the others around here. Julie wondered if that was a conscious effort. She considered remaining silent, since she could tell he wouldn't be as easily manipulated as Mark. What he might do to her, down here alone, was enough of a threat to make her speak though.

"Yes," she said.

"I was worried the fluids wouldn't be enough to get you going again. You lost a little blood, but I took care of you." He looked Julie over and asked, "How are you feeling?"

Julie was taken aback. "I'm not sure," she said. Nate nodded and looked at her with a cocked eyebrow.

"I see," he said slowly.

"What happened to my friends?" she asked. She was afraid of the answer, but she had to know.

"Oh, they're fine," the man said. "I'm more worried about you right now."

"Then why am I tied up?" She pulled her arms up, rattling the handcuffs as she jerked them back and forth.

"Hey, now," the man said, wagging his finger in a scolding gesture. "You know, the only reason you and your friends are even alive is because of me. If it were up to Les, they'd be hog feed by now."

Hog feed? She thought. *Holy shit, is that what they're planning to do to us? Oh my God, I could be hog feed?*

"Yes, I know, pigs, right?" Nate seemed to be misreading her. "Most people don't know pigs are omnivores." He was animated now, speaking with expansive hand gestures, leaning toward Julie eagerly. "You know where you are? This is the Goode Farm. My grandparents, they were pillars of the community. This farm, it used to be known throughout the whole state for our pork." He leaned back, arms braced on his knees. "My dad, though, he didn't know what to do with it. Almost let the whole thing rot. Until I stepped in and saved it." He sat back and smiled, not showing any teeth. "Without me and my pigs, the whole thing would fall apart."

"So what are you going to do with us?" she asked. Nate stopped what he was about to say and furrowed his brow. He closed his mouth and tilted his head as he considered how to respond.

"I apologize; I've been rude," he said finally. He looked at Julie and gave her as big a smile as he could muster, showing perfect white teeth. A movie star's smile. "I know who you are, but you don't really know me." He moved a hand forward and gripped hers to be comforting. His hands were huge and smooth, lotioned and manicured but powerful. Julie didn't move.

"Please, please, just let us go."

"Easier said than done. Things are complicated right now. You and your friends have put us in a bit of a bind. I'd be happy to let you go, but I'm not the one in charge."

"Who is?" Julie asked.

"My father, I suppose. But really Les, the one who brought you here; he's the brains of the operation. He's never had so many people here like this."

"We're not the first ones who've been in that room."

"No, no you're not," Nate said. He frowned. "I try to stay out of all that, but I don't have much of a choice. They make me do things. They've made me do a lot of things I don't want to do. I just had the bad luck to live here"

"So what's going to happen to us?" Julie asked. Her voice took an urgent tone as she pressed him. "To Eric? To Ricky?"

"I don't want anything to happen. But some of that's up to you." He leaned forward once more and put a hand on her bare arm. "I'm not a bad guy, you see. I helped you. I'm on your side." Julie saw something in his eyes that she'd seen in plenty of men before. Desire, longing, a need for reciprocation. His words turned her stomach, but she tried to hide it. She could use this, maybe. Hopefully.

"It's hard to trust someone who has you tied to a chair," she said.

"Trust needs to be earned," Nate replied. "I don't expect you to trust me right now either, but once you get to know me, you'll believe me when I say I'm one of the good guys." He held out an open palm to her magnanimously. "Like I said, you're alive right now because of me. Your friends are alive because of me. I think maybe together we can find a way to keep it like that." He leaned back in his chair, which shifted creakily under his weight.

Part Three

The Hard Way

13

Bud's Diner
Saturday, 4:53 p.m.

Brick parked in the same spot he'd used earlier in the day, strapping on his Smith and Wesson .38 before getting out of the truck. Most of the cars were different, but he noticed at least one was the same, a red Saturn SL sedan. He hoped that was Marcy's. He walked into the diner, which had about two-thirds of the customers who'd been in earlier. Marcy, he was happy to see, was still at the counter, wiping down a section of it with a wet rag. He grinned and sidled up to her, taking the seat directly in front of where she was wiping.

"You know, I just finished cleanin' that," she said, smirking at Brick as she put the rag under the counter.

"I guess I'll just have to be careful not to make a mess," he replied. "Uh, I heard you were getting off in just a few minutes."

"That so? I wonder who could've told ya that." She leaned in closer to Brick, close enough for him to smell the surprisingly pleasant mixture of grease and perfume she wore. "You have any luck finding your friends?"

"Not yet," he said. "I talked to the local PD; they were supposed to check in over here. You see anyone come in today?"

"No, and I'm not surprised about that. I ain't never seen two lazier people than our local police." She smiled wider now. "So, is Bud the only reason you came back?"

"I wouldn't say the only reason," Brick said. He leaned in some more, until the middle knuckles of his fingers were touching Marcy's bare arm. He noticed that her skin was smooth from years of shaving her arms. He liked that. He kept his own body shaved as well, most wrestlers did, unless they wanted to look like George "The Animal" Steele. "Is he still around?"

Marcy shrugged. "He comes in and out. He's out now, but he'll probably be back soon."

"What about Mason?" Brick asked.

"What about him?" Marcy asked. She stiffened a bit, looking defensive now.

"Nothing serious honey; don't worry. We're just concerned about our friends is all. I tried asking him about it, but I don't think he liked the way you and I were getting on."

Marcy laughed, her bosom heaving enticingly only inches from Brick's face. "Mason's had a crush on me since I used to sit for him a decade ago. Always trying to get me to go to a movie over in Ansted or one time even some fancy restaurant all the way out in Charleston." She met Brick's eyes with a devilish grin. "He always gets testy when he sees me interested in a man."

"I see. So what kind of interest might this be?" Brick smiled and met her eyes with his own, one eyebrow cocked.

"Well, it's quittin' time for me now. Why don't you come along and I'll show ya?"

Brick stood and, for a moment, considered declining politely. After all, he still didn't know where the other wrestlers were, and time was of the essence. His best option, however, was to talk to Mason, one on one, outside the diner. If Marcy really was that close with Mason, she might be willing to help Brick talk to the boy.

"Lead the way," he said. She started to come around the corner, and John seized Brick's elbow in alarm.

"Dude, what are you doing?" John asked.

"Just trust me," Brick said. "I'll hitch a ride with her. You take the truck, but for now wait here until Bud gets back. When he comes in, just ask about our guys, same as you saw me do."

"I dunno if I can handle that by myself." John was starting to look panicked now.

"Don't worry," Brick reassured him. "You've got this. I trust you. Besides, it'll probably come to nothing. Just take this," he said, pressing a folded twenty-dollar bill into John's palm, "and enjoy a meal." Marcy came up to him then, looping her arm through Brick's and leading him out the door. He gave John a quick wink over his shoulder as he left the diner.

It wasn't long before Bud arrived at the diner. John wouldn't have noticed if the waiter hadn't greeted the man by name as he came in. Bud was a tall wiry man with a slicked-back head of thinning white hair. He moved swiftly through the diner, pausing to peer curiously at John before ducking into the back. John had almost steeled himself to call out, but the door swung shut before he could say anything. He sighed and took another bite of his surprisingly tasty hot bologna sandwich. As the waiter passed by, John raised his hand to flag him down.

"Hey," he said. "Can you do me a favor?"

"Whatcha need, boss?"

"Can you let Bud know I'd like to talk to him when he gets a chance?

"You want to talk . . . to Bud?" The waiter peered quizzically at John.

"Yeah, nothing bad or anything." John didn't want the waiter to think he wanted to file some kind of complaint.

"Well, I guess so. I dunno how fast he's gonna get out to ya, though."

"Thank you," John said, "and can I get a slice of pecan pie?"

Without Brick to distract him, John spent the time alone watching the patrons. It seemed like every normal diner you might come across anywhere in America. He got no sinister vibes from it whatsoever. He did notice, however, a chair that had been pushed into the corner, its rear leg slanted at an odd angle. Under normal circumstances, it wouldn't seem odd at all, but paired with the blood spots under the counter, it seemed more sinister.

John was more than halfway through the pecan pie when Bud finally came out the door, sizing John up as he approached.

"Mikey says you wanted to talk?" he asked as he bellied up to the counter opposite John.

"Yeah, I just wanted to know if you were here at the diner at all last night?"

Bud looked at John closely. "I come by at least once most nights. Why?"

"Do you know if any large groups came through last night? Like, five people, four men and one girl?"

"No," Bud answered, a little too quickly. "Nobody like that came through."

"Okay, well . . . I noticed a broken chair in the corner over there. What happened?" John felt nervous asking about this. He wished like hell Brick was here with him, asking the questions. He'd know what to say. He'd know what to make of this situation. John kept thinking back on what Dante had said, about the drug dealers that liked to frequent this diner, and it made him nervous to press Bud too hard.

"I don't know. This is a diner. Chairs wear out. Why you wanna know?" Bud asked. Now he looked even more suspicious as his eyes narrowed.

"Well, I mean, I noticed that broken chair in the corner, and, uh, the floor over there seemed really clean—" Immediately John regretted saying anything. Brick knew, almost instinctively, when to reveal and when to conceal. But John had no idea how to do the same, and considering the way Bud was glaring at him now, he probably should have kept his mouth shut.

"I don't take kindly to the way this conversation is steering," Bud said. "Are you some kind of cop or something?"

"Well, no. Just looking for my friends is all."

"Sorry. There ain't nothing for ya here. How about you finish your pie and then go on back where ya came from. I've got actual work I have to do."

John Coors took another bite of pecan pie, just about the best he'd ever tasted, while keeping Bud's steely gaze.

"I'm sorry; I didn't mean any disrespect," he said after he swallowed. "I'll just finish my pie and take a coffee to go."

After he paid, John stepped outside. Steam rose gently from his cup into the crisp October air. He sipped coffee from the paper cup the waiter had provided, watching as an eighteen-wheeler hurried past on the road with a short gust of wind. A few autumn leaves lifted from the road and settled again. John looked at the parking lot, wondering what to do next. Whatever Brick was up to right now, John felt certain it was more fun than this. He hadn't learned anything substantive from Bud, but the man's agitation at the mention of the broken chair indicated that they may be on the right track.

Finishing his coffee, John walked to an overstuffed trash can by the pay phone and jammed the cup into it. As he turned to walk away, he slipped but caught himself. He lifted his shoe to remove a sticky plastic wrapper. He bent to peel it off, thinking he should throw it out before someone actually slipped and got hurt. As he turned to dispose of the wrapper, he noticed something shiny on the ground about a yard away from the other bits of garbage. He picked it up. Lipstick. Staring at it, his eyes widened; he turned back to Jack's truck, pocketing the lipstick and moving as fast as he could. He had to get to Brick and show him what he'd found. Black lipstick. The same type Goth Girl used.

14

Goode Farm
4:22 p.m.

The phone in the kitchen rang, startling Les, who was rifling through the meager contents of the refrigerator looking for something to eat. The caller ID came up "Unknown," and Les paused before answering. Not many people called the house, and he wasn't expecting any good news. He picked up the phone anyway with a curt "Hullo?"

"Why've I got some colored boy in my diner asking about who was here last night?" Bud McVeigh barked. Les squeezed his eyes shut in response to the headache he could immediately feel coming on.

"What are you talking about?" Les asked. It was a stall. He knew what Bud was talking about of course. He just wasn't ready to answer.

"Don't fuckin' play dumb with me. I know some serious shit went down. I didn't ask; I didn't wanna know any details." He coughed—a loud, wet sound that hurt Les's ear. "That's our deal. I don't ask, you don't tell. But goddam it, part of that deal is none of your shit gets smeared onto my shoes."

"How would anyone know to even come looking there?"

"How should I know? But apparently whatever you boys did last night, you didn't clean it well enough. You broke one'a my goddamn chairs and left blood on my fuckin' counter."

"That could be from anything," Les replied robotically. "What did you tell him?"

"What could I tell him? I don't know shit. I wasn't there."

"Did he ask about any of us?"

Bud coughed again, harder this time. "No. But I don't imagine it'll be long. Your little business is the worst-kept secret in Chimney Corner."

"That hasn't ever bothered you before."

"Ya'll never gave me a choice," Bud retorted. "Dunno why you even need me anyway. It ain't like you're making millions of dollars outta that farm. Who you trying to hide from?"

Les didn't bother to tell him. Bud wouldn't understand that it only took one IRS agent to ask one question about how Les could afford a new car and the whole thing would fall apart. No, they needed Bud to cover their ass, but it wasn't like he didn't benefit too.

Bud made a disgusted sound over the phone, like a wet cough crossed with a long sigh.

"Whatever you have to do, I don't want this shit running back to me. Find a way to shut this guy up, and make sure you bury whatever the hell else happened last night too."

"I'll find the guy," Les promised.

"Well, I know where you can start."

"Oh? Where's that?"

"There are two of them apparently. And my waiter says Marcy left with the other one when her shift ended."

"What?" Les asked in a harsh whisper. He gripped the phone tightly enough that his hand started to shake.

"Yeah. Had a few people complain to me about it, actually. Want me to have a talk with her about it when I see her next. Warn her about dangerous men and shit." Bud let out a sour wheeze of a chuckle. "Guess there's some people in town who still don't know what she's really like." Les was not amused.

"What was the one you talked to driving?"

"Big red truck. Hard for me to see, but I'd say it looked like a F-150 if I had a gun to my head."

Behind Les, at the entrance to the kitchen, Norm coughed to get his attention. Les turned to look at him, greasy-haired and bleary-eyed. Les turned back to the phone.

"I'll take care of it," he said to Bud. He hung up the phone and turned back to Norm.

"What's all that about?" Norm asked. Les struggled to come up with an answer. He was reluctant to tell Norm why Bud really called. Norm had a bad habit of shoot first, shoot later, and never ask questions. Les had always been the temperate hand on the throttle, keeping Norm from sending everything off the rails. Often that was done by leaving out key details that would have overly taxed Norm's fried brain cells. Les knew that if he told Norm about why Bud called, Norm's first instinct would be to kill the two Black men, and probably Mason too. That was something Les desperately wanted to avoid. Les decided evasion was the best option here.

"Bud just wanted to know what happened last night."

"What does it matter? He still gets his money from us." Norm's eyes narrowed with suspicion. "What did you tell him?"

"Nothing. Just that Mark must've had an accident." He shrugged and tried to squeeze past Norm, but Norm moved to block his way.

"I hope you aren't keeping anything from me. I really do. I'm not half as stupid as you think I am."

"That still makes you dumber than a box of rocks," Les replied.

Norm's eyes flashed. He always had more gumption right after he got lit. "Careful, Les. I'd hate to have to kick you out of that trailer."

"It's my trailer."

"No, it's *my* trailer. Ever since Louanne died, it's all fuckin' mine. My trailer, my house, my farm. So if I get tired of your shit, all it takes is one phone call to your probation officer and you'll be back at Mount Olive before you can take a piss."

Les sneered but said nothing in reply. Instead he shouldered past Norm and out the front door. He climbed into his Pontiac, not bothering to tell Norm or anyone else why he was leaving or where he was going. He sped out, kicking up gravel as he snaked down the roadway toward Marcy's house.

It was cool and quiet in the basement as Nate gave Julie a drink from a cup of water. She sipped greedily as the water trickled down her mouth and over her chin, embarrassed at her own eagerness but pushing that aside. She needed the water, especially now that Nate had removed the IV. Best to get as much as she could while it was being offered.

When she reached the bottom, Nate pulled the cup away and set it on the desk next to his computer. He put a piece of biscuit up to Julie's mouth next, which she took in with some reluctance. He stared at her as she chewed, studying her, and she watched his eyes trace over the shape of her body. She shuddered involuntarily.

"Excellent tone," he said. "Not bulky, not steroidal. Sleek, powerful." He sat back in his chair, folding his hands in his lap. "In a real fight, you'd dominate someone like Kristy or The Wrangler." He waited for Julie to reply, but she remained silent. After a few seconds, he went on anyway. "That's why you're so fascinating. I've heard the stories about how the people on top in wrestling, people like Hulk Hogan or Shawn Michaels, that they're rarely the ones who are the toughest in the group." He cocked his head, waiting to see if he could prompt a response from Julie. Still nothing. "While my brother was busy fantasizing about your opponents, I watched you, the way you sold their moves. You make people who couldn't knock out a child look like they put the world's worst beating on you."

"That's my job," Julie said finally.

"It hurts, though, doesn't it?" Nate asked. "When you get thrown onto a bed of tacks, that hurts, right?"

Julie didn't know whether to answer or not. It disturbed her that he watched her so closely, that it was he who recognized what she was putting herself through night after night. It would have been welcomed from just about anyone else. But it was this man, this clearly unhinged man, who was the first to say that to her. It made her skin crawl.

Nate stood up, towering over her as he inspected the skin that was uncovered on her. He touched one of the scars on her arm but pulled away when she instantly recoiled. The handcuffs jangled noisily in response. Instead, Nate got to one knee and examined the discolored old injuries to her knees and ankles.

"It's too bad I wasn't around to help with these at the time. I could have taken really good care of you."

He looked into her face, found the thin remnants of blade lines on her forehead, near the hairline.

"I heard wrestlers don't blade anymore. That you just use blood capsules and things like that." Julie turned away, uncomfortable with the attention. Nate stood up again before backing into his chair. "I wish you'd answer me. I told you I'm not the enemy."

"How do I know that?" Julie asked. "I don't even know if my friends are still alive."

"Well, what if I showed you?" Nate asked. Julie looked at him in surprise, wondering if she'd heard right.

"Yeah," Nate said. "I think that's actually a really good idea." He reached into his pocket and removed a key ring. On it was the key to the handcuffs, among others, and he unlocked the cuffs on her wrists. She rubbed at them where the metal had rested on her skin, but otherwise her hands felt fine. She nearly lunged forward, but with her feet still bound to the chair, she stood no chance of overpowering Nate. He held up a plastic zip tie.

"Let me see your hands, please." It wasn't a request. Julie considered resisting, but her need to see what had happened to the others won out. She proffered her outstretched arms, and Nate fastened her wrists together with the zip tie. Once she was secured, more uncomfortably than her handcuffs had been, Nate bent down on one knee behind the chair and pulled out a large pocketknife. He cut the ropes with it.

"Don't take advantage of the trust I'm giving you," he said.

He stood, pulling Julie up by the arm, and she nearly passed out as she came up—still dizzy from the dehydration and whatever Nate had used to sedate her earlier.

"Whoa, easy there. Lean on me," he offered. Julie fell against him involuntarily. "Are you going to be able to walk, or should I carry you?"

"I'll manage," she said, and forced herself upright.

Nate shook his head. "I'm not so sure about that. Come here; better safe than sorry."

He seized her around the hips and hoisted her over his shoulder. She resisted as much as she could, but it didn't amount to much. Nate carried her up the steps like she was a sack of flour. When they got to the door, Nate reached around Julie and opened it. She was immediately taken aback by the smell, a combination of stale laundry and rotted food. It was like a physical wall that pushed into her, and she might have tumbled right down the stairs if Nate hadn't been holding her. He let out a low sound, mechanical, like a child's imitation of a machine gun, and Julie realized that was Nate chuckling, a hollow and mirthless noise that sounded like a computer's rendition of laughter.

"Yeah," he said. "Don't mind the smell. My father and brother are slobs. The basement's the only place I can keep the way I like."

Nate tightened his grip on Julie and walked forward. She looked over her shoulder into the hallway, lit by a bulb that was about two shades dimmer than it should be for the area. Nate turned to the right, toward the front door, but as they were walking he twisted to the left without warning, taking her into a kitchen that looked like the ruinous aftermath of a hasty evacuation. Julie heard flies buzzing and heard the soles of Nate's sneakers crunching on a morass of grit from untold months of neglect. She'd thought the trailer home was disgusting, in a gross bachelor pad kind of way, but this was a literal biohazard. How anyone could conceivably prepare and eat food in here was mind-boggling.

She peered down at unidentifiable spills as Nate headed toward a side door, holding her breath as she passed too close to the sink. Water dripped from the faucet into a greasy pan full of shimmering liquid. She shuddered as they reached the door. Nate reached around her once more, turning the deadbolt latch, and the door swung open to show Julie a view of a weedy, unkempt lawn. Nate seized her by the bands of her tank top, steadying her, and then continued pressing onward.

Julie breathed deeply, enjoying the shock of cold, clean air as it filled her lungs. To the right was a wooden detached garage, the barn door fully open to show off the white van that had brought her here, surrounded by a bevy of mechanic's tools. Nate noticed her looking.

"I do mechanic's work on the cars we own," he explained. His chest puffed out slightly. "I'm faster and better than the closest three garages." He waited, hoping for Julie to acknowledge his skill. "And I'm self-taught. Took a shop class in high school then learned everything else on my own." Julie remained silent as they passed the garage and came around the back of the house.

There were not many people that Nate had even a modicum of respect for. He respected Les for the way he'd taken control of a shitty situation and made it work for him. He didn't respect Mark, but he still loved his brother, or at least came as close to love as he was capable. If he'd had the emotional range of a normal human, he'd have recognized his affection toward Mark was more akin to what one has for a beloved pet. And the less said about his father, Norm, the better.

Julie was someone else he respected, someone he saw as similar to him—a person surrounded by lesser-thans, a person thriving in an environment they were inherently superior to. He wanted Julie to see that in him, to see the way they were kindred spirits in that sense. Surely, once she saw that he was capable of mercy toward her friends, at least as much mercy as could be allowed, her attitude toward him would soften.

They walked onward, toward the hog pens in the back. Julie saw Les's trailer home to the left, and beyond that another trailer, an industrial cargo version with a window AC unit crudely affixed to a hole cut in the side. *That's where they cook the meth*, she thought. She could see that it was blocked from view by both the farmhouse and the trailer home. As they got closer to the pens, she could see three people sitting against the fence; her mind immediately leaped to Burt Knox.

"Where's Burt?" she asked. She feared she already knew the answer but couldn't stand not having confirmation.

"Fort Knox is no longer with us, I'm afraid," Nate said. He tried to sound sad about it. That seemed like the right tone to take. Julie didn't take any notice of his efforts. Instead her mind was roiling with the revelation of Burt's fate. She almost asked where the body was, but something held her back. She had a feeling she didn't really want to know.

Eric's haunches were numb, though he couldn't tell if it was from the way he was sitting or because his ass was pressed into ice-cold mud. He looked at Ricky and wondered how the hell the man could survive, sitting there in nothing but a pair of slacks. The angry bruises across Ricky's face and body were bright purple now. Eric wondered if the mid-forties temperature might be helping with the swelling, because he at least could see Ricky's eyes now.

To his right Terry was breathing shallowly through his mouth, doing everything he could to avoid aggravating his demolished nose. Blood trailed down his wrist in dry, caked rivers, and even from six feet away, Eric could see how raw and aggravated the skin on Terry's wrist was around the zip tie that held it to the fence. Terry had finally given up trying to free himself after an hour of increasingly frustrated efforts.

Eric reached up with his free left hand and gingerly touched the side of his head where Les had hit him. His vision blurred as pain poured over his head like a spilled drink. He inhaled sharply and then gasped. He'd almost forgotten the multiple kicks Les had given him with those steel-toed boots. Eric didn't know if his ribs were broken or not, but it felt like at least one or two of them were. He flexed his right hand, trying to keep the blood circulating through the pressure of the zip tie. He looked up to the dimming sky, watching the sun disappear too soon behind the mountains. It was about to get even colder.

His thoughts returned once more, without control, to his daughter. The last time he'd seen Lillian in person, not just spoken to her on the phone, was more than a year ago. He technically had no real visitation rights, but Cynthia had been kind enough to allow him to visit a couple of times, when Cynthia's brother was in town at least. Eric hadn't bother to fight for custody because not even he believed he deserved it. He'd patted himself on the back since then, congratulating himself for ditching the uppers and getting his temper in check. The lack of drugs gave him a convenient excuse for the weight gain, which had accelerated significantly in the last year or so. It was ironic to him that, a few years back, he might have been one of Les's customers. No wonder Jack had decided now was the time to pass the championship belt to Brick Lamar. Eric had always been a mess. Now he was a fat mess with graying temples.

Eric comforted himself by thinking of the improved relationship he'd forged with Cynthia since then. She'd never take him back of course—was already in a serious relationship with someone else, in fact—but she was warming up to the idea of giving Eric permission to see Lillian without being watched. And he'd earned that, hadn't he? He'd chosen making his daughter a part of his life over working himself into a frenzy to stay on top. Essentially, he'd given up his career for it.

He didn't feel much like he'd earned anything, though. He looked at the pigs, now resting peacefully near their pen, and considered that maybe being here, in the mud waiting to die, was what he'd actually earned. Maybe, a small and insistent voice at the back of his head whispered, it was better that Lillian never got to know him at all.

He looked at Terry, who seemed to be dozing fitfully. Eric didn't know how that was possible. He was exhausted as well, bone weary in a way he hadn't felt in years, yet his brain was buzzing so harshly he couldn't imagine drifting off. Ricky, on the other hand, was awake, digging quietly in the mud. Eric understood. He'd spent at least half an hour scouring the ground himself, looking for a rock, a stick, anything to use for a weapon, but had found nothing except pebbles and fragments of bone. Eric opened his mouth to dissuade Ricky from his efforts, then thought better of it. Everyone was coping in their own way, he supposed.

The sound of footsteps crunching through stiff cold grass brought Eric's head up, Ricky's too. Approaching the gate was Nate, carrying Julie over his shoulder. Seeing Nate holding her like that made Eric's blood run cold. He noticed an ugly black line of stitches on her left thigh, but otherwise she seemed to be in better shape than the rest of them. Nate walked her behind each of the other wrestlers. Her eyes went wide as she took in the state of the three, especially Ricky, whose battered body was easily the worst for wear.

"Oh, my God," Julie whispered. "What did you do to them?" she asked, turning to look over her shoulder at Nate.

"Not me," Nate replied. He looked at Ricky's body and Terry's ruined nose. "This is all Les's handiwork. He knows a few things about how to hurt someone." Julie curled her mouth in disgust and moved toward Ricky.

Damn, I forgot to bring out the other zip ties, Nate thought.

"Hey, Ricky," Julie called, "are you all right?"

"I'm not," he rasped. "They killed Burt. They . . . they . . . his body . . ." Ricky wanted to say more but couldn't talk through his shivering teeth. Tears began to leak from his swollen eyes, rolling slowly down puffy, discolored cheeks. Julie reached out with her bound hands but Nate kept his distance.

"I'm so sorry," she said. "I am so, so fucking sorry." She was crying now as well. She hadn't completely shaken off the guilt she felt from before, and seeing Ricky like this brought it bubbling to the surface once more.

"Okay, come on; I think that's enough," Nate said, turning away from the wrestlers and heading back where they'd come from.

"This is evil," Julie said. "These people, they didn't do anything to you. You have them tied up here, and for what? To torture them?" Julie felt nervous being that confrontational with Nate but couldn't help herself.

"The only reason they're still alive is because I said so," Nate retorted. Eric raised his head at this, and Nate met his eyes. "That's right. You and your friends are still alive because of me." He pointed first to himself then gestured at their free hands. "You have one free hand because I decided to be merciful." He looked at each of the wrestlers in a line. "So every moment you're still breathing, you should be thanking me. The fact that you weren't shot the moment Les brought you back here, that was me too." He seemed far more animated discussing this than when he was dismembering Burt, Eric noted.

"Why?" Terry asked. "Why are you doing this? What are you going to do to us?" He breathed shallowly through his mouth, his voice distorted by his crushed nasal passages. "If you're going to kill us, just do it already."

"I'm not going to kill you," Nate said dismissively. "Not her either." He indicated Julie with a nod of his head, and Julie blanched. Eric could tell how uncomfortable she was with the attention, how stiff she was in Nate's grasp.

"You don't touch her," Eric said, drawing himself up as much as his bonds would allow. He fixed Nate with a fiery gaze.

"You're in no position to demand anything," Nate replied. He looked at Julie then back at Eric. "I'll bring out some blankets. You'll need them if it gets below thirty tonight." He pulled on Julie's arm then, leading her back toward the farmhouse. She resisted and turned towards Nate.

"Please," she begged. "Please let them go. If you really want out, we can all run away right now; all of us, together!"

"I can't do that," Nate said. "I told you, it's complicated. Let me take you back inside first and I'll see what I can do. If Les was here right now, I'd get in a lot of trouble just for bringing you out here."

Eric, Terry, and Ricky watched them go, shivering as the temperature continued to drop.

15

Chimney Corner, West Virginia
5:42 p.m.

"I am truly sorry I can't stay longer," Brick said, inhaling the heady scent of Marcy as she pressed against his chest. He wasn't just sweet-talking. He'd been with more women than he could easily keep track of, groupies a lot of the time, but something about this woman drove him absolutely nuts. He knew that if he allowed it to happen, he could completely forget why he was even in Chimney Corner. But he wasn't going to do that.

Marcy hadn't been shy when they got back to her house, leading Brick straight to the bedroom after he said no to a drink. He stopped her halfway there and led her back to the living room. He'd never been one to say no to a woman, especially one as forward as this, but the pressing urgency of where Eric and the others might be weighed heavily on him.

"Hold on, sweety. I like you, and I like where you want this to go, but I have some stuff I have to take care of first, and I gotta talk to you about it."

"Well, I don't see why you can't stay a little longer," Marcy said. "I promise I'd make it worth your while."

"Oh, I have no doubt about that," Brick said with a laugh. "But I still need to find my friends. I need to talk to Mason about that."

"Mason?" Marcy asked. She pulled away from Brick and looked up at him suspiciously. "Why do you think he has something to do with it?"

"I need to know what happened at the diner last night. I get the feeling he knows more than he said earlier. He wasn't very talkative at the diner, though."

"Mason's a good boy," Marcy said. "He ain't never hurt a fly. I hope you aren't plannin' to do anything to him."

"No, of course not," Brick said with a shake of his head. "If you say he's not like that, I believe you." He leaned in closer to Marcy again, kissing her on the side of her mouth. "But he may have seen something he doesn't even realize is important."

"Well, I ain't never seen anything serious happen here. I don't think we've ever had a single murder, even."

"Is that so?" Brick asked. "Damn, I may need to retire here then." He grinned at Marcy. She smiled, standing on her toes to put herself up face-to-face with him, her chest pressed warmly against his.

"Are you sure you couldn't find a reason to come back sooner than that?" she asked. She leaned forward and flicked his lips with the tip of her tongue. He moved his hand from her shoulders to the top of her head and held her in place as he gave her a long, sensual kiss. His other hand scooped her bottom, steadying her, and she pushed more of her body into his. He broke the kiss and stared into her eyes, forehead resting against forehead.

"I think you just made a very strong case for that," Brick said. "But first, can you help me with Mason? Do you know when he's supposed to work at Bud's again?" She rolled her eyes in response.

"Ugh. You have a very one-track mind," she said. "And not for what I usually expect from a man." She arched her eyebrows. "I just hope you aren't leading me on, using me to get to Mason."

"No, baby, that ain't it at all. But I do have a job, and I was hoping you could help me out." He smiled and took his arms away. "And I was hoping I could make it worth *your* while later." He watched Marcy leave the living room and head for the kitchen. He followed and found her already mixing what looked like a very strong Bloody Mary.

"Just cause I'm a mountain gal, that don't make me stupid," she said. "I ain't some little girl that's gonna melt for a man with a hard . . . everything," she said, glancing up and down Brick's body.

"Look, Marcy, this really is serious. I'm worried my friends might be in danger, and I have good reason to think Mason knows more than he told me earlier."

Marcy sighed then relented. "I don't have Mason's schedule memorized, but I'm pretty sure he works most Saturday nights." She was about to say more when there was a knock at her door. Brick glanced down the hallway suspiciously.

"Are you expecting anybody?" he asked, stepping closer to Marcy. She looked at him with amusement.

"Are you worried about me, Brick? I've got a .38 in my bedside dresser. Never had to even show it to anyone, though."

"A woman after my own heart," he whispered in her ear. "I promise I will not leave this town before coming back over here." He gave her one more tender kiss as another knock came.

"Lord, they're persistent," Marcy said. "Probably some damn salesperson or something anyway."

"Do you want me to answer the door?" Brick asked.

"I think I can handle it, sugar," Marcy replied. She patted his rump as she walked past him, drink in hand. Brick admired the way she sashayed past, wondering if it was on purpose or just how she always walked. Brick heard the door open, and her wordless gasp of surprise was audible from the hallway. Putting a hand on his holster, Brick moved after her and came to the door as well. To his surprise, John Coors was standing there, eyes wide.

"Brick," he said, "we gotta find that guy right now. That Mason guy."

"Whoa, okay, calm down. He's gonna start his shift at Bud's in a few hours, apparently."

"No, that's too long. Ah, dammit, we've already taken too long. Look!" John pulled the black lipstick from his pocket and thrust it toward Brick. He looked over it, eyes widening in surprise. He knew exactly what it was.

"Where did you find this?"

"By the trash can outside the diner." He looked at Marcy. "You ever seen anyone in town who wears lipstick like this?" She shook her head. "They were there, Brick, last night. You were right. I think something bad happened. Something people are trying to cover up."

Brick turned to Marcy, whose face was pale with shock.

"We don't have time to wait for Mason. We need to know where he is right now. Do you know where he lives?"

"Um, yes, yes I do," she said haltingly. "I used to sit for him, after all. He's still living in the same house his momma owned, bless her soul." She went to the kitchen and came back quickly with a pen and a piece of note paper. "I'm gonna write down his address and directions for ya'll right now." She scribbled it down, then looked meaningfully at Brick before handing it over. "I still can't believe Mason would ever hurt anybody. Promise me you won't do anything bad to that boy. He's a good kid. He really is."

"I promise you," Brick said. He gave Marcy a very warm embrace, and she brushed his lips with hers.

"You be careful too," she whispered. "People who go looking for trouble are likely to find it." She handed him the paper.

"Trouble'd better hope I don't find it," Brick said. "You have my cell number, but I get terrible reception out here. I'll try to be in touch, though." Brick nodded and stepped out the door with John. They got into Jack's truck and pulled out quickly, fastening their belts as Brick shifted into drive. They were in such a hurry that he didn't notice a dull green Pontiac idling at the other end of the street, pulling into Marcy's driveway as soon as Brick was around the corner.

16

Goode Farm
6:20 p.m.

Eric grimaced as he readjusted himself. The light was scarce enough now that he had to squint to see Ricky or Terry, but he could hear them both. No one had come back out since Nate left with Julie, and Eric was starting to think no one would be coming anytime soon either. If what Nate said was true, that they were only alive because he was pushing for it, Eric had to ask why. He assumed it had something to do with Julie. Nate had brought her out here to see for herself everyone was still alive. Almost everyone. He didn't really understand why Nate had brought her out here, but he hoped Julie was still okay in the farmhouse.

He looked at Ricky, who gritted his teeth as a gust of wind blew past. It had dropped to about 50 degrees; not too cold, but with no sun and nothing to block the wind, it was damned uncomfortable.

Especially if you didn't even have a shirt. Ricky shivered violently. Wasn't it enough, Eric thought, losing Burt and watching what Nate did to the body? Did Ricky have to suffer half-naked in the mud too?

"I don't think he's bringing any blankets," Ricky said helplessly when he noticed Eric staring.

"I'm sorry," Eric replied. "I guess we shouldn't be surprised, though."

"I'm not," Ricky said. "I'm just counting time until we check out."

"That's a bit grim. We're not dead yet."

"Come on," Ricky said. "You know none of us are leaving here alive."

"Maybe you're not," Terry said. He spoke loudly so Ricky could hear him. "I still have some fight in me."

"How much fight, Terry?" Ricky asked. It almost could have been sarcasm, but Ricky seemed too tired for that. "Are you going to bite off your hand to get free? Are you going to rip your skin off sliding under the zip tie? Break your knuckles to make it fit?"

"I think," Terry replied, "seeing what happened to Burt fucked you up in the head a bit."

"Terry," Eric said. There was no energy to it, just the formality of verbalizing his distaste.

"No, it's true," Terry went on. "Not that I blame him. I mean, shit, I'd be fucked up too. I think I am fucked up, a little bit at least."

"You're not helping," Eric said.

"And what would be helping? Wanna do a pep talk, Eric? Wanna have a group hug, see if we can get Ricky feeling like he wants to live?"

"I'm not sure what you're suggesting instead."

"I'm saying we're only going to get out of here if we're realistic. Ricky's in no position to do anything, and as for you . . ." Terry trailed off as he examined Eric in the dim light. "You're breathing like you've got a few broken ribs. And you got that drunk slur going on. Concussion. If you could get up, I bet you wouldn't even be able to walk straight, let alone fight."

"I can fight," Eric said. He was shocked to notice some of the slurring Terry was pointing out.

"Ha, yeah, sure," Terry said. "It's going to be every man for himself. Whoever gets out of here first, he has to get to a car, a phone, get some help. I think I'm the only one who can do that."

"What about Julie?" Eric asked.

"What about her? We don't even know where that psycho is keeping her. And she was in better shape than all of us anyway. You want me to risk my ass to look for her? Nuh-uh. I get out of here, I'm gone like the wind, baby."

"They'll kill her," Eric said.

"All of us," Ricky corrected.

"That's a risk I have to take," Terry said. "It's a moot point if we can't get out of here, though. God knows I've been trying."

"We'd be better off finding a way to break the actual fence," Eric said as he probed the different knots and whorls of the wood. "It looks pretty damn old."

All three men turned as they heard another car starting up. Earlier they'd seen a Pontiac pulling away, and now they watched the white van that had brought them here pull away from the trailer home and head down the gravel driveway toward the road. They didn't see who'd gotten in, but when it was out of sight down the road, Terry met Eric's eyes.

"There's only two of them here right now," he said. Eric understood Terry's point and redoubled his efforts on the fence.

In the basement, Julie had been reconfined to the office chair once more as Nate stripped out of his sweat-stained shirt and pants. He was a frighteningly impressive physical specimen, with toned arms and a well-cut abdomen. He watched Julie to see if she was looking at him, and when he saw she was, he smiled. He approached her then, extending a hand toward her face once more, but again she pulled away from his touch.

Nate's face darkened, and for a moment Julie knew, she just knew, he was about to punch her, but then his demeanor changed and he turned around, grabbing a VHS tape off the shelf next to the TV.

"I have something I want to show you," he said. "Most people, like Mark, they don't like this, but I think you can actually appreciate it."

He put the tape into the VCR, and after a moment the screen blinked to grainy footage of a man chasing a woman down a strip of riverbank, tackling her, and graphically sexually assaulting her. Julie grimaced, not sure what she was watching. If it was a movie, it was the most realistic one she'd ever seen. It looked like someone was just using a handheld camera to film it.

The scene cut unceremoniously to a shot of the same woman, impaled vertically on a spike in the ground, the tip jutting from her mouth. Now the camerawork seemed more professional, as her rapist reacted with clearly fake horror to what he claimed had been done by the woman's native tribespeople as a result of the sexual act he'd forced on her. Julie's stomach heaved. She worried she would vomit, with no way to control where it landed, but Nate mercifully turned the TV off.

"I'm sorry; I guess I should have rewound it to the beginning. Have you ever heard of this movie? *Cannibal Holocaust*? It's a classic."

"Did you take the blankets out to my friends?" she asked him. She wanted desperately to talk about anything other than what she'd seen on that tape.

"I took them blankets already," he said with a dismissive wave. "Don't worry, I can't bring them into the house yet, but I have a plan. In a few hours, this will all be over." He motioned to the TV once more.

"You know, this movie is banned in, like, almost every country. It was real hard just to get a copy."

Julie stayed silent. She was desperate to get him talking about something else, anything else, but he seemed more animated now than she'd yet seen him. His eyes were positively glowing.

He walked over to her and placed a large hand on her chest, pushing the fabric of her neckline down to feel Julie's own heartbeat. "I can almost see your pulse going, up on your neck."

Julie looked down at Nate's hand on her breastbone. Her heartbeat quickened, and he looked at her with large eyes filled with disappointment.

"You still seem so afraid of me," he said. Behind him, the VCR automatically ejected the tape.

"Why wouldn't I be? You just showed me a snuff film, for God's sake."

Nate stepped back, furrowing his brow. He shook his head. "It's not a snuff film. Although I see why you'd think that. The Italians actually dragged the director into court because they thought he'd really killed people. He had to bring the actors into court just to prove they were still alive!" Nate seemed impressed by this. Julie pursed her lips, not wanting to encourage more discussion of that tape.

"I don't know why it bothers you so much if it's all fake. I mean, it's not really any different than what you do, right? The more real you can make it, the more you can get people to think you're actually hurting each other, the better, right?"

"There aren't many people who actually believe it's real anymore," Julie said. She chided herself for engaging, but she felt personally attacked being compared to what she'd just seen on that video.

"Okay, yeah, but then why do it at all? Why throw yourself onto a pile of thumbtacks? Why let someone hit you in the head with a baseball bat wrapped in barbed wire? If no one thinks it's real, what do you get out of it?"

Because that's what you have to do, Julie thought. It was either that or resign yourself to the bra-and-panties matches that were glorified stripteases.

"I have to say, I thought you of all people would be able to appreciate *Cannibal Holocaust*," Nate said. He seemed genuinely disappointed.

"I don't enjoy watching women get raped," she said. She shook her head. Why couldn't she keep her mouth shut? What was she trying to prove?

"It's just one scene," Nate argued. "It's not like the whole movie is about that."

"Kind of a coincidence that you just happened to be at that part on the tape, then," Julie said. The words were out of her mouth before she could stop herself. She was annoyed with herself, but a small, triumphant part within her was crowing about shoving Nate's face into his depravity.

"I'm not into that," he said flatly. "You really think I'd do that to you?"

Julie kept quiet this time. She sensed she may have pushed him too far, but she wasn't going to test it again.

"You know, I don't have to rape anyone. I've had women before. You think, what, I get some kind of kick out of the idea? Or that's the only way I can get sex?"

Oh my God, Julie thought. She leaned back as Nate came closer, bending down to be eye to eye with her.

Julie swallowed hard over what she said next. "I'm sorry." She stared directly into Nate's eyes. "I haven't had a lot of good experiences with men." Nate nodded knowingly.

"Well, I'm not one of those men. I'm not just going to hurt you for no reason."

"I've had men tell me that before. Then they tried to force themselves on me. I have good reason to be afraid."

He leaned back and opened his arms palms-up. "Haven't I demonstrated that I care for your well-being?" He quickly turned and removed the tape hanging out of the VCR. "To answer your question;

no, I don't plan to hurt you. I thought I'd already made that clear." He slipped the tape back into its sleeve and replaced it under the desk.

Julie thought hard about how to proceed. She had to walk him back from where he was, get him calmed down.

"You're right, Nate," Julie said. "I think I misjudged you. You seem like a very smart, very capable man. You've treated me well. I just don't know why I'm still tied up."

"If I'd intended to do anything awful, I would have already. I could force myself on you, if I wanted to. You couldn't stop me. But I already know that, and you already know that too, so what would be the point?" He leaned closer now, close enough that she could see the light freckles across both cheeks and the bridge of his nose. "But what if I didn't have to force you? What if you just realized we have so much in common?"

"We do?" Julie asked. How on earth, she wondered, could this man possibly see any similarity between them?

"Don't be so surprised. I've watched you on TV. You have a dedication few others can match."

Julie didn't understand where he was going with this, but she didn't interrupt.

"We both excel in environments we don't belong in. I don't want to be here propping up my father's meth business, and you don't want to be wrestling in pudding matches for the rest of your life. We could both leave here and make something better."

Julie frowned, irritated at his summation of her life's work.

"I want to go, but I can't leave my friends behind," she said.

"Of course you can't," he replied irritably. "And like I keep saying, the only reason Les didn't kill the rest of you is because of me. Me!" He sat back once more, animated, gesturing wildly with his hands. "They don't have to die. I can save you. I can save all of you." He reached out and put his hand over hers. She somehow restrained herself from flinching. "And I'm really not asking for much in return."

"I know, but then why can't we go now? You said Les isn't here, so what's stopping us?"

Nate felt panic creeping into him. The moment was slipping away. This was all wrong, not at all how he'd planned for it to go.

"It's still dangerous. I don't know where Les is, and he always has a gun. I'm worried if he sees us, he'll kill us both." This was a wild exaggeration, but it slid out of his mouth like the gospel truth. He took a deep breath. "At this point, I can't stand the idea of losing you like that."

And there it is, Julie thought. *There's the lever.*

"I'm actually glad you feel that way," she said. "I was surprised you weren't already spoken for."

"Around here?" Nate snorted. "You must be joking."

"So you've never even had a girlfriend?"

"I don't really want to talk about it." He was red in the face now.

"Oh, I didn't mean to . . ." Julie's mind raced. This was her chance. This was the way she could get out of these handcuffs and save her friends. Maybe if she played along with Nate? It couldn't hurt, she supposed. She looked at him, summoning every bit of knowledge she'd accumulated about being in character. Wrestlers were actors, after all. She was going to play the part. Her eyes widened, and she focused on memories that would make her happy in order to hopefully dilate her pupils.

"It's okay," Nate replied. "You're curious about me, I get it. That's how I know there's something connecting us, you know? I felt it as soon as I saw you in the yard. It's like this was meant to be."

Meant to be, Julie thought. *He really is crazy.* "I can see it," she said. "And, well, I'm grateful for the help you've given me. I mean, you saved my life, right?"

He smiled then, a lopsided sort of thing, and leaned forward with his hand still on hers. *Oh God, is he going to try to kiss me?* Julie thought. She prayed she could keep from retching if that was the case.

"I did save you," he said. "I'm glad you see it that way." He leaned closer, closed his eyes, and Julie could see that, yes, he did intend to kiss her, and what the fuck? How divorced from reality did he have to be to think *this* was the way to a woman's heart?

His lips began to press onto hers, and she steadied herself for the inevitable tongue she was sure he'd push in, but just as he made full contact, there was a loud, insistent pounding on the door to the basement. Nate's eyes flew open, enraged, looking directly into Julie's, which had never closed. He jumped to his feet, knocking over his chair, and flew up the stairs.

▬

"What?" Nate hissed as he swung the door open. His father stood on the other side, and while normally he would have cowered before Nate in such a mood, for once he stood resolute. He backed off just far enough to give Nate some room and motioned hurriedly for him to step out.

"Close the door," he whispered, which Nate did. "Good." Norm looked down the hallway towards Mark's room; the door was closed. They could hear the heavy bass of whatever music Mark had on from where they stood. "Okay," Norm said. "I have a problem. *We* have a problem," he corrected himself. "It's one that only you can solve."

"If Bud's complaining about the pork again," Nate began, but Norm cut him off.

"No. Nothing like that." Norm continued to whisper, as if fearful that someone might hear him. "Bud called here a little bit ago, talked to Les. I don't know about what exactly."

"What's that have to do with me?" Nate asked.

"Because he tore off in the Pontiac right after. Pissed as hell." He sighed. "He tol' me Bud was askin' about last night. But I think he wouldn't be runnin' off like that if that's all it was. I think someone said something to scare Bud."

"Who would be saying something?"

"I don't know. But the only other person who knows anything is Mason, right?"

Nate nodded slowly.

"Now, I ain't surprised people'd already be lookin' for those wrestlers. Les isn't some master criminal after all. He couldn't even rob a liquor store without getting caught." Norm looked back toward Mark's room again. "If someone went to Bud, it won't be long before they get to Mason."

"I thought Mason doesn't know anything."

"That's what *Les* told me. But he's always had a soft spot for that kid and Mark. Even if Mason doesn't know what happened to the wrasslers, he knows Les was there at the same time. He knows we made Bud close the diner. He's too dumb to put it all together, but I'm not willing to bet anyone else would be that stupid."

"Okay." Nate bent down lower, bringing himself face-to-face with Norm. "So what do you want *me* to do?"

"I want you to go to Mason's house and fix this," Norm said. "Do I really have to walk you through it?"

"No. But that's not what I do. You know that. I deal with the pigs, I deal with the bodies; that's it. I want no part of any of this other shit."

"You listen to me," Norm said. He was angry. It surprised Nate. He could barely remember the last time Norm had been visibly angry with him. "This is still my house, my rules. I tolerate you doing the bare fucking minimum around here. I tolerated it when you kicked me in the nuts, changing your name to Goode. But understand that if I go down, you go down. We all do. You are no fuckin' angel. You'll go to prison too if we get caught."

Nate stood up and crossed his arms. He scowled at Norm, hoping to cow him into submission as usual. It didn't work.

"Don't you try to intimidate me, son. If you don't get out there and handle Mason, I'll put a bullet in you first then go do it myself."

Nate stopped scowling and raised his eyebrows. Norm had never been brazen enough to openly threaten Nate before. He took in Norm's bloodshot eyes and shallow breathing and chalked it up to injectable courage. Still, Norm had a point. If Mason spoke to anyone, if there was a cavalry coming to save the day, Nate's hastily-assembled plans to be Julie's savior would crumble to ruins.

Nate had wanted to get out for a long time now, but didn't have the means to. He had money saved away in the bank, yes, but it wasn't much. It wasn't enough to pick up and start a whole new life. Norm didn't give Nate that much pay. Norm considered Nate's room the majority of what Nate earned.

Les's plot to take off had accelerated Nate's own plans, though. He wasn't going to be the asshole left behind holding the sack. He didn't start any of this, and he sure as hell wouldn't be taking the blame for it. He just needed more money, Les's preferably.

He knew Norm didn't have much money, because he flushed it all down the drain on food and prostitutes. And lately he'd been using more of the product than selling it. Mark was the same way, for the most part. Only Les seemed to have the cash on hand to get the hell out. Nate wondered for the first time just how much Les was making off their business.

That kind of money, combined with Nate's own stash, would make it possible for Nate to extricate himself from his family before he got in any deeper. And Julie represented the best opportunity to do that.

It would never work if someone else made the save, though. Then Nate would be seen as just another part of the business, regardless of whether he ever handled the drugs or not. He didn't recoil at the idea of killing Mason, or anyone really, but he didn't want to endanger his own freedom in the process. He'd have to be very careful about how this was done to make sure he could still walk away with his hands clean.

"No need for threats," he said to Norm. "I'll take care of it." He opened the door to the basement and walked in, turning on the first step to say one more thing. "By the way, I changed my name because it's still called 'the Goode Farm.' That's what everyone in town knows us by. It makes things look more official. If you were smart, you'd've already changed your name too. The only Whites in West Virginia are criminals." He closed the door before Norm could respond. It was petty, but Nate did enjoy getting the last word, especially with Norm becoming so assertive with him. That would not do. No, that would not do at all.

He walked back down the stairs, where Julie sat exactly as he'd left her. She was staring at the heart he'd left on the table, which pleased Nate. He'd never shown anyone the kinds of experiments he occupied his time with, and seeing her shock, even if it was tinged with horror, made him swell with pride. Finally he had somebody to share his discoveries with. Soon she would learn to appreciate the genius behind the work, much the same way people learn to enjoy the bitter bite of alcohol that precedes drunken bliss.

"Sorry for the interruption. That was just my father," Nate said. It was amazing to him how immediately comfortable he felt around Julie. If he believed in heaven, he would believe she was divinely sent, at just this moment, to save him from a life of tedium with his family. "There's an errand I have to run, but don't worry. I won't be gone long."

"What do you have to do?" Julie asked, her voice tinged with worry.

"Nothing important. I mean, important to you. Nothing to do with your friends. I just have to go deliver something. Don't worry, though. The door to the basement is locked, and only I have the key. No one else is going to bother you."

Honestly, that was the last thing Julie was worried about. She was more concerned about her friends, but she smiled and played along with Nate.

"Thank you," she said. "I appreciate that." He smiled back at her, and then moved in quickly and planted another kiss on her. This time no one interrupted, and Julie had to feign passion and restrain her gag reflex, meeting Nate's tongue with hers as he pushed it into her mouth. After a few seconds that felt like an hour, Nate pulled away and wiped his mouth. He looked at Julie expectantly, and she did her best to appear pleased with him.

"I'll be back," he said, and Julie tried to chuckle. She gave him a weak, forced smile, and he nodded before pounding up the steps and leaving the basement. Julie sighed and settled in, trying to gather her strength for when the moment to strike would come.

17

Chimney Corner, West Virginia
6:03 p.m.

Les guided his Pontiac into Marcy's narrow driveway, barely clearing the road as he parked behind her Saturn. He stepped onto the cracked concrete driveway and closed the door carefully before walking up to the front door. His Desert Eagle was still tucked neatly into his waistband against the small of his back.

He'd watched the wrestlers leave like hell was on their tail, and he was keen to find out exactly what Marcy had said to them. Les wasn't looking forward to having to kill Marcy, but he was prepared to do what he had to do. He knocked lightly on the door and waited. She couldn't pretend she wasn't home.

After a few minutes Marcy came to the door, pulling it open as far as her security chain would allow. It wouldn't deter Les of course;

he could kick the door in with hardly an effort, but if it let her feel comfortable, then all the better.

"What are you doing here, Les?" she asked. He couldn't quite tell, but it looked like Marcy was wearing a sweatshirt with no bra. It brought back pleasant memories that were, unfortunately, almost two decades old now.

"Would you believe I was just in the neighborhood?" Les smiled in what he hoped was a disarming way. "No, I guess not. Listen, I saw who just left your house. I wanted to know what the deal is with you two."

"I don't see how that's any of your business," Marcy said. "Why do you wanna know, anyway?"

Les braced himself against her doorframe. "Well, I was concerned when I heard you left Bud's with some Black guy no one had ever seen before."

"What? You're worried I can't handle myself?" She arched an eyebrow at him.

"Well, maybe just a little," he said.

"We gonna play this game? You want me to believe that you came up here outta concern, all worried about me?"

"Yeah . . ."

"I ain't even gonna pretend you did this outta the goodness of your heart. The whole town knows what you do up there on the farm now." She shook her head. "Your grandmamma would be disappointed that's the best her grandson can do. Or her great-grandson either."

"Mamma Goode ain't around no more; that's the problem. It's up to me to look after Mark."

"And you done such a bang-up job—get outta jail and turn him into a fuckin' meth head." She saw the anger flash in Les's eyes and decided to pull back. "I'm sorry. I like that boy's all. I used to like *you too*, Les. Before the armed robbery and all."

"People make mistakes. That was over a decade ago."

"Yeah, but you keep makin' the same mistakes. Every day." She shifted her position and began to close the door. "Good night, Les."

He stopped the door with his foot, imposing it in the space left by the security chain. "Wait," he said. "I need to know what you said to that guy."

"What makes you think I said anything? I just thought he was cute and invited him back here."

"I heard he and a friend were asking questions and then you left with him," Les said.

Marcy rolled her eyes. "I didn't say nothing to him, or his friend."

"I just need to know what they were asking you." Les sighed before going on. "Look, you say you like Mark so much, and I think he's in trouble with these guys."

Marcy considered Les for a moment, then unfolded her arms as her scowl softened. "They're trying to find some missing friends of theirs. Apparently they didn't show up this morning at work. Do you know if any groups was in the restaurant last night?"

"I don't know anything about any wrestlers," Les replied.

"I never said they was wrestlers, sweetheart." Sweat started to bead on her brow. "I think I'm done talking now."

She moved to close the door, but he still blocked it with his foot.

"Les, I don't want to have anything to do with this. I didn't say nothing to him, I just thought he was cute. Offered him a drink but he politely declined, like a gentleman. So don't get me wrapped up in your trouble, just let me go back to my screwdriver."

"Marcy, I can't let you do that," Les said, holding her gaze with his. *God, she's still so beautiful,* he thought. He hated having to do this.

"You can't?" she asked him.

"You know why," he said.

"No, I don't. Not really. But I don't wanna know, either." She stared into Les's eyes before finally letting out a resigned sigh. "They wanted to know where Mason lives."

"Shit," Les whispered. The gun in his waistband felt a lot heavier now.

"I know that look," Marcy said. Her brows knit in concern. "What are you gonna do?"

"Nothing," Les said. "Just trying to keep these kids outta trouble."

"Then maybe you should rethink the kind of business ya'll are in." She tried to close the door again, but Les wouldn't move his foot. She looked back up at him, trying to hide her fear behind a practiced weariness she used on every asshole customer at Bud's. In the back of her mind, Marcy estimated how quickly she could get to the phone and call Brick, or 9-1-1 at least, before Les broke in. She didn't like the answer.

On the other side of the door from Marcy, Les raised his right hand to his waistband.

"What are you gonna do, Les, kill me?" she asked him. He looked at her, hand on the pistol, and considered. He hated loose ends. But this was quickly spinning out of his control. Marcy was the last person he'd ever want to hurt. She's the only person he was going to regret leaving behind. He removed his hand and stepped back in resignation.

"I'm hurt you even asked," Les said. He searched her face for regret about it, but saw none. He sighed, wishing for the millionth time that he'd made different choices in his life. But you play the hand you choose to keep, and he had to make the best of it. "Good night, Marcy."

She closed the door in Les's face without replying.

Brick Lamar drove without his sunglasses for the first time since John Coors had gone on the road with him. It had become dark enough now for the sunglasses to be worthless, but it was still disconcerting for John to see Brick's eyes, wide and alert, darting back and forth as he took in everything they passed. They were on a residential street, the homes mostly dilapidated trailers set up on permanent foundation blocks. The area was surrounded with forest that was nearly overrunning the street, giving it a secluded and natural feel.

They pulled up to a home that looked like it had been decorated by a grandmother in her mid-sixties. Suncatchers and wind chimes dangled from the porch awning. A cardboard cutout of an old woman's behind stood in front of the flower bed, meant to look like someone was working out there. A weathered wreath with yellow flowers hung on the front door. Brick pulled the truck into the driveway behind a light blue Impala that John remembered from earlier at the diner.

"You sure this is the place?" John asked as Brick turned off the engine.

"Unless Marcy was lying to me," Brick replied.

"Maybe he still lives with his mom."

"No, Marcy said she passed away a few years back." Brick got out of the truck, followed by John, and they approached the front door. Brick pushed the doorbell but heard no sound from inside. After a few seconds, he tried knocking instead. They heard footsteps approaching from inside, and the door swung open to reveal the young man Brick had spoken to earlier at the diner.

Mason was dressed for work, even though his shift wouldn't start for another two hours. He'd opened the door without thinking of who it might be, and when he saw Brick and John out there, he nearly swung the door shut again in surprise. He regarded them with large, fearful eyes until Brick smiled at him and nudged John with his elbow, prompting John to smile as well.

"Hello, Mason, how are you tonight?" Brick extended his hand and Mason took it instinctively. Brick pumped it up and down as he went on. "I'm sorry to barge in like this, but I needed to talk to you and wanted to do so privately if that's okay."

"Um, privately for what?" Mason asked. He had not forgotten the way Brick had been flirting with Marcy earlier, and his resentment combined with his unease from last night made him hesitant to cooperate.

"Well, about last night, really." Brick stepped forward without releasing Mason's hand, moving into the house with John close behind. "You see, I'm pretty sure my friends came through here last night, and I'm also pretty sure they stopped at Bud's for a bite to eat."

"Your friends . . ." Mason looked over Brick more closely now than he had before. "Holy shit, you're Brick Lamar!"

Brick raised his eyebrows and glanced at John with a look that said, "How do you like that?"

"Yeah, that's me. You probably know John Coors too, then." He let go of Mason's hand and gestured to John.

"Yes, I do. Well gah-damn, I can't believe I've met Jiggolo *and* Brick Lamar!" Mason clapped a hand over his mouth, immediately regretting having said anything. Already Brick and John were both on high alert.

"You've met Jiggolo?" John asked. "When? Last night? At Bud's?"

"Um, shit, um, yep, they was here last night. Whole pack of 'em." Mason's heart was hammering at his chest. He could imagine Les's face, twisted in fury for talking to *anybody* like this. Mason was a shit liar, though. Always had been.

"Where did they go?" Brick asked, holding up a hand to restrain John from saying anything else.

"I dunno. They ordered their food, Jiggolo and Fort Knox and all them, but then they left soon as I went back to make it."

"They left without eating anything?" Brick asked. Mason nodded.

"Uh-huh. Just up and left. Didn't even get me no autograph."

"You closed up and went home early last night. Why? No customers?"

"Um . . ." Mason's mind raced. He hadn't anticipated anyone asking him this. He could say Bud told him to, but what if Bud tried to say it was all Mason's idea instead? Les hadn't told him what to say, had he? His face contorted as he tried desperately to remember.

"Okay," Brick said, taking note of Mason's agitation. "How about this: Was anyone else in the diner last night besides Jiggolo, Fort Knox, TJ Azz, Goth Girl, and Ricky Chalmers?"

"Um . . ." Mason didn't understand. The way the guy talked, was he a cop? A cop *and* a wrestler, like Big Boss Man or the Mountie? He didn't want to get in any trouble with cops. Not when he didn't do anything wrong. "My buddy Mark was there. And Les. His uncle. Well, not really his uncle, I guess. Mark's momma was Les's cousin, so that makes Les Mark's uh, uh . . ."

"His second cousin," Brick said. "Or something. But that isn't important right now, Mason. What's important is, did they all leave at the same time? Your friend Mark, and Les, and our friends?"

Mason cringed, not sure of what he ought to say. Les scared the piss out of him, but Les wasn't here right now and these guys were. He didn't really know what had happened, but he had a feeling something might have. He didn't want to risk getting himself in trouble.

"I honestly don't know," Mason said. "I was told to just go on home." Mason paced around the small living room, walking round a scuffed wooden coffee table. "I don't know nothin' else; please don't ask me nothin' else."

"What are you so scared of?" John asked. "Did someone threaten you?"

"Les's always threatenin' me. Tellin' me to keep my mouth shut, to not pay attention to stuff, to not talk to no body. But now here I am, blabbing away!" Mason was becoming more and more agitated as he went on. Brick stepped in, trying to calm things down.

"Hey, listen; it's okay, Mason. No one knows we're here. And I'm not going to tell anyone what you told us. We just want to find our friends."

"Where does Les live, Mason?" John asked.

"Um, I can't tell you that. No way, nuh-uh. They's gonna kill me if I do, I know they will."

"It's a small town," Brick said. "We'll figure it out anyway. But it'll be a lot easier if you tell us." He leaned over, bringing himself face-to-face with Mason. "If they did something—*if*—then by not telling us, you'll be an accessory. Do you really want that?"

"It's true," John said. "Withholding information that could potentially save a life is a criminal offense."

Mason's chin quivered as he wrestled with what to do. His fear over what might happen if he told was conflicting with his fear of what would happen if he went to jail. He remembered how different Les had been after he got out of prison. Mason didn't want to know what caused that change.

"They all live at the Goode Farm. On Cemetery Road." He sighed. "I don't know the exact address. But they's just about the only farm out there. That and the old Baptist church." Mason collapsed heavily into his couch, all the strength leaving his body.

"Thank you, Mason," Brick said. He looked around the room, then picked up a pencil and a sticky-note pad. He signed his name on the yellow paper and handed it to Mason. "For your help," he said, and Mason smiled for the first time since they'd arrived.

"Ah jeez, thank you! I'm gonna get this framed and put up on my wall!"

"You're welcome. Come out to one of our shows some time; I'll get you ringside seats." They turned to leave, and Mason waved happily. Once they were outside, Brick's expression turned serious again.

"We need to get to the motel," John said. He pulled out his cell and tried to dial 9-1-1, but the signal was barely making it through.

"What are you doing?" Brick asked, and slammed the phone shut in John's hand. John looked at him in shock.

"What are *you* doing?" he said. "We've got to get someone over there in case that's where Eric and them are."

"Yeah, but listen to what you said: In case. The cops wouldn't be able to search the property, even if they did take you seriously. They'd have to knock, ask their questions, and then—*if* Eric and everyone are out there, and *if* they're still alive—what will those guys do to them as soon as the cops leave?"

"So what do you suggest?" John asked.

"You were right about one thing. Someone needs to get over there. That's us. If I sneak around and see something, you can call 9-1-1 from there; then the police would have probable cause to enter the property."

"Good thinking," John said. Brick put an arm around John.

"Let's get on the road. We're losing light by the minute. Get out the map and find me Cemetery Road."

Norm stood at the front window in the living room, watching Nate drive off the property in the Astro van. As Nate turned onto Rural Route 47, Norm turned around and headed down the hallway to Mark's bedroom. The heavy bass from Mark's speakers still resonated through the walls, so Norm didn't even bother knocking before bursting in on Mark. He sat on the bed, leafing through one of those auto magazines that feature tricked-out cars and chicks in string bikinis. He had his stash and supplies out on the bedside table, a lighter and glass pipe lying next to the clear crystals. Norm grunted as he forced the door open enough to accommodate his entry, pushing it against a pile of clothing on the floor.

"Whoa, what the hell?" Mark asked, sitting up and setting the magazine on the floor by the bed. "Maybe knock or something?"

"Cut the shit," Norm said impatiently. "I need you to get out to the pens and take care of those three assholes now."

"What do you mean?" Mark asked dumbly.

"I mean, I just sent your brother on an errand so that *you* could go out there and get rid of the problem *you* created." He sidled up to Mark's bed and seized him by the upper arm. "Come on. I don't know how long it's gonna take him, but you probably have forty-five minutes or an hour at most."

"Um, I ain't never actually killed someone like that b'fore. Uncle Les is the one who always done that."

"Well, now it's time for you to man up and fix your own fuck-ups, okay?" Mark offered little resistance as Norm pulled him to his feet. "Go get the .45 out of the desk and shoot them in the head. It's real easy, one-two-three."

"I dunno," Mark said. "I think Nate'll be pissed if he gets back and they're all dead."

"Who gives a shit? What's done is done. Ya think he's gonna, what, kill you for it or something?" Norm shook his head in disgust. "You and Les are so fucking scared of Nate. It's embarrassing."

Mark crossed him arms defiantly, pulling away from Norm's grip. "You're scared of him too."

Norm's face contorted with fury as he came nose to nose with Mark. "I ain't scared of nothin', you got it? I ain't scared of Les, and I sure as hell ain't scared o' my own flesh and blood!" He backed away, his face reddening with exertion.

"Then why don't *you* go kill them, you so tough and shit?" Mark said with a grimace.

"'Cause I give the orders round here, you ungrateful fuckin' shit. I let Nate think he's got a say, but he don't, you got it? The only one who has final word in this house is me! So if I tell ya's to get your ass out there and shoot those fuckers in the head, you will goddamn do it right the hell right now, okay?"

Mark dropped his arms and his eyes, sufficiently cowed. "Yeah, Dad, I gotcha," he said. He left the room without another word, and Norm listened for the sound of him fetching the pistol from the desk in the living room. After he heard the front door open and close, he reached into his pocket and pulled out his keyring, holding up a small bronze key. He walked out of Mark's room and eyed the door the basement, where the keyhole that fit the bronze key sat in the silver doorknob that Nate had foolishly assumed only he had access to.

—

Nate left the unfortunately conspicuous white Astro van at the closest parking lot to the road leading into Mason's neighborhood. In a town of about two thousand people, just about every vehicle stood out, and Nate had no intention of being seen near Mason's house. He parked in front of a pawn shop, a common destination for either Les or Mark. Leaving the van, he began the fifteen-minute walk to Mason's home.

Nate had been considering whether to follow through on this as soon as Norm broached the idea. He wasn't some mercenary, a thuggish killer that didn't blink an eye at knocking off potential rivals. That was more Les's department, although Les had made it very clear multiple times that he wouldn't harm a hair on Mason's head unless absolutely necessary. Nate didn't have quite as stringent a policy when it came to Mason.

It wouldn't be hard, Nate imagined, to either cover up the murder or at least make it appear that someone else had done it. He could take care of this, make sure no one else pieced it all together, and still come out the hero at the end.

Nate was pleased to see Mason's car in the driveway, letting him know Mason was still there. Nate was quite familiar with the vehicle, having worked on it for Mason's mother many times over the years. Mason hadn't wanted to bring his car around anymore; no one really wanted to, not since what happened to Louanne's Tahoe. Ah, well. The hit to his reputation was small potatoes. He still felt pride in his accomplishment. It took a certain level of genius to make something look like an accident.

Nate knocked lightly at the door, a gentle rapping meant to put Mason at ease. Mason was at the door in less than a minute, cautiously speaking out.

"Uh, who is it?" he asked.

"It's Nate, Mason." Nate put his hands behind his back. He knew Mason couldn't see the gesture, but Nate found it helped him sell the overall image in his own head. "Can I come in for a minute?"

"I'm pretty busy, Nate," Mason replied. "Maybe we can talk at the diner? I'll be headin' that way in just a few hours."

"Not in a few hours. Not at the diner. I need to talk to you now." Nate struggled to keep the irritation out of his voice. Yes, he could force his way in without much trouble, but that would hardly fit with his plan for Mason to have some kind of accident, or just disappear.

"About what?"

"About the wrestlers from last night," Nate said. "I need to know if you've heard from them since they left the diner." Nate hoped this would confuse and disarm Mason enough to open the door. Within a few seconds, he was rewarded with the sound of a deadbolt being thrown and the door swinging inward. Mason appeared at the door. Nate wasn't surprised to see him dressed for work so early. He was very much a creature of habit.

"Come on in," Mason said. "I didn't realize they was all missing."

"Thank you," Nate said without emotion. He turned back to Mason and reached over his head to close the door. He threw the deadbolt as well. "Now, we need to talk about last night. Specifically, what you know, and who you told."

"Well, all I know is, I came and took the orders. And after I went to cook 'em, Les come in and tells me they changed their mind and I had to go on home," Mason said. "I didn't even get to say goodbye."

"Did anyone talk to you about it? Ask you questions about it?"

"N . . . n-n . . . no?" Mason said. He really was a terrible liar. Nate sighed. Now he had to force the answers out of Mason. He didn't need this.

"Who did you talk to, Mason?" He walked around the room, interposing himself between Mason and the door as he did so. Out of the corner of his eye he saw a yellow sticky note with a signature on it proudly tacked up on the wall. He studied it carefully.

"Brick Lamar. Hmm. I didn't know he was in town. When did he give you this?" He gave Mason a sideways glance as he waved the sticky note around. "I thought you said you didn't talk to anyone today."

Mason started sweating now and began to back away. "I'm sorry, Nate. I really didn't say nothin'. I don't know nothin'! Please, come on, I'm beggin' ya, just listen to me, please!" He was moving toward the rear of the house, toward the back door. In a few quick steps, Nate was on top of him, grabbing him by his work polo.

"You're lying, Mason. I need to know exactly what you told Brick Lamar. You can tell me now, or I can start breaking every bone in your body, starting with your little finger." He seized Mason's flailing, sweaty right hand, grabbing it by the wrist with his right and the pinky finger with his left. Nate bent it backward until it stopped, then bent it a little further. Mason's face turned white as he screeched in pain.

"Okay, okay!" he said. "I'll tell you everything! They was here, all right? And they made me tell 'em who was at the diner last night besides Jiggolo and them others. So I told him it was Les and Mark, but I swear I didn't say nothin' else 'cause I don't know nothin' else! Les made me stay in the kitchen till they all left!"

"Did you tell them that part?" Nate asked. Mason yelped and swatted ineffectively at Nate's arms.

"No! I just told 'em that everyone was gone when I left!" He was stammering now, sweating. He was pathetic, and it disgusted Nate.

Nate let go of Mason's hand, and Mason scrambled to the kitchen table and sat down, cradling his wrist. Nate shook his head dismissively.

It wasn't even going to bruise. He stepped up behind Mason and wrapped his right arm around Mason's throat and his left across the back of his head, pressing it forward. He hooked his right arm to compress Mason's carotid artery and waited. Mason struggled at first, but quickly lost strength. Within a few seconds, Mason's body was limp against Nate's arms. He held the choke for a while longer, counting in his head. When he reached sixty he let go, and Mason's body tumbled limply from the chair. Nate checked for a pulse and found none.

Nate nodded and moved to Mason's mother's room, which Mason had left more or less untouched since she'd passed away. On a dresser opposite the bed was a small collection of scented candles. He selected one, Granny Smith apple scent, and carried it into Mason's room. Thin gauzy sheets hung over the only window in Mason's room. Nate set the candle down on the side table in front of the window.

Nate carried Mason's body without much trouble into the bedroom and laid him out on the bed, taking the time to remove the work shirt and pants and hang them back in the closet. He tucked Mason in like a child, then pulled a packet of matches from his back pocket and struck one. Nate lit the candle on the side table, taking the time to inhale its aroma. It really did smell like apples. Amazing. He took one of the flimsy curtains and laid it along the edge of the jar, where it quickly caught fire.

Nate left the room. There was no need to supervise the rest. If there was one thing he knew about trailer homes, it was that they were basically livable tinderboxes. In a few minutes the whole house would be engulfed in a perfectly natural, very tragic accident. No one would second-guess an idiot like Mason accidentally burning his house down.

Nate walked quickly through the back woods to the parking lot where his van was. In the dark people would notice a fire burning almost immediately, and he wanted to be as far away as possible when that happened. He got back to the van without incident and started it up. This is it then, Nate thought. No turning back from here. He pulled out of the parking lot and drove back to the farm, taking care not to speed and draw unwanted attention.

Les sat in his Pontiac for several minutes, unsure of what to do. He could go to Mason's, but he knew he wouldn't make it there before those wrestlers did. And what would he do then? Kill the wrestlers? Kill Mason? No. It was time to cut his losses. He had to get back to the farm, he had to get Mark, and he had to haul ass outta town. The jig was up, of that he was sure, and he had only one option left. Let Norm and Nate figure it out when the cops came roaring up the drive. He'd make sure to be at least a couple of states over by then.

He sped down the road toward the farm, hands gripping the wheel, heart racing.

18

Goode Farm
6:27 p.m.

Eric watched Mark approaching the pens with dread. He anticipated that the only reason Mark or Les would come out here would be to finish things off. He steeled himself for what was to come, feeling his leg shake uncontrollably. Terry stared at Mark as well, body tense. Their breath puffed in the cool air. Only Ricky seemed completely unconcerned. He shivered in the mud, curled in a fetal position, not even paying attention to Mark as he opened the door to the pens and walked in. Eric saw with dismay that Mark held a revolver in his hand; not the Desert Eagle he'd been wielding before, but still plenty intimidating.

Mark first walked up to Ricky, who still seemed only barely aware of Mark's presence. Mark raised the pistol and pointed it at Ricky's head. He pulled back the hammer with his thumb and took careful aim.

"Really? You're cocking the hammer?" Ricky's voice, clear and crisp in the cool night air, startled Mark.

"Huh?" he stammered. His arm wavered as he squinted, unsure of how to respond.

"It's bad enough," Ricky went on, "to be shot by a dick-less turd like you, but you can't even be manly about how you shoot me." He shook his head. "Cocking the hammer. Good God. Are you gonna hold the thing sideways too? Have you ever fired a real gun, or just watched it in movies?"

"Ain't no way someone like you tells me I'm not manly," Mark said. He was angry now. He raised the revolver once more, hammer still cocked.

"So . . . what . . . you're trying to scare me with that? Big tough guy, shooting the tied-up man from ten feet way. At least the other guy could fight."

"You shut the hell up," Mark said. He fired, and the sound was deafening. He was furious to see Ricky was still alive, and actually laughing at him.

"You missed? Oh my God, how pathetic! Go ahead. Keep shooting; I'll freeze to death before you hit me."

Eric watched the scene unfold with wide eyes. Ricky was a talker, one of the best in MAW, and he'd seen few better that could rile up a crowd. He was working Mark like, well, a mark, but why?

"I'll get plenty close, then," Mark said. He stepped forward again, adjusting his aim so that the barrel was lined up between Ricky's blackened eyes. Ricky threw his head back and laughed.

"Are you serious? You're scared to get closer than that? My hands are tied. What are you afraid of? Come on, bitch, be a man." Ricky stretched out his leg and flicked some mud onto Mark's shirt with the toe of his shoe. Mark said nothing, instead moving forward and swinging out with his foot, hitting Ricky's sternum with a disconcerting *thwack*.

Ricky wheezed and then began to laugh again. It started, Eric noticed, as his phony "character" laugh, but soon morphed into real guffaws, trailing off into light coughing.

"Shut up!" Mark said, dropping to his knees then. He grabbed Ricky by the throat, cutting off the last bits of laughter, and pressed the barrel of the revolver into his forehead.

"Is this close enough, you fucker?" Mark asked. Ricky's face contorted into a rictus grin before answering.

"Yeah," Ricky said, and then slammed his free left hand into the side of Mark's neck. Mark stumbled back, firing the revolver as he fell ass-first into the mud. The revolver went off two more times, deafeningly loud. Eric watched, uncomprehending, as Mark twitched and thrashed in the mud, dropping the gun as he clawed at his neck. Eric saw blood spurting out in an arc from Mark's neck, and more of it collecting beneath him in an expanding pool. As Mark flopped onto his side, Eric could see what his fingers were clawing at: A mud-stained chunk of broken bone jutted out from Mark's throat, right where the artery was. Ricky had had one shot and knew just where to aim it.

Eric looked toward Ricky and saw him slumped forward, unmoving, his head an odd shape. It wasn't surprising that Mark's wild shot had landed, but it still tore at Eric regardless.

"Jeez, Louise," Terry said. He looked at Eric, then at his own hand. "We have to try to get out of here, now, before anyone else is the wiser." He reared back with his left hand and brought it down with a sickening crunch on his own right hand. Eric heard Terry scream through pursed lips, trying not to make too much noise.

"What the hell are you doing?" Eric asked.

"Ricky just sacrificed himself for us. He was right, there's no way out unless we take some desperate measures." He brought his fist down once more, and now Eric could see the way Terry's right hand was mangled. Terry sucked in air through his teeth and did several quick breaths as he steeled himself for what came next.

Terry gritted his teeth and squinted, bracing his feet against the post as he pulled back. His hand compressed around the zip tie. The plastic slid up, millimeter by agonizing millimeter, bunching up the skin as it went. The color drained from Terry's hand as well as his face, but he didn't relent, even as rivulets of blood began to appear once more around the plastic. He let out a primal groan as he pulled. Then, with a terrible ripping sound that nauseated Eric, Terry yanked his hand free. He bit down on his left hand and screamed into it, muffling the cries of pain. Eric could see flaps of skin hanging off Terry's right hand as blood poured onto the mud.

"Holy shit," Eric whispered. Terry's eyes were wide, his left hand still in his mouth as he breathed in and out around it. Fresh blood had started to leak from his broken nose as well.

Standing unsteadily, Terry gazed at his mangled right hand with uncomprehending stupefaction. Gingerly he pulled his shirt over his head with his left hand and wrapped it tightly around his right, grimacing in pain. He shook his head a couple of times and took a few shambling steps toward Mark, who had finally stopped moving. He got down on one knee next to the corpse and rifled through the pockets, pulling out a pocketknife.

"I was hoping for some car keys, but this will do."

Terry half-stumbled to Eric and bent down, flipping open the knife. "Hold still," he said. "I'm not so good with my left hand."

The lock on the basement door rattled and swung open. Julie braced herself. This could be her chance. Her opportunity to turn the tables and get out of here. She craned her neck to watch for the heavy, deliberate steps Nate took and was shocked to see instead an overweight man with unkempt black hair and a stench that was partly BO and partly something else, almost like ammonia. Had he pissed himself?

"Well, well, well," Norm said. "It's like Christmas morning."

"Where's Nate?" Julie asked. How perverse, it seemed, to wish for him to be here for any reason.

"He's taking care of something for me. Just like you're going to do." He came forward and pulled a zip tie out of his pocket. Julie thought if she never saw another zip tie again she could die happy. With his other hand Norm held up his key ring and singled out a slim silver one. "Did you know all handcuffs use the same key? I don't know if that's brilliant or stupid." He unlatched her left wrist and she reared it back, preparing to snatch the keys, but he decked her before she could. The keys in his hand drew shallow cuts on her cheek. She'd never been struck like that by a man, and the shock of it dazed her almost as much as the blow itself. He dropped the keys and seized her wrist, dragging it to her handcuffed one and tying them together with the zip tie.

Once that was done he bent down, with some effort, and undid the duct tape around her ankles and the legs of the chair. Finally he stood back up, bracing himself on the chair to stand, and undid the second handcuff.

"Come on," he said, pulling her up. "We're goin' someplace a little more romantic." He led her up the stairs much more roughly than Nate had done. Clearly this man had no concern for how Julie thought of him. Was this Nate's father? Probably. How many other people could there be in this house? She went up the stairs nervously, wondering how the hell she could take advantage of this situation.

"It's not fair, Nate keeping you all to himself," Norm said. She could smell his breath. It reminded her of a stale cat box. "It's my house, and everything in it belongs to me. Including you." They emerged into the hallway and Norm jerked her to the right, toward another open door. This one led to a stairwell for a second floor.

"Nate isn't going to like this," she said lamely. Would Norm even care what Nate thought? She wanted to believe what Nate had said about his ability to sway the decision on whether to kill them or not. But these were criminals, and Norm clearly wasn't of anything close to sound mind and body. He opened the door opposite the basement entrance, revealing a long, straight staircase. Her leg ached as she considered what would happen next.

Before they could move, three quick shots echoed through the house. Both Norm and Julie jerked their heads in the direction of the pens. Julie's heart sank as she realized what those sounds probably meant.

"Finally," Norm said. "Gonna make my boy a proper man yet." He began to pull on Julie again, then stopped.

"Wait a second," he said. "That seemed too close together, right? Like, if you were shooting three people it'd normally go bam . . . bam . . . bam, right?" His brow knit in concentration. "Did he just fuck it all up?"

Before he could say or do anything else, Julie struck. She swung her head backward, connecting solidly with Norm's face and causing him to stumble back. Spinning on her heels, she shoulder-checked him while he was still off-balance, causing him to trip and fall on his side. Julie tried to run past him, but he was quicker than she anticipated; he grabbed her by the ankle, causing her to tumble down as well.

"Oh, you bitch, you're gonna pay for that!" he said, blood staining his front teeth. He dragged himself on top of her, and with her hands tied there was little Julie could do under Norm's 230-pound bulk. He raised his fist and brought it down onto her forehead, bouncing her head like a basketball against the wooden floor. Julie saw stars from the impact and tried to roll away, deflecting another blow to her shoulder. As she rolled back, she arched her neck forward and bit down on Norm's ear as best she could. All she got her teeth on was the ear lobe, but that was enough to make Norm shriek and yank himself away.

Julie tasted blood and spat out a chunk of flesh with revulsion. Norm was on his knees now, cradling his bleeding ear with one hand.

"God *damn* it," he howled, bracing himself on one hand. Julie kipped up to her feet and remembered what Terry had said to her about the zip ties back in the van, a million years ago. She raised her bound hands, pulled them as far apart as she could, and with as much strength as she could muster, brought them down hard against her knee.

Nothing.

Norm was starting to get up now, grimacing and swearing at her. In desperation she did it again, and again. As Norm stood up and locked eyes with her, she did it one more time and gasped in shock as the plastic snapped and let her hands free. Whether Norm noticed or cared about this, Julie couldn't tell. He just barreled forward with a look of fury smeared across his face, and Julie did the only thing she could. She ran.

"I don't see a 'Cemetery Road' on this map," John said. He clenched his fist in frustration.

"Follow the roadways a bit. Sometimes these little roads, they have multiple names," Brick said.

"Where are you going?" John asked. "I haven't even found the road yet."

"Headin' to the police station. This is a lot more than I anticipated when Jack asked me to come take a look over here. I was thinking, I don't know, a bar brawl or a drunken fender bender. Not this, whatever *this* is." Brick guided the truck too quickly around the curves, bearing down on Main Street faster than John liked.

"I get wanting to report this, but they didn't seem too eager to help us earlier," John said. Brick glanced at John, eyebrows cocked.

"I know there isn't much chance they'll take us seriously. And even if they *do*, what then? They need a warrant to go on someone's property; warrants need probable cause, signed off on by a judge." Brick gestured expansively to the night outside. "How many judges do you think are available for that right now, out here?"

John said nothing. Brick scowled before going on. "I didn't bring you with me to put you in a dangerous situation. I just thought it might be nice to get you some extra cash."

"I appreciate that, but there are five other people who might be dead if we wait for the law to catch up."

"They might already be dead. Which means we need to be careful, or we could end up dead too. We should at least see if anyone else is on duty. Someone besides the asshole from earlier. At least then there'd be some record of a report." Brick pulled up to the police station, which was dark and empty. No cars sat in the lot; no lights were on inside or outside the building.

"This doesn't look promising," John said. Brick shook his head.

"Two cops, right? For the whole town? Jesus." Brick stepped out of the truck, followed by John. Brick tried the front door in vain, not surprised in the least when it held tight. He turned, tight-lipped, to face John.

"Call 9-1-1," he said.

"Okay, but we haven't been able to get any reception out here."

"Just try, dammit!" Brick yelled, shocking John into pulling out the flip phone. He dialed and waited, shaking his head when the call wouldn't go through.

Before Brick could say anything else, another car pulled into the parking lot. For a moment, Brick hoped it was the patrol car, but instead the streetlights caught a glint of purple paint as the Caddy slid into the spot next to Brick.

"You know, there's other places to see in Chimney Corner besides the police station," Dante said. His windows were rolled down, and he was alone in the car.

"We were trying to report something," Brick said. He put his hands on his hips. "You know where the patrol officer is right now?"

"No idea," Dante said. "I make it a habit to stay as far away from the police as I can, y'know?" He leaned over and raised an eyebrow. "What's got you so fired up anyway, big man? Someone lookit you the wrong way?"

"We think the people at Goode farm might have our friends, or at least know what happened to them," Brick said. Dante stopped smiling.

"Mm, yeah, well good luck with that." He started to roll up the window, but Brick put his hand on it.

"Wait," he said. "You mentioned something earlier, about that diner. That it was no surprise people might go missing there. And now you look like you might still know something. You want to say anything else?"

"Nope," Dante replied. "I ain't got a death wish. Real sorry about your friends, but I can't help you."

"Okay," Brick said. For a moment, he looked like he was going to walk away, and then he lunged in through the open window. He opened the door, seizing Dante by the lapels of his jacket and hauling the skinny man out.

"What the hell, man?" Dante said as he got his feet planted. He reached into his coat and pulled out a .38, but Brick was ready for it and slapped it halfway across the parking lot. He seized Dante by the shirtfront once more and slammed him onto the hood of the Caddy.

"Brick, what the hell are you doing?" John said. He ran up to Brick, but stopped short of putting a hand on him.

"We don't have time for his bullshit," Brick said. He glared down at Dante. "Talk. What do you know? Who are these guys? What do they have to do with that diner?"

"Man, I can't say shit. They find out it was me, they gonna kill me. Won't be the first brother they made disappear."

"And what do you think *I'm* gonna do?" Brick said, pressing his fists harder into Dante's chest.

"All right, all right! Jesus!" He looked from Brick to John and back to Brick again. "Hell with it."

"You know more than you let on yesterday," Brick said.

"I had ideas. Soon as I heard about Bud's, yeah, I had some ideas. It was all just speculation."

"Then why didn't you say something to us sooner?"

"Look, it ain't none of my business. What am I gonna get digging into White man shit? You know what happens when a Black man does that. I ain't some hard-ass gangsta. Just a simple guy trying to make a living." He struggled in Brick's grip. "Come on, man, lemme up. Like I'd really stand a chance against you anyhow."

John put a hand on Brick's rigid bicep. "Yeah, Brick, let him up, before someone sees us, okay?" Reluctantly, Brick let Dante up. The pimp brushed off his jacket theatrically before continuing.

"I used to take girls out there, to their farm, once or twice a week."

"I thought you were scared of them," John said. Dante's eyes flashed angrily.

"Hey, now; I ain't scared, just know when to keep my mouth shut is all. Besides, I didn't have no reason to be scared back then. The only Blacks disappearing round here were dealers and shit. No one really cared too much about that."

"But you don't take girls by there anymore," Brick said.

"Naw. Few months back my girl Nikki, she don't come out that morning when I go to pick her up. Instead, the big guy they got out there, he comes and tells me Nikki decided she done quit. I say that sounds like bullshit, but then he gives me this look, ya know, and I realize I'm in the middle of goddamn nowhere arguing with a dude that can snap my neck like a twig. So I just nod and leave." Dante crossed his arms and leaned against the car. "Ain't never seen or heard from Nikki again. But I stopped taking girls out there after that."

"You didn't go to the cops?" John asked.

"Bitch, please." Dante laughed. "No one ever did contact me from the farm again. Fine by me."

"And they own that diner?" Brick asked. He crossed his arms as he looked down at Dante.

"No, Bud owns it. But he got somethin' going on with those guys; I just don't know what. You don't ever see 'em there except at night, like late at night."

Brick looked at John, a worried expression on his face. This was even worse than they'd anticipated. If these people were the ones who'd taken Eric and the others, Brick didn't have much hope for what had become of them.

"How many of these assholes are there?" Brick asked. Dante thought about it for a second before responding.

"Just the four of 'em, I'm pretty sure. Only two of 'em are really scary, though. Les is a hard-core felon, and the big guy, Nate, he just seems like a silent serial killer. You know, real *Friday the 13th*, Jason-type shit."

"And the other two?" John asked. Dante shrugged.

"Just seem like a couple of methed-out crackers. At least, that's what my girls said." Dante stood up straight. "So, am I done now?"

"Yeah," Brick said. "I think so."

"Just one more thing," John called out over Brick's shoulder. Brick turned in surprise.

"You can tell us how to get to Cemetery Road," John said.

"Ah, yeah; you ain't gon' see it by that name on the map. It's just north'a town, past the Baptist church. Look for 'Rural Route 47.' It's only called Cemetery Road in Chimney Corner." Dante walked to where his pistol had landed and picked it up, examining it carefully. "Man, you done scratched the grip," he complained to Brick.

"You could have said something to us earlier," Brick said.

"Yeah, well, I enjoy breathing. Honestly, I already regret sayin' anything, but . . ." Dante shrugged. "I'm thinkin' I like Charleston better anyway." He put the car into reverse and began to back away. "You watch your back, brother." Dante waved out the driver's window as he pulled away, and in a minute he was gone, disappearing around the corner in a cloud of exhaust.

Brick and John got into the truck and took off, heading deeper into the mountains.

—

Les was uneasy as he pulled into the farm's driveway. The van was gone, which could mean that Mark was gone, but Les doubted it. He thought it more likely to be Nate or Norm, which he would prefer, as that would make it easier to just grab Mark and run. He'd have to collect the money first, though, and whatever clothing and other essentials he could fit in the Pontiac. Traveling light was going to be the name of the game. Les wasn't sure how long it would take before those two wrestlers found their way to the farm, but he anticipated a few hours at the most.

Les parked the Pontiac by his trailer and got out, looking toward the house. Mark was probably in his room, hopefully not high off his ass. He should probably go fetch him first, tell him to get started on an overnight bag. Les started to walk toward the house and was halfway to the front door when he heard the kitchen door on the side of the house swing open with such force it hit the wall with a sharp crack. Les quickened up his pace, then set out in an all-out run when he saw Goth Girl hightailing it for the woods.

Les pulled the Desert Eagle out of his pants as he ran but didn't bother trying to shoot. It was too big and powerful; he'd have to take a shooter's stance to fire it properly, and Goth Girl was too far ahead already to aim effectively. His only hope was to catch up to her. As he rounded the corner of the house he collided with Norm as Norm stumbled out the side door as well, hand clutched to his head. They both fell to the ground in a heap of limbs, and the Desert Eagle fired off as Les braced himself during the fall. Goth Girl didn't even look back.

"What the fuck?" Les yelled as he extricated himself from Norm. "Seriously, Norm, what the fuck is happening here?"

"She broke the zip ties; it isn't my fault," Norm said as he struggled to his feet.

"Why was she out of the basement at all?" Les asked. "Where is Nate?" He looked at the open door. "And where's Mark?"

"Mark's in the pens, taking care of the wrestlers. I was gonna take care of the woman."

"He's what?" Les's stomach lurched. Everything was going sideways. He had to get control quickly, had to get out of here before anything else went wrong. He started to jog toward the pens, leaving Norm behind.

"What about the woman?" Norm called after Les.

"Fuck it," Les said. "She's your problem now."

Julie needed weapons. Or car keys. A phone. Anything. She could barely see two feet in front of her as she struggled through the thick underbrush. She had to be careful—the ground was incredibly uneven, threatening to snap her ankle with one wrong step. Julie wondered what animals might be out there, trying to reassure herself that it was too cold for snakes to be active. She stopped to look over her shoulder, and was relieved to see that no one was pursuing her. Someone had fired on her of course, but whoever it was must have decided she simply wasn't worth it, which was a relief.

She tried not to veer off in any direction, as she didn't relish the idea of getting lost in the woods. She could hear a creek running not too far ahead, and that made her cautious. She knew that creek could be at the bottom of a very painful fall down a ravine. No, if she was to survive, she had to swing back around to the farm, get a car, and get to the road.

Julie stepped as quietly as she could through the brush. Her upper thigh throbbed where Nate had stitched her up. She'd been through worse pain and still finished her matches, though. Gritting her teeth, Julie walked forward, entering a clearing that led out to the pig pens. She stopped, not wanting to expose herself, and watched for any signs of movement. Part of her, a larger part than she wanted to admit, screamed at her to run into the night, to assume the others were dead and save herself. Then she thought of Eric, shoving her ahead of him and telling her to run.

She looked both ways before going any farther. She didn't see any movement out there, but she didn't want to walk in blind, either. Crouching down, she felt around the ground until her hands wrapped around a sturdy branch, thick as a baseball bat and almost as long. Picking it up, she hefted it in both hands before continuing on to the pens.

Rural Route 47 was pitched in early-evening shadows and getting darker. Brick had the high beams on as they rolled down the dirt road, bouncing noisily along.

"Do you think we should call Jack?" John asked. The closer they came to the Goode farm, the more knotted his guts felt. It was all starting to seem so real, and the suffocating darkness along these steep gravel roads heightened the sense of isolation.

"Did you manage to magic up a signal, Merlin?" Brick said. "Even if we could reach him, we need visual confirmation that our guys are out here. Otherwise we don't even have a reason to call out the police."

"Okay, so what's the plan? I don't think these guys will let us walk up and knock on the door."

"This is going to be pure recon; observe and do not confront. I'll scout the area, locate our people, if they're out there, and get them out."

John looked intently at Brick. "So what am I supposed to do then?"

Brick said nothing else, and soon he turned off the headlights. The sudden loss of the road in their headlights lit up John's nerves. The truck slowed to a crawl in the darkness.

"What's going on?" John asked.

"Farm's coming up. I don't want anyone seeing us." It was almost full dark now. John wondered how the hell Brick was even keeping the truck on the road. Suddenly they stopped just short of a gated entry road barely visible in the moonlight.

"Take this," Brick said. He handed John the cell phone. "I doubt you'll get a signal, but we can try at least. If you hear anything, any yelling or gunshots or something like that, do not wait for me. Just get the hell out of here and call for help."

"I'm not going with you?" John asked.

"Are you serious? You can barely sell a worked punch. You go in there, you're gonna get your ass killed. No, I'm not risking your life on this. That's final." Brick's tone brooked no dissent. John almost let out a "Yes, sir!" in reply.

John felt sick to his stomach. Privately, he was desperate to not be here, to be as far away from West Virginia as he could get. Alaska sounded nice. Or maybe Russia. But he drew strength from Brick's presence. Brick was a good name for him. He was solid as a rock wall, unflappable. John was sure Brick had seen hairier situations than this in his time with the armed forces. It would be okay. And if what they'd deduced had been accurate, Eric and the rest desperately needed help.

"Wait here," Brick said. He checked over his pistol, making sure it was fully loaded and ready to fire. "Do not, under any circumstances, come in there after me. If shit goes south, I need you to haul ass."

"Okay," John said. His voice was barely above a whisper. Brick nodded, then reached out and grasped John by the shoulder.

"You've done good. I'm glad I brought you with me." And with that he was gone, disappearing into the gloom.

Les's heart raced as he approached the pens. He wanted to be in the wind. He should already be packed and on the road. That woman was gone, out in the woods, and that alone was reason enough to haul ass outta the state. Out of the country, really. He'd have to switch up cars as soon as possible, dump the Pontiac in the woods where no one would find it for a while.

Les figured he'd work out how to proceed once he got to the pens. At this point, he'd rather not be the one to kill the wrestlers. No need to add more murders to his sheet if he was already fleeing. Les hoped to God that Mark hadn't worked up the nerve to shoot them yet either. But it was so damn quiet. If Mark was out there, he should hear voices, he thought. Something at least. Sound carried pretty well out here.

The gate to the pens stood open. Les could hear the soft snuffling of the hogs to his right and shivered. He hated being out here. He looked to his left, along the fence, and swung his penlight in an arc. It illuminated, in sections, his worst nightmare.

There were two bodies in the mud, one still tied to the fence and the other not. Les could see the imprints of where the other two wrestlers had been, but all that was left of them were the cut zip ties lying on the ground. Les raced to the body not tied to the fence and rolled it over on its back. His breath caught in his throat as the penlight illuminated the pale, bloodless face of his nephew, eyes wide and unseeing, a long jagged segment of bone protruding from his neck.

"You motherfuckers." He didn't know if he was talking about the wrestlers or his own family at this point. Les had invested his entire sense of purpose into caring for Mark, in trying to save him from the influences of his worthless father and psychotic brother, but it had all come to nothing. A stupid fight in a shitty diner, ending in blood and mud for all of them.

Gunshots blew up the darkness, three of them, and Les saw one slam into Mark's skull and deform it. Les rolled away instinctively, turning off the penlight and raising his gun as he came up in a crouching position. He tracked where the shots must have come from and fired once, not wanting to waste the nine shots he had loaded. It pinged off the concrete wall of the slaughter room, and he heard someone cry out. Shifting his aim slightly, Les fired two more times, and as his ears rang with the percussion of the shots, he realized he was now firing blind and deaf. He had to retreat to the trailer, get his money, and get the hell out of there. He came up to a crouch and ran as fast as he could out of the pen, making for the trailer where his safe was buried.

"What the hell are you doing?" Terry asked as Eric fired three rounds from Mark's revolver.

"I'm trying to shoot that asshole," Eric whispered. Before he could say anything else, a shot rang out and he heard it hit the wall next to him. He cried out in surprise.

"Shoulda let me shoot, then," Terry grumbled. "Even with my left hand..."

Two more shots came before Terry could finish his complaint, but both missed. They weren't sure what was hit.

"We have to move," Terry said. They began to crawl to the right, around the table where Burt had probably been dismembered. Eric tried not to think about that as they crouched next to it.

"He's not firing anymore," Eric said. "Why not?"

"I don't know. Maybe he doesn't know exactly where we are. Maybe he doesn't have enough bullets to keep shooting wildly, so he won't waste them." He gave Eric a dour look. "Which is what you should have done."

"I've never fired a gun in my life!"

"And now we're out of bullets. Great." Terry looked around, thinking. "Maybe he's heading back to the house, to get that other big fucker."

"We have to get out of here." Eric peered around the table. He could see lights from the house and the trailer where they'd originally been held. Suddenly he saw a shape move through the light of the porch lamps on the trailer.

"I see him," Eric said. "He's going into the trailer."

Terry pursed his lips. "Maybe he's getting more guns. Guys like these always have a shitload of guns."

"Should we head to the house, then? Maybe we can find a phone, or another gun, or even car keys."

"Are you insane?" Terry whispered. "We don't know who's even *in* that house! We should haul ass into the woods, take our chances there."

"You need something more than a shirt for that hand, or you're going to bleed to death."

"Your concern is touching," Terry said.

"Did you see if that van came back at least?"

"No. I mean, no, I don't see it."

"Okay. Then we should head for the street. It's our best bet."

"If we see or hear anything, and I mean anything, we run like hell, okay?"

"All right."

They started to move then, Terry being careful not to bump his right hand on anything. It was heavily wrapped in Terry's shirt, but the pain was still extreme enough that Eric could see it written in the lines on Terry's face. Eric held up the revolver. He wished it was loaded.

They had just made it out of the gate of the pen when they heard the loud gasp and shriek of a woman, followed by quick steps coming from behind, crunching through the leaves. Eric and Terry looked toward the sound and saw Julie running toward them, between the pens and the farmhouse. Another man, one they hadn't seen before, was moving toward her from the side of the house. Eric and Terry ran to her as fast as they could.

The sun had set behind the mountains, but dampened daylight still seeped out around them, lighting Brick's way enough to see where he was going. Directly ahead was a ramshackle two-story house, with chipped paint and an overgrown front porch. Closer, on his left, was a trailer home of the type he'd lived in himself as a young boy.

Brick decided to avoid the house for now. The trailer was smaller, faster to search, and their layouts didn't vary too much from one to another. If he was lucky, he'd find Eric and the others tied up in there. Or their bodies, he thought as he prepared for the worst. He approached the building slowly, quietly, careful not to give away his position. His knee ached from climbing the fence that circled the property. He heard nothing, which seemed odd. It was dark, but still a bit too early for your average person to be tucking in for the night. He approached the window near the rear of the trailer. As he reached the window, he heard gunfire erupt from the field beyond the trailer.

Brick dropped to the ground, assuming the shots were meant for him, but as he listened he realized two different guns were being fired. Maybe at each other? He couldn't be sure, but whatever it was, he had to establish that Eric and the rest were here. He moved around the corner of the trailer to the back, avoiding the porch lights. He heard someone approaching, running in fact, and listened as he pounded up the wooden steps and opened the door. Brick prepared to follow whoever it was, but as he rounded the other side of the trailer, he heard a woman cry out.

Is that Julie? he thought, and began to move in that direction.

John Coors immediately regretted his insistence on coming out here as soon as Brick disappeared over the fence. It would be bad enough if Eric, Julie, and everyone else was in danger or already dead, but even worse if Brick ended up in trouble. He opened up the flip phone Brick had left him, the blue light of the screen so bright in the darkness that it made him squint. He tried calling 9-1-1 but got no signal. He tried Jack Meyer, but still nothing. He went back and forth between the two, his heart hammering his ribcage as he tried to keep an eye out for any flashes of light from the farm. His efforts to get a signal, however, were futile.

"How the hell do they survive up here?" he wondered aloud as he tried once more to reach 9-1-1. When that failed again, an idea occurred to him. At the bottom of the screen display were three letters: "SMS." He didn't know what they stood for, but he was aware that you could send brief typed messages to people through these phones. He didn't know how it worked really, but it was worth a try.

He opened the SMS menu and selected Jack as the recipient. A screen with a cursor popped up, and John began to type. It was slow going, as he had to use the letters on the number pad and that required pressing some of the buttons three times to get one letter. After several minutes, he had the message he wanted to send to Jack:

"Maybe found our guys. Call 9-1-1. Send Police. Goode Farm Rural Route 47 Chimney Corner WV."

He pressed "Send" and waited. The message attempted to send. And attempted. It was trying to find the signal. John sighed. He brought the phone up to his face to call 9-1-1 when he heard gunshots in the distance. He'd never heard actual gunshots before, but he'd read that it sounded like a car backfiring and, honestly, what else would make that sound out here at night? His heart raced as he tried once more to call 9-1-1, but still nothing. He checked the SMS message, which was still attempting to send, and was about to attempt 9-1-1 again when the door to the passenger side opened and a hand reached out from the darkness and seized him by the shirtfront, yanking him out the door.

I should have locked the doors, John thought desperately as he fell face-first onto the gravel roadway. Sharp rocks stabbed into his cheeks as he tried to stand up, but a huge booted foot kicked him in the temple and knocked him over again.

"Who the hell are you?" Nathan Goode asked as he leaned down and pressed a knee into John's neck. Whether he expected an answer or not, John couldn't tell, but he was incapable of saying anything with a knee on his throat. He felt panic clawing at his brain but fought it off, instead angling a punch into the crotch of the man kneeling on him. The thick stretched seam of the jeans protected Nate from the worst of the blow, but it was enough to give John leverage to roll away. He stood up quickly, his eyes widening as Nate stood up too.

Nate was easily a head taller than Brick Lamar, maybe even taller than Burt Knox, and at least as wide. He didn't hesitate, moving forward with a swift left jab that staggered John. John recovered quickly, though. He may not have been a trained fighter like Brick, but John was still an athlete, and he knew how to take a punch. John stepped forward, goading Nate, and juked as soon as the big man shot another jab at him. He ducked inside Nate's reach, giving him three quick jabs to the gut. He'd hoped to hit Nate's diaphragm, knock the wind from him, but John had to settle for a few bruising blows instead. It gave Nate an opportunity, though, and he took it, ramming his elbow hard into John's spine. John's fingers spasmed from the impact, and he ducked out of the way of another vicious shot. Nate had overcompensated and put too much force into the blow. Without John there to absorb it, Nate staggered and nearly fell over.

John was on him quickly then, scooping under Nate's left arm and hoisting him up bodily in one fluid motion. It was a move used in both professional and "real" Olympic wrestling, and it was an easy way to bring Nate to the floor. Nate landed on his back, which is what made this one of the safer moves in pro wrestling, and John was on him instantly. He straddled Nate and began raining punches down on him. He saw a cut open across Nate's cheek, but was surprised when Nate reacted by shooting his arms forward and seizing John by the head. He jammed both thumbs into John's eyes.

The pain was instantaneous and crippling. John had, of course, taken worked shots to the eyes in the ring before, but the pressure from Nate's monstrous thumbs was something else entirely. Stars exploded in the darkness as Nate pressed inward, and John scrambled backward, pulling his head as hard as he could to break Nate's grip. He blinked, trying to see, but it was mostly darkness that swam in his vision. Nate was quick to follow up, backhanding John across the cheek, but John retaliated with a wild swing that somehow, miraculously, connected at the base of Nate's throat. Nate backed up, gagging, and John moved toward the sound, fists balled and ready. He threw another punch, but this one went wide and Nate caught his arm. Nate's strength was astonishing. John tried to pull free, but Nate only tightened his grip. He swung John face-first onto the hood of the truck. Nate didn't let go, instead pressing his shoulder into John's back and pinning his chest to the truck.

"Where's the other guy?" Nate asked, almost calmly. He wrenched John's arm backward, bracing his own forearm against John's elbow. John grunted, sweat trickling down his brow as he attempted to break the hold.

"F-f-fuck you," John said, pulling his arm with all his might. Nate had the leverage advantage though, and without much effort he wrenched John's arm once more, snapping the elbow against his forearm.

John screamed, and Nate responded by dragging John to the open driver's door and laying his head down on the door frame. John tried to push back, scrabbling for purchase with his feet, but Nate held him steady with a boot between the shoulder blades. John heard the door creak as Nate grabbed hold of it, and an instant later felt the literal head-splitting impact of the door against his temple. He was in too much pain to cry out even, and Nate followed up with a second blow from the door, which left John swimming at the fringes of consciousness. He barely felt Nate picking him up and chucking him into the frigid creek running alongside the road. The shock of the freezing cold water forced a gasp from him. As he breathed in, the water came through his mouth, into his lungs, and he coughed involuntarily, trying in vain to expel the liquid he'd just drawn into his lungs. Fear scrabbled through John's brain as it screamed for oxygen, fear like he'd never experienced in his life, and as the engine of the truck roared to life on the road above him, John's last thoughts surprised him—they weren't about his father or mother, nor about his life being cut short. Instead, he found himself wishing he'd locked that fucking door.

Nate didn't stop to admire his handiwork. He worked quickly, hopping into the truck and pulling up to the farm's front gate. If Coors was here, the other one Mason told him about was most likely around somewhere too. Somewhere on the farm. He swore under his breath, wishing he'd brought a gun. Nate approached the front gate, unlocking the padlock and sliding it open. It was well-oiled and rolled smoothly.

Nate was glad he'd decided to park the van down the road. He knew after talking to Mason that if those other wrestlers weren't at the farm yet, they soon would be. Better to approach with caution, he'd thought. This had proven prudent. It didn't mean, however, that he would abandon his carefully laid plans.

Whoever else might be dead mattered little to Nate as long as Julie was still alive. Nate could finish off everyone else, blame the deaths of all the wrestlers on Norm, Les, and Mark, and still be the hero of the day. How could Julie hate or reject the man who saved her life, after all? Yes, things could still be salvaged. When he heard the gunshots coming from the farm, he raced through the gate.

Nate drove the truck up to the farm. The biggest danger was that other wrestler, Brick Lamar. Nate was aware of him, though only tangentially, through what he picked up watching the show with Mark. Nate knew Brick was a large, intimidating man, but Nate was on his home turf and had the advantage. He watched from the driver's seat, keeping an eye out for movement. He saw something large making its way from Les's trailer, and before it could get far, Nate threw on the headlights, illuminating Brick in the blinding high beams. Brick stared, hand visored over his eyes. The tires squealed in the mud as Nate hit the gas.

Eric and Terry ran toward Julie, and Eric made a point to hold the gun out in front of him. Loaded or not, who would know? It didn't occur to him that the others might just shoot first.

They saw Julie in the bright moonlight, twisting to avoid Norm's oncoming charge. Terry, still suffering the effects of degloving his right hand, lagged behind Eric as they approached, and Eric threw himself bodily at Norm, who had both hands clasped over Julie's wrists. A large branch lay on the grass between them. Norm reacted sluggishly to Eric's approach and barely had a chance to release Julie before Eric speared him into the ground. Eric straddled Norm and began raining blows onto his face. Norm grunted in pain, twisting around as he tried to get away, but even though he had a weight advantage, Eric had the better positioning and held him steady between his clenched thighs. Behind him, Terry was helping Julie to her feet. Eric glanced over his shoulder to look at Julie, who was stumbling a bit as she leaned on Terry.

"Are you okay?" he asked. Before she could answer, the sound of a knife tearing through cloth and flesh interrupted them. It felt like a shovel had been jammed into Eric's guts, but when he looked down he saw that it was a tactical knife, held by Norm. The cold wash of pain overtook Eric and he exhaled with a loud *Ough!* He began to move, but Norm yanked the knife out first. Its serrated edge tore bits of viscera and ribbons of fabric from Eric as it went, and the cold numbing changed immediately to a molten wave of pain that made his vision blur.

Shit, Eric thought. *He fucking got me.* He pitched backward as Norm shoved him off. Norm got on his knees and raised the knife, ready to stab again, but Terry knocked him over with a stiff Clothesline to the side of Norm's head. Terry grimaced as the impact jostled his makeshift bandage but followed through with a lunging stomp that crushed Norm's elbow into the ground. Terry went in for more, but Les interrupted. He raised the massive Desert Eagle and aimed it two-handed. Eric cried out a warning to Terry. Too late, though.

Les pulled the trigger.

Nothing happened.

Everyone stood frozen as they watched Les try again and again to squeeze the trigger. Eric couldn't tell what was wrong, but the gun simply wouldn't fire. Les frantically slid open the chamber and began pulling at something. Acting fast, Terry turned on Les and ran into him with a full-body shoulder tackle. They went down in a tangle of arms and legs. Eric got to his feet, holding his wound shut uselessly as blood oozed through his fingers. He stumbled forward, every step agony, and threw himself at the struggling men as well. Terry was trying to wrestle the gun away from Les, determined to rip the man limb from limb, even with only one good hand.

Les swung his left elbow into Terry's temple. Terry, all adrenaline and rage, held on anyway. Eric joined the fray by grabbing Les's right hand and wrenching it backward in a modified wristlock. He'd learned the move during a tour with Stampede Wrestling, from none other than a young Bret Hart, but had never used it in a legit fight before. Hart had warned Eric to use the move with care because it could do serious harm, but he showed no concern now, twisting Les's wrist with all his considerable might. He felt a crunch in Les's wrist as Les screamed and dropped the Desert Eagle. As it hit the ground the shell that had jammed the slide popped out. Enraged, Les pushed both men away and lunged toward the gun with his good hand, but Eric stopped him with a right hook to the cheek that split the skin and gushed with thick red blood. *I'm busting you open the hard way, you bastard*, Eric thought triumphantly. Les stumbled back, shaking his head a few times, then lunged forward with a left-handed uppercut to Eric's abdomen.

Eric thought being stabbed was painful, but it was forgotten next to the blossoming agony of impact from Les's punch as it struck his wound. Blood seeped out like water from a sponge, and Eric felt lightheaded, watching it splatter to the grass. Les prepared to strike again, but Terry caught him off-guard with a stiff forearm to the crotch from behind. A classic heel move in the ring, but this time of course, Terry wasn't pulling his punch. Les gasped and clutched his groin, falling to his knees.

"Ah, you motherfuckers," he growled, but Terry didn't give him a chance to say more than that, laying Les flat with a big boot to the face. He was preparing to do more when his attention shifted to the sound of gunshots coming from the direction of Les's trailer. All three men looked perplexed as they wondered who the hell else was out here to shoot at.

Brick couldn't figure out what John was doing. He'd told John to stay at the entrance and wait. This was not the time to be playing hero.

"What the hell?" Brick whispered. Maybe John heard the gunshots and came running. It occurred to Brick then that there was no way John could get through the gate without a key. As he thought of that, the high beams flashed on and blinded him. The truck roared to life and leapt toward him.

"Oh shit," Brick said. "That ain't John." He tried to move out of the way, but the truck was too close. It clipped Brick in the hip, spinning him around and smacking him with the side mirror. He fell to the ground and barely rolled out of the way of the truck's wheels. His hip and shoulder felt like they were on fire, and he crawled away as quickly as he could.

"Son of a bitch," Brick groaned. He'd been shot before, but this was surprisingly worse. His bones below the waist felt out of joint, like they were grinding against each other. He struggled to his feet then realized he no longer had his gun. He must have dropped it when the truck hit him.

The door to the truck opened and closed as its driver stepped out. Brick could tell from the way it sounded that he was a big one. Brick, still woozy from the impact, swayed a bit as he turned to face Nate, barely illuminated by the trailer's porch light. Brick raised his fists, sizing up his opponent. Nate moved with fluid confidence, no fear at all evident in his gait.

Brick stepped forward, getting close to Nate, and struck out with a feinted left followed by a hard right punch into the diaphragm. Nate whuffed loudly and stumbled back, his eyes widening momentarily in surprise. Brick suspected he'd never been hit that hard before.

Semper fi, motherfucker, he thought as he moved in again. He moved like he was going to throw another body shot, then came around with a quick jab to the jaw that landed with a solid crack. Now Nate was looking angry as well as surprised. *Good*, Brick thought. His fear of what happened to John fueled his rage. He focused that rage onto the big bastard standing in front of him.

Nate attacked with a straight punch. Brick was shocked that someone so big could be that fast, but Brick was even quicker. He moved out of the way of Nate's stiff straight strike, dropped under the swing and hooked Nate's right leg, trying to hoist him in a fireman's carry. Nate then widened his stance and brought a fist down hard at the base of Brick's spine. His hip screamed in agony, and Brick let go, stumbling back as quickly as he could.

"Huh. I thought you'd be tough. MAW champ and all that doesn't count for shit, I guess," Nate taunted.

Brick grimaced as he stepped wrong on his bad knee, and Nate struck again, hitting Brick with a swinging roundhouse to that knee. Brick gasped and fell, rolling quickly out of the way of Nate's stomping feet.

Nate stepped forward as Brick rolled toward the trailer home. Brick fell backward and came up on his feet, surprising Nate with a low forward kick to the kneecap. Nate went down grimacing, reaching for the injured knee. Brick, ignoring the pain in his own hip and knee, ran forward with a solid kneecap to the side of Nate's head. There was a squirt of blood as Nate's ear ruptured, splitting along the cartilage. Nate rolled onto his back, glassy-eyed. Brick approached to take advantage while Nate was still woozy. As he knelt down over Nate and raised his fist to finish him off, he heard a scream, a woman's scream, and turned to look in its direction. Before he could determine where it had come from, he heard a gunshot, followed by another scream. Without hesitation, he stood up and ran in that direction, leaving Nate lying on the ground behind him.

Julie watched Norm struggle to his feet as Eric and Terry rushed Les. Norm was holding the knife, momentarily forgotten by the other three men and trying to take advantage. Thinking quickly, Julie grabbed the same oak limb she'd brought out of the forest with her and swung it like a baseball bat, cracking Norm in the head as he tried to run past. He fell to the ground again like a sack of dirt, and Julie was on him in an instant, stomping down again and again on his back.

Norm rolled over with effort, swinging wildly with the knife and grazing Julie's forearm. She ignored it, blood flying from the fresh cut as she slammed the branch into Norm's hand. She heard a satisfying crunch and Norm cried out, dropping the knife. Both tried to get to it, and they reached the knife at the same time. Norm growled at her as he tried to yank the knife out of her hand, but she wrenched it away and raised it high.

Norm's eyes opened wide as he watched her. She thought of what they'd all endured and brought the knife down again and again with such fury she paid no attention to where she was stabbing until the knife slipped from her hands, slick with blood. Her hands trembled as she looked at the now-unseeing eyes staring up at her, and she found herself unable to look away until she heard the gunshot from where Eric and Terry were fighting Les.

The momentary halt of their fight gave Les just the time he needed to duck away from Terry and make for his gun. Eric watched him go for it and struggled to get there first. Les was faster. He grabbed the pistol and fired it in Eric's direction one-handed, the aim thrown off but still true enough to graze Eric's shoulder. He winced as the bullet slit open the side of his right arm but kept pushing forward, seeing Julie and Norm struggling from the corner of his eye. Terry managed to reach Les, but before Terry could try to get the gun, Les seized Terry's bad hand and squeezed. Terry screamed through gritted teeth and swung a very weak left hook to Les's ribs that Les easily shook off.

Les raised the pistol to Terry's temple and with a determined look on his face pulled the trigger. Terry's skull seemed to ripple like a pond with a stone thrown into it; his body collapsed to the ground instantaneously. Les didn't hesitate, swinging the pistol around once more to finish off Eric. Eric moved quickly, grabbing the gun and jerking it sideways as Les fired again.

Eric came in close to Les, chest to chest, holding the pistol over their heads. He couldn't hold it for long; his left hand couldn't overcome Les's right, but he knew he wouldn't have to. He stepped forward, positioning his leg behind Les's, then twisted sideways. It was a modified Russian leg sweep. It was good for putting an opponent on the ground, what the pros called a transition move. Les fell backward hard, the gun falling from his hand. Eric gripped his right foot. He braced his own foot against Les's left knee and pushed the right leg sideways. He felt it spasm in his hands. It wasn't a complicated move. Doink the Clown used it as a joke, calling it the Stump Puller. However, Eric knew sometimes the simplest moves hurt the worst.

Les howled with pain and reached for the gun. Eric threw himself on top of Les as he put a hand over the Desert Eagle. With Eric on top he was able to put Les's arm in an elbow lock. Les dropped the gun as his arm bent backward, and Eric immediately released Les and lunged for the gun. He seized it, turning on Les and firing it point-blank into his midsection.

The recoil was intense. Eric had never fired a gun, but had thought he at least understood that part of it. He was wrong. The gun flew back, out of his hand, and he dropped it as he felt the recoil from his wrist all the way to his shoulder. Les curled into a protective ball.

"That's for Terry," Eric said.

"Eric!" Julie said as she came up to him. She was covered with blood, but Eric was glad to see that it didn't appear to be hers. He tried to stand, but fell to one knee, then let Julie help him to his feet.

"We need to get out of here," Julie said. Eric picked up the Desert Eagle.

"Have you ever shot a gun in your life?" someone asked from behind them. Eric whirled around and, to his shock, saw Brick Lamar approaching them.

"Brick? Is that you?" Julie asked. The big man nodded. Julie raced forward and embraced him.

"Thank God! Is anyone else here?"

Brick's lips thinned to a straight line. "I had John Coors with me. I don't know what happened to him."

"We really need to get Eric some help. Did you see anyone else? Someone even bigger than you?" Julie asked.

"I did. We fought."

"Do you have your cell phone?" Eric asked. "We might not have much time."

"No. I left it with John."

"There's a phone in the house. As long as the house is empty, we can go in there," Julie said.

"What about the big guy?" Eric asked.

"If he's already on the move, he might sneak up on us. At least in the house we can call for help, lock the doors," Brick said. "It's not much better, but it's something. And we do have that gun."

"Yeah," Julie said. "We need to get into the house."

Julie and Eric followed Brick into the house, leaving the other three bodies behind.

—

Nate rose to his knees and stared in the direction Brick had gone. He didn't like the sound of those screams one bit. It was a woman's, and that meant Julie was out there somewhere. Which meant Nate had to confront Les and the others, and also pray the wrestlers were already dead. He still held out hope of a future with Julie, but for that to work, she'd have to believe Les or Mark or even Norm was responsible for the deaths of her friends. And everyone else would have to be dead to corroborate that story. He saw Brick's gun lying in the grass and grabbed it. No more playing around.

He approached the back yard of the house without even a hint of stealth. It was about as bad as Nate had expected. Norm, Les, and the wrestler named TJ Azz lay motionless in the grass. All appeared to be dead. Nate was about to leave when a weak cough from Norm made him stop.

"Nate?" Norm asked. Nate approached his father and knelt next to him. Norm was in a bad way, his shirt crimson with gore. Blood seeped from wounds onto the ground, enough that Norm's face was ashen-white. He was alive, but not for long. Nate doubted that he could survive even if they had an ambulance sitting right there.

"Where's everyone else?" Nate asked. He dreaded the answer.

"I don't know." Norm gurgled. "They all escaped."

"That's unfortunate. Let me guess; you let Julie out of the basement?"

Norm just stared. His breathing became more shallow.

"Well, you always were useless. No wonder Louanne wanted to leave you." He waited for a response, but none came. Norm's eyes had glazed over into a death stare. Nate stood back up and looked toward Les, who was curled up on the ground. Curious, he approached slowly.

"Les? Still alive?" Nate asked.

"For now," Les replied softly. Nate rolled Les onto his back, looking at the tennis ball–sized hole in his guts.

"You're dying," Nate said.

"I'm surprised you care," Les replied. He looked at Nate with a glassy stare.

"You were going to leave. You were going to take Mark and just leave me here with him," Nate said, indicating Norm's body. "I guess that didn't work out so well for you."

"So you knew," Les said.

"Of course I did. You were never half as smart as you thought. I still liked you, though. You should have trusted me. Not just with this, but with everything. You could have taken me too."

"I couldn't trust you. Not after what happened to Louanne."

"Everything I ever did was always to look out for myself. You taught me that."

"So . . . so you did cause that accident?" Les tried to sit up, grunting, red in the face, and then fell backward.

"You're the only one that never even considered it might have been accidental. Guess that makes you smarter than everyone else in this town." Nate looked back at the house the wrestlers had retreated to, and realized he'd have to act fast if he was going to salvage anything. He turned back to Les.

"I have to take care of this mess. And I can't run the risk of you actually surviving and contradicting my story." Les started to say something in reply, but Nate cut him off as he covered Les's mouth and nose with his hands. Les gave a feeble effort to push Nate away, but it was hardly noticeable. Blood spurted violently from the gunshot wound as Nate waited for Les to stop breathing.

With that part taken care of, Nate began walking toward the farmhouse. He had to finish this.

Julie and Eric entered the old farmhouse through the side door into the kitchen. Brick took the Desert Eagle from Eric and waved them on.

"You two call the police. I'm going to secure the house."

Julie nodded as Brick walked into the entry room. She and Eric turned to walk through the kitchen.

Julie was prepared for it from earlier, but the kitchen's disheveled state took Eric by surprise. He grunted as he stood up more fully and scowled at the mess surrounding them.

"Oh, my God," Eric whispered to himself.

"Yeah, I know," Julie said. "I think I remember seeing a phone in the hallway. We can call for help from there. Come on." She pulled out one of the kitchen chairs and helped Eric into it. There was a roll of paper towels on the table, and Julie pulled some off and pressed them into Eric's hands.

"It's not much, but it's what we have."

"I'm sorry," he said. "I guess I wasn't much good for saving you."

"Oh, stop it," Julie said. "I'm not some damsel in distress. We're rescuing each other."

Eric smiled ruefully as she grabbed his wrist.

"I need you to stay awake, okay? Just hang in there until we get an ambulance out here." She went to the hallway where the old rotary phone was mounted to the wall. Julie grabbed the receiver and began dialing 9-1-1 before realizing there was no dial tone. The hair stood up on the back of her neck.

"What the hell?" she asked.

"What happened?" Eric asked from the kitchen.

"It's dead," Julie said.

"What do you think's wrong with it?"

"I don't know. It was working before; I heard it ringing."

"Maybe someone cut the line."

"Without a phone, there's no reason to stay here," Julie said. She was feeling like she was stuck in a horror movie.

"And go where?" Eric asked. "I can barely walk." He stumbled into the hallway and sighed as he leaned against the wall. "What we should do is find some car keys."

"Just wait here a second," Julie said. "I'll be right back."

"Wait!" Eric called. "Where are you going?"

"To look for keys," she replied. "Just sit tight and try not to bleed to death."

Julie moved deeper into the house, toward the bedrooms. She glanced at the basement door, then thought better of it. Julie had a feeling that Nate didn't keep any keys in there, especially not when she was supposed to be down there as well. The last thing she wanted was to get pinned down in a room with no exit. Especially *that* room.

She turned from the basement and moved on. At the end of the hall were doors on opposite sides. She ducked into the one on the left. Inside was a living space that had no real personality. It was barren—no TV, no stereo, not even any pictures on the wall. Besides the bed and the dresser, the only personal item immediately visible was a well-worn paperback sitting on the nightstand. Its title was *Let's Go Play at the Adams'*, and on the cover was a door opening to reveal a young brunette in a nightgown, tied in multiple looping cords of rope to a wooden chair. She was gagged and terrified, eyes brimming with tears.

"What the fuck?" Julie said. She'd never been so revolted by a book before. *This must be Nate's room*, she thought. She considered going through the dresser drawers, but couldn't bring herself to go any further into that room. Only as a last resort. Instead, she turned to the other room across the hall. This one was more in keeping with the rest of the house, a pit of filth and degeneracy. An unkempt bed was flanked with a nightstand filled with rolling papers, powders she couldn't identify, lighters, and even a syringe. Sellers and users, apparently. Julie crept into the room and began searching for any keys, but realized it would take longer than they probably had to find them. Brick had a gun, and it would help if she did too. If they killed Nate, they would be able to leisurely search the whole house for keys.

And the bodies, but she didn't want to think about that.

Julie abandoned the idea of continuing to search Mark's room when the first few drawers she opened held nothing of use, deciding instead to arm herself with a knife from the kitchen. She emerged from Mark's room, turning toward Eric. He was pale, his hair wet with sweat and his athletic shorts slick with blood. Panic seized Julie by the throat. After watching Burt die slowly, she had no illusions about what has happening now to Eric.

Bracing herself, Julie approached Eric and put an arm around him for support once more. He looked at her with glazed eyes.

"You look pretty good with those bangs outta your eyes," he said.

"Now I know you're in bad shape," she said as she helped turn Eric toward the kitchen. "Let's see if we can find a knife." Eric pulled a revolver out from his waistband. She raised her eyebrow at the limp way Eric was holding it. "Can you even lift that thing?" she asked.

Eric's gaze hardened and his body firmed up as he stood straighter and lifted the gun to hold it pointed upward. "I can muscle through," he said. "Or are you forgetting I was the longest-reigning heavyweight champion MAW ever had? I'm a pretty hard bastard."

Brick came down the stairs leading to Norm's bedroom.

"Well, champ, if the phones are out, someone's gonna have to go outside."

"You find any keys?" Julie asked.

"No, but those bodies outside might have some. If not, the keys to Jack's truck might still be in the ignition." He glanced at the revolver Eric was holding.

"No bullets left," Eric said. "Sorry."

"Well, shit." Brick frowned as he considered what to do. "Keep it anyway. Look for more ammo. There's gotta be some in here. I'm gonna take this," he said, holding up the Desert Eagle, "and see if I can get us a car." He walked back through the kitchen and paused at the door.

"Lock up behind me. Then stay away from the windows." He opened the door and was out in one fluid move, hampered only slightly by his bad knee. Julie rushed to the door and locked it, then went back to Eric, who was braced against the kitchen counter

"You know, I was in Terry's car because of you," he said. Julie looked in his face, which was pale and slick with sweat.

"I kind of figured that. I bet you regret it now."

"Naw. You might . . . might be dead otherwise. My wife always said I was a selfish prick. At least I can die knowing she's wrong for once."

"You aren't going to die."

"I don't need any of that bull right now, but thank you." Eric breathed in and winced from his broken ribs. He coughed wetly, spraying droplets of blood on the floor.

"Okay, then, how about this: No bullshit, you pull yourself together and stay alive, I'll let you take me out to dinner." She put her hands on either side of Eric's face and lifted him up to look in her eyes. His mouth twitched into the tiniest of smiles.

"You sure know how to motivate a guy. But just so you know, I'm gonna hold you to that."

"I know," she said. She leaned in and gave him a quick kiss at the corner of his mouth. "Come on, let's get to the living room. I'll lay you down on the couch while I look for ammo." They made their way out of the kitchen and turned as the front door swung wide behind them.

The porch light outside was alive with a sea of small insects, but most of the space was filled with the dark shape of Nathan Goode. He looked at Eric, then Julie, and his mouth twisted as he raised the pistol he'd stolen from Brick Lamar.

He didn't speak, just fired, and the sound was deafening in the confined space. Eric fell over, the bullet taking him mid-shoulder, and dragged Julie down with him. Nate stepped forward, his face a mask of fury, and Julie scrambled to pull the gun out of Eric's grasp. She did so just as Nate reached the entry to the hallway and brought it up to aim at him.

"Don't fucking move," she said, and Nate did as she asked, freezing in mid-step. His expression changed to one of confusion as he eyed the gun in her hand.

"That's . . . hmm. That's Mark's gun." The corners of his mouth twitched. He didn't drop his own gun, though.

"Let us go, Nate," Julie said. "You were trying to help, you said so yourself. Let us go and that's what we'll tell the cops. Everyone else is dead. You don't have to go to jail for what everyone else did. We can just end this."

"I was so stupid," Nate said. He stepped forward, looking from Julie to Eric, who was rolling on his side and trying to get up. He turned his attention back to Julie. "Stupid and naive."

"Nate," Julie said, "You're not stupid. Just, you know, misunderstood. Please, put the gun down. Please?"

Eric could hear what Nate was saying but couldn't make sense of it. He was focused instead on the fire in his shoulder and the ache in his midsection. It was almost impossible to move. Fresh sweat broke out over his forehead as he made the effort.

Eric never thought of himself as hard, not in the same way he thought of people like Terry. He didn't like to work stiff, he never took more bumps than he had to, and he never bladed unless Jack insisted. He wanted to see himself as the hero of the day; he wanted to save Julie, but all he could do was get beat up, stabbed, shot, and now lie on the floor bleeding to death while a psychopath moved in for the kill.

What did it mean to be hard? Eric believed his whole life that it meant a willingness to throw yourself into dangerous situations, to shrug off pain like it was nothing. Maybe he'd been wrong. Right now, he could be the hard man. He had two holes in him, broken ribs, a concussion, but if he could stand up, if he could not shrug it off but instead overcome it, he could be the hard-assed hero he'd always wanted to be. With all the will he could muster, Eric braced his hands against the floor and pushed up.

"Nate, I appreciate the way you helped me, helped all of us," Julie was saying. She didn't get a chance to finish, as both she and Nate turned their attention to Eric, who lunged awkwardly to his feet, stumbling a bit before bracing on the wall. Nate responded almost instinctively, bringing Brick's gun around to fire, but paused when he saw Julie pull the trigger on the revolver first.

It clicked harmlessly.

"I knew it," Nate snarled. He slapped the gun from Julie's hand and moved to strike her with the butt of his pistol, but she gave Nate a strong front kick to the groin. Nate doubled over in surprise. Eric seized the moment. Even though the holes in his body felt like they were ripping him to pieces, it didn't stop him. He would be hard. He grabbed Nate by the shirt and yanked with all his might, treating Nate like an opponent who was sandbagging him. Eric wrapped his arm around Nate's head, pinning it to Eric's waist. Nate tried to pull away, but Julie kicked him in the ribs. Without hesitation, Eric dropped Nate in a real DDT, smashing the top of Nate's head into the floor under his own weight.

Done properly, a DDT is one of the safest moves a wrestler can do. Done improperly, or "botched," it becomes a lethally effective way to incapacitate someone. Eric had never botched one, but he did this time, jamming Nate's head too low and driving it into the wooden floor as hard as he could.

Nate dropped his pistol with the impact, grabbing the top of his head as he moaned in pain. Eric tried to stand but couldn't get his legs to support his weight. Julie was there then, hoisting Eric up as she moved him to the front door. He remembered, somehow, to grab the gun Nate had dropped.

"Let's go," she said. They staggered out the front door, moving around the side of the house toward the back yard where Les's body was. Within a minute they heard the side door to the kitchen bang open as Nate crashed through.

He bellowed inarticulately with a rage unseen before then. There was a flash, and the muzzle of the revolver lit up his face as he fired. Of course, Eric thought dismally. Of course he'd know where the bullets were.

The encroaching darkness was a saving grace, making it harder for Nate to aim, but he wouldn't have to work hard to catch up to them on foot. Already he was on the move, stomping across the grass in a quick trot. Eric hoped he'd continue to fire blindly, wasting his six shots, but Nate wasn't going to make that mistake.

"Can you shoot him?" Eric asked. Julie shook her head.

"If I try, he might get us first. We don't stop unless we have to." They continued on, Eric trying not to lean on Julie too hard. The pain in his abdomen was excruciating now. He thought for a minute he'd managed to piss his pants, until he realized it was the fresh blood flowing down his body.

"I'm not going to make it much farther," Eric gasped. "Just drop me and run."

"No way in hell," Julie said. "That didn't work out well for either of us last time."

They continued on, with Nate fast approaching. He stopped, took aim, and fired again. Eric could feel the air as the bullet passed. A second bullet came, then a third. This one found its mark, knocking Julie off her feet as Eric fell heavily on top of her.

"Shit, I'm sorry," he said as he tried to roll off. She struggled under his weight, trying to get out and stand up. Nate's steps were coming fast now. Julie's right calf soaked Eric's shirt with blood. Eric tried push himself off her, but his adrenaline had finally run out.

"I'm sorry," he whispered to Julie again. "I'm so fucking sorry." He gave one last effort to move and failed, his arms buckling as he collapsed onto Julie.

Julie heard Nate's footsteps. He was taking his time now. No need to exert himself at this point. Julie looked at Eric's pained, blood-smeared face and felt a wave of empathy for him so strong it made her head spin. She knew he was going to die, and she knew that if he'd just tried to run earlier instead of coming to look for her, he might have made it out of here, and her heart swelled to know he'd done that.

"Thank you," she said, and kissed his cheek. She turned her head to face Nate, wondering if she might be able to talk him down. She doubted it, but it was all she had.

Nate was close now, and as she craned her head she could see him emerge into the sickly yellow glow of the exterior porch lights. A disturbingly triumphant smile lit his face.

"Just you and me now," he said. Then his leg twisted at an odd angle as a bullet tore through the meat of his thigh. Brick approached quickly, a snarl on his lips, and Nate responded by firing a few shots of his own. Brick ducked down but dropped the Desert Eagle when a shot clipped his arm. As he reached to pick it up, Nate lunged forward, raising the gun once more. Brick threw himself forward as well, colliding with Nate and knocking them both to the ground. Brick managed to brace himself on top of Nate and rained hard elbows into his head, not stopping until Nate's face was a crimson mask, a river of blood from his split forehead running into the mud. Panting, Brick fell backward, landing face-up next to Julie.

"I hear sirens," he said. He stayed quiet afterward. They watched Nate, waiting for him to rise once more like a demon, but he remained motionless until the police cars and ambulances arrived.

Eric was loaded into an ambulance, still alive somehow but barely. Brick sat on the bumper of one of the cop cars, watching as they struggled to get Nate onto a stretcher as well. Once they did, Brick stood up to get one more look at him. Nate appeared to be awake, but he stared vacantly toward the sky.

"Got you, motherfucker," Brick said. As the EMTs moved the stretcher away, Brick noticed something wrong. Nate's head, rather than staring upward, was turned towards him. His eyes were open, clear, and full of malice. They stayed on Brick until he was loaded into the back of the ambulance and driven away. Brick clenched his fist and walked shakily to Julie.

"They think Eric might make it. He lost a lot of blood, so it's going to be touch and go," she told him. "It's good they got here when they did."

"Yeah," Brick said. "I guess Johnny was able to get a text message out to Jack after all." He grimaced, thinking about John and the way the paramedics had found him, beaten and dumped in a canal like trash.

"I'm sorry about John," Julie said. She glanced at Nate as he was loaded into an ambulance. "I actually hope that bastard lives. Someone needs to pay for all this."

Brick watched the EMTs closed the door on Nate, kept watching as the ambulance pulled away with its lights flashing. "Yeah," he said. "Someone should."

Julie glanced toward the ambulance they loaded Eric into. "I think I'm going to ride to the hospital with Eric, if they let me."

"They aren't trying to put you on a stretcher too?"

Julie gave him a wan smile. "I'm actually in the best shape of all of us. I hate to say it, but that might be thanks to Nate."

"Well, you get going then, before they leave without ya." Brick winced as he steadied himself before reaching out and giving Julie a reassuring pat on the shoulder. She put her hand over his and gave it a gentle squeeze before heading to Eric's ambulance. Brick watched her argue her way into the back, taking a seat next to the EMT who was looking over Eric. She reached out and took his hand. Brick could see her mouth moving as she spoke to him.

"Sir, we have a stretcher for you," another medic said, indicating the one at his side. It was set at waist height. The EMT, young, White, and eager, clearly felt intimidated telling Brick what to do.

"Are you kidding me?" Brick said. He stood up defiantly, then gritted his teeth as the pain from his hip flashed through him. He sat back on the bumper, defeated but still defiant.

"It didn't feel this bad when I was whooping that guy's ass," Brick grumbled.

"Adrenaline will do that, sir," the medic said. "But I really need you on the stretcher, or I'll get in trouble. So, um, please?"

In spite of everything, Brick had to smile. He moved unsteadily to the stretcher and lay down.

"All right, pal, let's get going." A second medic came over then, and the two of them wheeled Brick to one the few ambulances still on the property. He imagined some would probably be there until they could determine no one else was alive. But Brick knew that answer already. The only thing left on this farm was death.

He closed his eyes, allowing himself to relax for the first time in hours. The stretcher rattled as they loaded him in, but there was a comfort in that. It meant safety. It meant things were done, the nightmare was over.

And it *was* over.

Brick looked out the back windows as the ambulance drove away and saw Jack's truck left where Nate had gotten out after trying to run Brick over. Beyond that, he saw another crowd of people gathered around the canal outside the entrance of the property.

"John . . . ," Brick whispered.

As he closed his eyes again, he saw John sitting by him in the truck, laughing, and Brick knew he'd be seeing John's face whenever he closed his eyes for a long, long time. And that seemed fair, that seemed right.

Some things ought never be forgotten.

ACKNOWLEDGEMENTS

As has been said many times, books don't come from only one person/place. There are so many people who made this possible. First my wife, Lisa, my first reader. who spent countless hours butting heads with me over editorial choices and without whom this book would probably not even be complete, let alone published. Also, thank you to John Dufresne, Les Standiford, and Lynne Barrett, who all helped kick me into shape and took a chance on me when I really didn't deserve one. Thank you as well to my publisher David LeGere, who plucked me out of nowhere and gave me my shot.

And finally, thank you to my parents, who always encouraged me, even when it seemed like a hopeless long shot.

ABOUT THE AUTHOR

David Sangiao-Parga has been a pro wrestling "mark" since he was a small boy. He's been to live shows, met a wide variety of the performers (From Jerry Lawler to Ric Flair to Mick Foley and John Cena), and is widely read on the ins and outs of the industry. He's also a child of the Midwest, and has spent a great deal of time in towns just like Chimney Corner throughout his life. He is a graduate of the MFA program in creative writing from Florida International University, and currently lives with his wife and four children in Davie, Florida.